ALSO BY ZOË CASS

*Island of the Seven Hills*

# The Silver Leopard

# Zoë Cass

# The Silver Leopard

RANDOM HOUSE
NEW YORK

Library of Congress Cataloging in Publication Data

Cass, Zoë.
The silver leopard.

I.   Title.
PZ4.C3418SI3 [PR6053.A824]    823'.9'12    76-14180
ISBN 0-394-40816-0

Manufactured in the United States of America

2  4  6  8  9  7  5  3

FIRST EDITION

# The Silver Leopard

# I

THE GREAT drawing room of Quern Lodge held a score of friends, men and women, talking quietly and drinking coffee or malt whisky. Some had driven many miles, for Highland houses are set far apart, separated by moor and mountain, loch and torrent. Julian Bennet and I had come farthest of all, our station wagon gulping down the miles between London and Skerran in north Argyllshire during the dark hours of the night while we took turns to drive and doze. We had rolled to a halt in front of the gray stone house at eight o'clock this morning, surprise guests and perhaps even unwelcome.

In the early light of this strange day, twisting lochs and rivers had worn chiffon scarves of mist, insubstantial and ghostly. Shreds broke free, and caressed by zephyrs of wind which died as soon as they were born, crept between pine and rowan, clinging like gossamer to leaves and branches. The mountains, soaring above wooded glens into a clear, pale sky, restored my spirits with their grandeur. In spite of my mood of sorrow, I had been glad of the glory of that morning which, had she been alive, my mother would have loved.

After nightlong hours of engine noise, the silence in the car was intense, but outside, doves called softly, birds chirruped, and in the distance we could hear cattle, some of Robb Morrison's famous herd, no doubt.

"Caroline, you are home." Julian, my business partner and good friend, spoke with irony. He was looking at the closed oak door, the glittering, faceless windows of Quern Lodge.

"Yes." I left it at that.

"Why don't we go back to the village and have breakfast in that little hotel we passed? I suppose we could change there, out of our trousers and pullovers and into something a little more formal, in time for the funeral." I winced at his last word. "Someone will have seen us arrive. Why don't we just go and ring the bell?"

Reluctantly Julian got out of the car when I did; we rang the bell and the door opened. The housekeeper, Mrs. Munro, looked the same as when I had last seen her over a year ago; her black hair was drawn severely behind her ears as usual and her round black eyes looked at me impassively. She greeted me as Miss Westwood, which is my name, but there had been a time when she addressed me as "Miss Caroline."

I introduced Julian Bennet and after a murmured greeting Mrs. Munro said in her practical way, "You've had a long drive, you'll both be wanting breakfast."

We walked into the paneled, polished hall where Highland targes, dirks and claymores, ancient shields and weapons which had been well used in distant, bloody battles, decorated one wall like a huge metallic wheel.

We washed in a roomy cloakroom on the ground floor, like strangers, but Mrs. Munro herself served us with a delicious breakfast of porridge and cream, bacon and eggs, and hot rolls. "The daily help does not come from the village until nine," she explained.

I asked after the health of Mrs. Munro's son, a dimly remembered boy who had gone to college, and was told that he was well. She said nothing of his progress. Then, at last, I brought myself to inquire about my half sister and brother, Flora and Cosmo Cunningham.

"They're fine, Miss Westwood, considering what has happened. They ride early every morning, today no exception, but they will be back soon, I'm thinking." Her soft Highland voice until now had betrayed no emotion, but suddenly her black eyes filled with tears and pain. "Miss Caroline, I'm that sorry about your mother's death."

She left the room before I could reply, and in any case I could have found no words with which to answer. My mind was filled with sadness, regret and questions which I would not ask.

Flora and Cosmo returned soon after Julian and I finished breakfast. They were astonished to see us and I thought I detected hostility in Cosmo's greeting, but there had been time only for a brief and stilted conversation before guests began to arrive.

Now, a few hours later, the sad ceremony at the village church was over, debris from the luncheon which followed littered the empty dining room at the back of the house, and here in the drawing room, not out of any sense of duty towards Flora and Cosmo but because most of the guests had been my friends also, I moved among them, exchanging a few words, accepting messages of sympathy. Hardly anyone, I was glad to see, was dressed in mourning, which my mother had hated. I had changed into a cream-colored linen suit with a blue scarf tucked into the neck.

Julian caught my eye and gave me a brisk, encouraging smile, though he looked as tired as I felt. Mr. McNab of the snowy whiskers, who had driven from Oban in his elderly Rolls, was talking earnestly to him and I wondered what the retired owner of a fleet of trawlers could have to say to a young London antique dealer.

The log fire, sparking and crackling in its bed of soft

5

gray ashes, cast a glow over apricot chintz, pale carpet and azure walls, yet I felt chilled. The house was colder than my London flat and I was in that shivery state which comes with emotional and physical exhaustion.

Beyond the tall windows, September sunshine lay like liquid honey along the rose border, its warmth hazing the blue loch and distant purple hills. There is a dense quality in autumn sunlight not noticeable at any other time of year. I longed for its healing quality on my skin and thought that out there my sense of shock and confusion might at least be muted. I longed for an end to this ordeal so that I might leave the house and walk through the long, sloping birchwood to the edge of the water, with only Julian for company.

I thought of my mother, Margaret Westwood Cunningham. Until yesterday, a short yet endless time ago, I had not known that she was dead, or even that she had been ill. Julian and I had been attending auction sales in Hereford and Gloucester and we had been away from London for three days, during which time I had not even glanced at a newspaper. In any case, I don't read the death column—does anyone at the age of twenty-seven?

We had returned to London yesterday afternoon with the firm's station wagon filled with splendid things which we unloaded at our antique shop in Beauchamp Place. Then, tired and very dirty, we parted and went home to bathe and change. Among the usual assortment of mail waiting in my flat there were two telegrams, one telling me that my mother had had a stroke, the other telling of a second, fatal attack and giving details of the funeral arrangements. Both were worded in the bleakest terms, and sent by my half sister, Flora. For various reasons Flora and I did not get on well, but I was shocked by the tone of those telegrams.

I called Quern Lodge at once and my half sister answered the telephone in person. "Why bother to come at all?" she had asked with cold anger. "There is nothing you can do now."

I swallowed an indignant retort and bit back the explanation I had been about to give, of my absence from home. There would be time to account for that later, if it mattered. But even while I was saying that of course I would be coming to the funeral, I heard a *click* at the other end as Flora hung up, and I doubted that she would have heard my protest. I considered calling her again, but I did not want to add to the distress Flora and Cosmo must be feeling, and in any case I was stunned with shock and knew that, on my part, cool coherence would be difficult. So, instead, I telephoned Julian to let him know that I intended to drive to Scotland overnight.

"You are not going up there alone." He had been at his most decisive.

"I must go to my mother's funeral. I must!"

"Calm down, Caroline. Of course you must. But I am coming with you."

"Oh, Julian, I'd be so grateful."

The relief had been intense and, sensing my panic, Julian told me exactly what to do. At that moment, firm instruction was what I needed more than sympathy. "Fill a couple of flasks with coffee and soup. Pack some cheese and biscuits, fruit, anything you have."

In less than two hours, without fuss, he was with me and we set off on our long drive.

Now that we were here at Quern Lodge and my mother gone forever from its cool and beautiful rooms, I felt my grief the more keenly because it was shadowed by guilt. Mother and I had quarreled bitterly two years ago, before her second husband died. We had quarreled because my

7

mother was obviously unhappy with Angus Cunningham and I wanted her to leave him, but she wouldn't. She talked of the children, meaning Flora and Cosmo, but they were children no longer. I could only conclude that she was still at least half in love with Angus or hypnotized by his powerful animal attraction. I wondered with bitterness if her love would vanish and her disgust match mine if I told her that he had made a determined pass at even me, his stepdaughter. No reasonably attractive woman was safe from Angus Cunningham when he was drunk, which was often.

But of course I never told her of that—it would have been too cruel—and she and I made up our quarrel after a fashion. I even went back home a month later, for Mother's birthday. There'd been a lavish party on board my stepfather's yacht, with champagne and whisky flowing, a lethal mixture. That night Angus Cunningham had gone overboard and drowned. It was late October and unusually cold; the man had been swept out to sea and his body recovered days afterwards, washed up on a rocky islet, mutilated by fish and sea birds. Some fishermen found him and brought the remains back to the mainland.

There had been an inquiry, of course, with a verdict of accidental death and, mercifully, I had been able to keep from my mother the sordid details of a struggle I'd had with my stepfather on the night of the party. He had brooded and glowered at me, swaying on his feet and looking utterly evil, before pursuing me. I had managed to break away from him, using every bit of strength I possessed . . . Even now, I cannot bring myself to think of that terrible night without shuddering.

I hated Angus Cunningham but was sickened at the thought of anyone suffering so horrible an end. For my mother it must have been hell. She could never speak of it and would leave the room if anyone mentioned that hideous night and the days of waiting which followed. Such an appalling birthday, and she was to have only one more, for which she came to London and stayed with me. It was reasonably happy, I think. We went to the theater and were determinedly cheerful.

Dear heaven, if I had only known how little time there was left to us, I would have visited her more often. We were incompatible in many ways but we loved each other. The ache in my throat was hurting unbearably. Two strokes, three days apart, had taken my mother's life. If I had known about the first one, I could have come in time to see her alive once more.

My father, Saul Westwood, a farmer, died with other skiers near Zermatt when I was only two years old. I cannot even remember him and I have no full brothers or sisters. Mother sold the farm and we lived with my grandfather at Invercorrie Castle, eight miles from Quern, until my mother met and married Angus Cunningham, of the easygoing charm and dissolute ways, who had bought Quern Lodge. He had little money and the Lodge was in a state of disrepair, but my mother had enjoyed restoring it, grudging none of her income and dipping heavily into capital to make the house and garden more beautiful than they had ever been. It was at her insistence that the sporting rights to moor and river should be let; and my stepfather sold off some land to the Forestry Commission so that there was money for the education of his children. My father had provided for mine. I went to boarding school and left home at eighteen to start learning about antiques at Sotheby's. I'd met Julian Bennet there and eventually we opened our own business.

Flora Cunningham, my young half sister, seemed to enjoy simply being at home, but Cosmo, at eighteen, had been planning a year's travel before going to Glasgow University. It seemed unlikely that Mother's death would alter Cosmo's plans. There would be enough money, I supposed. I looked at them now and thought how astonishingly alike they were. The boy was taller, though a year younger, but both were slim, blond, tanned and blue-eyed, as our mother had been. They were also blessed with effortless charm, like their rogue of a father.

I wondered if they would stay on in Quern Lodge. Mrs. Munro had implied that it was difficult to get resident help. There was still a small staff living in at Invercorrie Castle, I believed, but my grandfather, Ian MacRobert, though seventy-eight years old, was a man still to be reckoned with in Skerran. Indeed, in all of northern Argyllshire. Formerly a landowner with large estates, he had sold most of his land to the Forestry Commission, keeping only Invercorrie. He now whiled away the time with his silver collection.

When my mother married again, he had reacted furiously, shutting both of us out of his life because he disapproved of the marriage and was unaccustomed to having his wishes disregarded. The births of two more grandchildren did nothing to soften him. Poor, lonely man. I knew that whether directly informed of Mother's death or not, he would have heard of it. News travels on every breath of wind in the country and he would have seen the announcement in *The Scotsman*. But he had not been at the funeral, which meant that he was either unable or unwilling to attend. I gazed through the window, dreaming of the time when we had lived at the Castle. So long ago, such happy times, before Angus Cunningham came into our lives. All the quarreling started with him.

I sensed the nearness of Robb Morrison even before he spoke, and when I heard his voice it was as deep and compelling as ever, so that I wished, passionately, that we were meeting under different circumstances. It was a long time since we'd met and talked.

"Caroline, it's good to see you. I understood you were not coming to the funeral."

I returned the intent gaze, lifting my head and staring at his full, strong mouth, brooding gray eyes, bony jaws, nose and brows. He had changed so little. I wondered if the same could be said of me. Outwardly, perhaps, I looked the same, but my heart was dry and barren.

Robb's eyes were hooded and, in shadow, dark as slate. His brown hair was very thick and neither curly nor straight, but something in between, so that it looked rough. He was as attractive as ever. Robb was one of the reasons for my leaving Scotland. When I was eighteen I had believed myself deeply in love with him, but he was eight years older and had no eyes for me. There had been a dark-haired beauty in Fort William, but he had not married her, it seemed.

Robb's remark puzzled me. After a murmured greeting, I said, "Did you say that you understood I was not coming? Why? Did someone tell you that?"

His brows lifted, then drew together. "Yes. I can't remember who it was, though. Flora, I suppose."

"She was indulging in wishful thinking, perhaps." Immediately I wished I had not voiced my bitter thoughts aloud.

"You can't mean that."

I sighed and briefly explained the circumstances of the business trip, my telephone call and Flora's reaction. I caught a momentary flash of compassion in Robb's eyes, and with that quick decisiveness which I remembered so well, he said, "One shock after another. How rotten for you, but I am sure Flora is glad you have come."

11

I glanced at him in amazement and wondered how much he saw of Flora and Cosmo these days. Changing the subject, I said, "I wanted to ask Dr. Farr about Mother's illness, but I don't see him here."

"No, he has been away for some time, visiting his daughter in Australia."

"Then he wasn't here when it happened?" I felt the most intense anguish for my mother, denied the care of old Dr. Farr when she needed it most.

"There is a substitute, a Dr. Staines."

"Is he good?"

My anxiety must have shown. Robb said, "Caroline, can you imagine Dr. Farr leaving his patients in the care of an incompetent doctor? I'm sure everything possible was done."

"Yes, of course." I swallowed hard.

"How are you? You must have driven all night to get here."

"We did. Julian came with me, you know. He's been wonderful. You must meet him." With an effort, I focused my attention on the social niceties of the moment and looked round the room. Julian was with Mr. and Mrs. Abercrombie, but he excused himself and came over to us, his brown eyes flickering from my face to Robb's.

The two men were almost equal in height, about six feet, but where Julian was slim and very elegant, with fairish hair and an easy grace, Robb was broader and more solid.

I introduced them with a word of explanation. "Julian Bennet is my partner. Julian, this is Robb Morrison, a neighbor and friend of the family."

They nodded and murmured a few words of greeting before Julian said, "Caroline, you haven't had any coffee. Let me get some for you." He lifted a finger and a girl who had helped Mrs. Munro at lunchtime came over, carrying a square cut-glass decanter of whisky in one hand and a jug of coffee in the other.

"More coffee, sir?" She lifted the jug towards Julian's empty cup.

"Yes, but, first, will you please bring a cup and saucer for Miss Westwood."

She brought them at once from a side table, filled my cup and then refilled Julian's. He had the knack of making everyone do what he wanted, instantly and willingly. It made being with him very pleasant, and his attention was not lost on Robb.

"Whisky, Mr. Morrison?"

Robb gestured with his tumbler, a lovely thing of modern Caithness glass, still half full. "No, thank you, Jean. This will be enough for me."

"Have I seen her before?" I murmured as she moved away.

"Probably not. Her name is Jean Jamieson. She works at the local hotel as a trainee, so I suppose she is on loan to Mrs. Munro for today."

"I see." As I sipped my coffee, I began to feel warmer, less frayed. Robb touched my arm and indicated an ox of a man who had just entered the room. He would be in his late thirties, I thought, and had a fine head of wavy red hair, worn rather long, with curly sideburns and a beard. "That is Dan Drummond, her employer."

"Well, I certainly haven't met *him* before. He's not the kind of man one would forget."

"If you say so." Robb looked sardonic. "He made a lot of money on North Sea oil rigs, I'm told, and took over the hotel back in the spring. He seems to be doing well enough there and he is liked in the neighborhood." After a pause, Robb added in an expressionless voice, "He comes to Quern Lodge a lot."

"Perhaps there's an attraction," Julian observed with a slow smile.

"Perhaps." Robb was looking impassively at the small knot of people who had gathered round the new arrival. It included Flora and Cosmo, and Drummond was greeting everyone in a deep, rumbling voice.

While I watched, Jean Jamieson poured a generous glass of whisky, put it into her employer's hand and glided away. The group moved together into a dark corner of the room but Dan Drummond's red hair flamed in the shadows, and close to his massive shoulders I could see Flora's pale, smooth blond cap.

Robb moved, turning his back towards the room and his face to Julian and me, giving us all his attention. Instantly, the past swooped up to me. In my childhood, personal attention was something I seldom enjoyed. My mother married again when I was seven and became much occupied with her new husband and their two children, one following rapidly after the other. Also, the transformation of a sullen gray house into a beautiful home took up much of her time. This was natural enough, but I had lost the companionship of my grandfather as well, and I still felt bitter towards him for that. Sometimes, however, during my solitary wanderings on the moor, I would meet Robb Morrison, who was not too old or too lofty to spare a little time for a lonely child. He had worn this air of close attention then, I remembered, and it had won from me a kind of devotion. Later, I bestowed my childish heart on him, but he hadn't accepted the gift, being far too well principled to take advantage of anyone so young. I went away to school and returned, still cherishing a dream of unrequited love, but I grew out of it and imagined now that Robb had never known of its existence.

My adult path had led far away from the moors and

mountains of this remote corner of Scotland. A lovely land, but insular. In London—gritty, competitive, dirty and crowded though it was—I became my own woman and felt alive.

"You are partners in an antique business, I understand?"

"That's right." As I answered, I felt Julian's long fingers slide under my elbow. He knew I was tiring, my troublesome left knee aching after the headlong race northward and from too much standing. But there was a tinge of possessiveness in the action. If Robb noticed it, he gave no sign.

"Do you specialize?"

"Not really, though Caroline is good at small stuff—porcelain, glass and silver particularly. I deal mostly with furniture."

"Not pictures?"

"Oh, we both go in for pictures if something interesting comes our way, but a lot of our time is spent in searching for specific items for our clients. It can be very absorbing."

"Baffling, too, I should imagine, if you can't find what they want."

"That doesn't often happen."

"Really?" Robb's dark eyebrows lifted in surprise.

I smiled. "The knowledgeable collector likes to do his own searching, it's part of the fun. And there are some who follow the fashion. Oh, yes, there are fashions even in antiques and the trick is to spot the next one and be ready with a few desirable pieces. Not too many, of course. The trend may change and we don't like to be left with stock on our hands."

"It all sounds very complicated. I'll stick to my cattle and timber."

"And your own antiques. Let me tell you, Julian, Ardnacol House holds some very beautiful old furniture."

Julian's dark eyes sparkled with interest, as I had known they would, and Robb promptly invited us for a pre-lunch drink on the following day.

"Thanks, but unfortunately we shall be returning to London tomorrow." My partner did not even glance in my direction as he refused the invitation, so although I had plans of my own I said nothing.

"A pity. Some other time, then. And now, if you will excuse me . . ." He glanced at his watch, drained his glass and set it down. "Caroline, you have my sincerest sympathy. Let me know if there is anything I can do to help."

As he moved away, Julian said casually, "Nice chap."

"Yes."

"Known him long?"

"Since I was about seven years old."

"The boy next door?"

"Only in the literal sense."

I watched Flora's violet eyes lift to Robb's when he went to say goodbye, and even from a distance I could see her expression of melting intimacy. Did she plan to capture him? I wondered cynically. My half sister was nothing if not ambitious, and Ardnacol land joined to that of Quern Lodge would make a handsome heritage. She was welcome to both estates. Only the recollection of my grandfather as he had been when I was little, and the magical memory of his mysterious castle, perched on a rocky spur which thrust out into a sea loch, held me still to this land. Other memories drove me away from it. Before I went south, I must see Ian MacRobert of Invercorrie again, but whether to lay ghosts or arouse long-dead emotions and settle an old score, I scarcely knew.

A fleeting glimpse of an expression I saw then on

Cosmo's face made me catch my breath. His emotion showed for only a moment and was gone.

"What is it?" Julian's hand tightened under my elbow. He must have heard my gasp of surprise.

"Nothing," I replied. But the glance Cosmo had given his sister had changed from approval to contempt, and the smile she threw him in return as she turned from Robb Morrison back to Dan Drummond did nothing to soothe her brother's angry spirit. He looked at that moment far older than his eighteen years and I wondered if his sister recognized this angry maturity. Perhaps she did, for after a moment she detached herself from Dan, followed Cosmo and thrust a hand through his elbow. Robb was leaving the room, with a word here and there to acquaintances as he went. Flora paid him no more attention but walked with her brother towards the fire. They stood together in pride and dignity with their backs to the flames, and as if a signal had been given, visitors drifted towards them and there began a general leave-taking.

"Let's go outside," I murmured to Julian, putting my coffee cup on a table, "I feel stifled in here."

"Don't you want to talk to those two?" Julian inquired.

"Later." I led the way out of the handsome room, into the long hall with its waxed floor, stained-glass window and mounting of ancient weapons on the wall. We went out through the open front door, where I stood for a moment, drawing in great breaths of sweet, pollen-laden air. Bees hummed in the climbing roses which clung to the stone walls, the sun fell warm on my face, the ever-present crooning of wood pigeons filled the air, and all these things, as much as the presence of Julian, combined to calm me.

I smiled up at him. "Let's walk to the lochside," I suggested. "There is a way through the silver-birch wood, over there." I nodded to our left, and we passed through an archway of clipped yew into an orchard where ancient apple trees writhed low to escape the prevailing wind and find shelter behind the yew hedge. A few moments later we had left cultivation behind us, thrusting through a belt of pines and into the grove of silver birch, all brilliant light and dappled shade, with winding paths, outcrops of gray rock patched with ochre lichen and turf so fine and green that it formed a carpet. I took off my cream linen jacket. Underneath it I was wearing a sleeveless blue top, and as we emerged from the wood the sun burned my bare arms. It was almost too hot.

"Is your leg hurting?" Julian asked.

"Hardly at all," I lied.

A month ago we'd had a car accident on Park Lane, in London. Julian had been driving and was unhurt. A carelessly driven truck hit my side of the car and I spent nearly three weeks in hospital with injuries to knee and thigh. Scars and sore muscles, with weakness in the knee, still reminded me of the mishap. Julian blamed himself, but it had not been his fault and I did not want him to feel responsible.

We crossed a narrow road to reach Loch Skerran. Our footsteps clicked on the tarmac, pressed softly on a stretch of turf starred with daisies, pink clover and yellow celandine, crunched on a pebble beach and came to a halt where the clear water gently lapped the shore.

"I wish I had brought a swimsuit," I said in an attempt at lightness. Then, after lifting my eyes from the glittering water to the hills on the other side of the loch and finally to the great blue sweep of sky above, I bowed my head again and burst into tears.

"Well, it's about time," Julian said, and I had never heard his voice so husky. He took off his elegant gray jacket, spread it on a flat stone and sat me down upon it.

Then he sat beside me, drew me close and, with one hand behind my head, held my ravaged face against his shoulder. He did not say a single word, just sat there like the rock of ages while I shook and shuddered with sobs, my tears soaking his shirt. Finally an awful calm stole over me. My head was throbbing like a steam hammer but the tumor of pain inside me had burst, bleeding away a torrent of fury and bitterness. I sat up, palming my cheeks and eyes, and rather shakily I said, "I'm sorry. I must look a sight."

Julian lifted my chin with one hand. His pleasant, well-bred, all's-right-with-the-world-and-if-it-isn't-we-won't-let-it-show expression, so very English, had given way to one of honest, genuine concern. It quite shocked me and I gulped.

Musingly he said, "Your eyes are exactly the color of the loch, intensely blue." Then, forsaking such foolishness and returning to cool normal, he added, "But your toffee-colored hair is horribly disheveled and your thin little face streaked with eye stuff. May I suggest a wash in the lake?"

"Loch," I murmured automatically.

"That's my girl. Go wash your face and I'll provide a hankie to dry it with."

Half laughing, I knelt on a rock which was exceedingly hard, leaned precariously out, dipped cupped hands and splashed my face. The loch was icy and I caught my breath. "Oh, I'd forgotten how cold the water is here." I turned at last. "Better?"

Julian nodded, holding out a white handkerchief with a gray border. "Better. Slightly pink but definitely better."

I dried. "Poor Julian. How embarrassing for you."

There was a silence. I stopped mopping and looked at him. He was frowning at me.

"I'm not unfeeling, you know. Under this flippant exterior I hide a caring heart." He became serious, even grim. "It may come as a surprise to you, but I have been extremely worried. Do you realize that until now, so far as I know, you have not shed one tear for your mother?"

"I know." I twisted his hankie. "I loved my mother even though we didn't always get on, and she loved me, I think. There are so many things I regret and I am appalled to realize that now I shall never be able to make up for being cross and casual with her. I'm not unfeeling, either, Julian."

"I know that, little idiot."

A childish, hiccoughing sob shook me, but it was the last. I had finished crying. Julian took my hand and I looked at him in inquiry.

"We'd better go back to Quern Lodge and talk to your half sister and brother, don't you think?"

"I suppose you are right."

"And you must see the family lawyer before returning to London."

For a moment I could not think what he was talking about. I had not even thought about inheritance, bequests or a will. My mother was only forty-nine and I knew little about her affairs, but I now realized that as her eldest child I might have duties and obligations, so I sighed agreement.

Julian drew me to my feet, put my jacket round my shoulders, picked up his own, shook it and threw it over his arm. Since yesterday he had devoted himself entirely to me and I was grateful, but I remembered that he was expecting me to return with him to London tomorrow, whereas I had other plans which had nothing to do with lawyers but everything to do with my grandfather at Invercorrie Castle.

Silently, apprehensive about going back to the Lodge, I walked with Julian, not through the grove this time but up the long driveway to the house. Our feet made a great noise on the gravel and, as we approached, I could see that the front door was open, waiting for us.

# 2

FLORA AND COSMO were alone, one on either side of the fire in the drawing room, and on a low table by Flora's side there was a tray. Silver caught the firelight and gleamed with that subtle, rich glow not to be found in any other metal—to my way of thinking, gold plate is vulgar by comparison. Delicate blue and white china stood on the tray and I saw that there were four cups and saucers, two already used.

Cosmo stood up and in a gentle tone he reproved his sister. "There," he said, "I told you that Caroline would be back soon."

"So you did," Flora replied lightly, and I refrained from pointing out that it didn't take a genius to figure that one out, with our dusty station wagon standing in the drive. I felt angry with myself for being so much on the lookout for trouble with these two. We were no longer children, the days of their ganging together against me were long past and, in any case, I was well able to look after myself. Yet the sensation of being on the defensive against them was still with me.

Flora rose and put one long, slender finger on the bell-push by the fireplace. Mrs. Munro came almost at once and was asked to bring some fresh tea. Unobtrusively she removed the tray and returned with it a few minutes later, together with dishes of buttered scones, small cakes and shortbread. I had little appetite; Cosmo tucked in hungrily, presumably for the second time, and Julian did justice to the homemade food. Flora ate nothing, I noticed. She drank another cup of fragrant China tea with a slice of lemon floating in it, and as she drank I was aware of her scrutiny of both Julian and me. She was trying, as so many people did, to size up our relationship. It puzzled those who did not know us well because it was not a sexual relationship. We both believed that to mix business with that particular pleasure led to disaster—we had seen it happen. We were fond of each other, but that is too insipid a relationship for marriage and would suit neither of us. Our partnership in business went smoothly and outside the business we dined together occasionally or went to a theater. Apart from that, we went our own separate ways, embarking on other relationships if we wished to, though neither of us was promiscuous.

We knew each other very well and sometimes I wondered if our warm understanding might grow into something hungrier, but for the present we were happy as we were. All the same, I recognized danger in this too-comfortable situation. We might in the end drift into a marriage which would be suitable and happy but not at all what I wanted, though it might do for Julian—his nature was calmer than mine. I had been a repressed child and knew that deep inside me there was an intense need for passionate fulfillment. I felt sure that Julian was not the man who could give me that.

"We must apologize for running out on you," I said, as Flora poured a second cup of tea for me.

"Not at all." She was too polite, her level blue gaze overcool and perceptive. She had seen that my eyes were still pink from weeping and was contemptuous of my weakness. Flora was completely in control of herself and I admired her for it.

Julian, while carrying on a conversation with Cosmo about sailing, was watching Flora covertly, and unwilling respect softened his finely shaped mouth. In spite of himself, I felt, he was thinking less harshly of the young Cunninghams.

To Flora, Julian said, "Has Caroline explained to you that she received both your telegrams at about six o'clock yesterday evening? That she knew nothing about her mother's illness until then?"

"No, she hasn't." The brilliant eyes widened and turned in my direction. "Why didn't you tell me?"

Dryly, I replied, "You didn't give me much chance. I could have explained that Julian and I had been away at auction sales for a few days, but you hung up on me."

"I am so very sorry," she said softly, her voice filled with distress, and then she administered one of her body blows by adding, still in that same gentle voice, "You used to be such a loner when you lived here, but that doesn't mean that you would be heartless now that Mother has died. I should not have jumped to conclusions."

Cosmo smiled at his sister in sly appreciation of her outwardly handsome apology. Julian looked gratified, while I met her full in the eye, conveying, I hoped, that I understood this ploy to the full but was not going to put myself in the wrong in front of witnesses by saying so. Armed truce, then, for the moment.

"In that case, you had quite a drive to get here in time." Cosmo sounded cross; he finished eating a piece of shortbread and wiped fine sugar off his fingers.

"There was plenty of time so long as we didn't spend much of it sleeping." Julian placed his cup and saucer on the small table, and Flora, with a muffled exclamation, sprang up and reached for the bell-push.

"I shall ask Mrs. Munro to make rooms ready for you. You will stay the night, of course?"

23

"Thank you. No." My prompt refusal brought an awkward silence. Julian's glance almost bored a hole through my head but I didn't even look in his direction. I had no intention of staying in this house for even one night. The tourist season was sufficiently far advanced for it to be fairly sure that we would find rooms somewhere. True, there were few hotels in the area, but Dan Drummond's place in the village, only two miles or so away, might have accommodation. All I knew was that I wanted a long, long night's sleep on neutral ground, where I need not be on my guard, before embarking on any attempt to see my grandfather.

"We are returning to London tomorrow, anyway," Julian said briskly. "But thank you for the offer, all the same."

"The lawyer is coming tomorrow morning. You will want to be here for that?" Cosmo's remark was a question.

"It might be as well for you to see him," Flora urged.

Julian replied, on my behalf, that of course I wanted to see the lawyer and would help in any way that I could.

"Oh, good." Flora sounded genuinely relieved and I softened a little towards her. She was only nineteen, after all, and the prospect of all the legal affairs to come must be a daunting one. Julian was right. I would try to help and, in that way, atone for some of our earlier prickly encounters. There was no reason why we should not work together, the three of us, on whatever had to be done. It was not their fault that they'd had a drunken rake of a father.

As we drove away, after agreeing to return at eleven o'clock the following morning, Julian said mildly, "Was there any particular reason for your not wanting to stay at Quern Lodge?"

"Did you want to stay?"

"No, but it would have been simpler, that's all."

"Yes, it would." I moved restlessly in my seat. The sun

had been shining full on the car and it was hot in spite of a window having been left open. "We should have stayed, I suppose."

"Do you miss your mother so much while you are there? Does it upset you? Is that why you don't want to stay the night?"

I shook my head. "It isn't that. The house is full of all sorts of memories for me. Not all of them are happy, and I just wanted to get away."

"Caroline, dear, memories can never be all happy."

"Wise, wise Julian." I gulped in cool air from the breeze we set up by our own motion, and gazed at the blue loch as we drove past it, moving towards the village. In all the two-mile drive we saw no one on the road or in the grove or on the moors. To our right lay the loch, and across, on the other side, where mountains swooped upward in a curve first smooth and then craggy, clefts in the rock face held narrow silver plumes where water gleamed in a vertical fall.

The rowan berries were a burning orange and the pines nearly black where they were shadowed by a great cliff. At the edge of the loch on the far side there was a spit of land and a sliver of golden beach with two small boats upturned on the sand. In a fold of the hill, hidden from us, there were two or three crofts; the boats belonged to the crofters who would fish from them. For generations their working lives had been spent in the same way, but now, in the evenings, they probably watched television like the rest of us and the wonders of the small screen would help to lure their young people away, if help were needed. Few stayed where the living was poor, but some returned to find peace. I mused as Julian drove, wondering if I could ever endure living up here again, thankful that I was un-

25

likely to be put to the test, for the beauty of the country called me still.

We had driven past the hotel on our way up but I had scarcely noticed it. Now, as Julian stopped the car on a graveled forecourt, I inspected it with interest. The long, low building had been painted white, the window frames black, and bay trees had been set along the front in square wooden tubs. There were window boxes and climbing roses, lamps hanging on iron brackets from the walls and an inn sign swinging lazily in the faint breeze. The sign was beautifully painted in scarlet, blue and gold, and showed a set of regimental drums. Underneath the painting the name hung suspended from two short, thick lengths of chain: THE DRUMS.

Julian laughed. "A suitable name when the landlord is named Drummond. Has it always been called that?"

I shook my head. "I can't remember that it had any name other than The Inn." Doubtfully I added, "I suppose it is a bit overdone, but it looks attractive, don't you think?"

"If it has a couple of rooms, Caroline, and a good menu, it will look very attractive indeed."

"A menu! Julian, we have done nothing but eat all day."

"I ate at breakfast time; no one makes breakfasts like the Scots. But since then I have been picking at things and I want to sit down at table, eat some good hot food, share a bottle of decent wine and then fall into bed for about twelve solid hours of sleep. Listen to that silence," he added, "there won't be a sound to disturb us at night, not a sound."

"You'd better go and make sure they have rooms for us before you indulge your imagination any further."

"I'll do that." Grinning, he swung himself out of the car and disappeared through the white-painted door with the shining brass knocker, also in the shape of a drum.

Yes, it was a mite overdone—larger than life, like the landlord, Dan Drummond of the fiery red hair.

Julian was back in no time, smiling blissfully. "Two single rooms, dinner from seven-thirty onwards, everything shining with polish and a welcoming, buxom Scots lady at the reception desk. How's that?"

"That," I said, getting out of the car and helping Julian to get our things, "sounds like the answer to our prayers."

A man emerged and took the two small bags from Julian's hands. "If you'll just leave your keys in the ignition, sir, I'll move the car round the back for you." He was small and quick, and spoke with a strong Glasgow accent. No Highlander, this one. A stranger in Skerran, like his employer.

I lay on my bed for an hour, planning a hot bath before dinner. Pleasant sounds floated in from the garden at the back of the hotel—a mower with the attendant smell of newly cut grass, bird song, gentle voices fading away as their owners strolled further from the building. Exhausted by the events of the past twenty-four hours, so deadly tired that I was able to thrust all thought right out of my mind, I drifted off into a deep sleep and was awakened by Julian knocking on the door and calling softly but in some alarm, "Caroline. Caroline, are you all right?"

I stumbled to the door and opened it, smiling, still in a daze of sleep. I had been running, running away from rough water, over the moor, towards something utterly delightful, but I could not remember now what it had been. The dream was fading, as dreams do, leaving only a tantalizing thread behind, a fragile link which was breaking even as my mind tried to hold on to it. Something, or someone, had been beckoning to me, but the last vestige of the vision faded, leaving only Julian there, smiling his nice, bland smile, his equable disposition restored by the realization that I had been asleep.

"I'm sorry. If I had known you were resting, I wouldn't have called you yet—there's no rush. Would you rather stay here for a little longer?"

"No, I'm fine. And I know how hungry you are. I'm going to take a quick bath, though, so have a drink while you wait for me. See you downstairs."

"Right." He turned at once and made for the dark oak staircase which led from the center of the carpeted hall down into the reception area.

I collected my washing things and a towel from the basin in my bedroom and made for a bathroom. The Drums had private bathrooms but they were not attached to small, single rooms. However, the bathroom I found was well appointed, the water was hot and there was some decent soap. Refreshed by bathing, I dressed again in my pale suit, the only garment I had with me apart from trousers and sweater, and went downstairs.

The bar was crowded and, in the country, people dressed up in the evenings, it seemed. The women wore stylish clothes of every material from tartan to velvet and were very smart. Men were more casually dressed. It was impossible to tell residents from visitors, but many had come in for a meal, I fancied.

Julian raised a beckoning hand and I joined him as he stood to make room for me at a small table with a polished granite surface. It was real granite, not a plastic imitation. I ran my fingers over the cold pink-and-gray-speckled surface appreciatively. "Nice," I said.

Before Julian could order a drink, I became aware of a large presence standing in front of me and lifted my eyes to meet those of Dan Drummond himself. They were a light, bright gray, an unusual color in Britain but often seen among Dutch people.

"Good evening, Miss Westwood," he said, "I was sorry not to talk to you this afternoon. I hope you will be comfortable here."

"Thank you." I was glad that he did not fuss or make banal expressions of sympathy over my loss. For the moment I had managed to push grief into the background, and although it would return, I hoped it would not be for a little while yet.

"May I bring you a drink? We have a special whisky for our friends, for the ones who appreciate good malt." He smiled and I smiled in return, glancing at Julian's glass. "I see you have supplied some to this table already. I'll have the same, thank you."

He brought it himself on a small wooden tray and bowed before returning to the bar. There was someone serving there, but Drummond was not above lending a hand while being pleasant to visitors. He was an impressive man. One could imagine him as a clan chieftain of old, leading his band of ragged warriors into battle and slaughtering the enemy with the kind of weapon now mounted on the wall at Quern Lodge.

"Have you fallen for him?" Until Julian spoke, I was unaware that I had been staring, and as I tilted my head in Julian's direction I replied dryly, "Really, Julian, do you think it likely?"

"I'd say it is not impossible." Julian answered in the drawl he adopted sometimes when trying to appear disinterested. I had heard it in operation at many a sale, when dealers were prowling round the goods on offer and circling their rivals, wary and defensive, pretending indifference.

My mind conjured up a picture of Drummond with Flora at his shoulder, as I had seen them that afternoon, and lightly I said, "I wouldn't want to poach on Flora's preserve, now, would I?"

"Flora . . . Do you mean that she and that man have something going? He is old enough to be her father."

"That might be part of the attraction."

"Because she has lost her own father, you mean?"

"No, not that. Some girls like older men."

Julian chuckled. "If that is on account of feeling safe with them, the theory might fall apart with that one."

Julian was right. Dan Drummond exuded a pleasantly compelling animal attraction. I could feel it, and I had never thought of myself as being particularly susceptible on chance acquaintance. I took a long time to get to know people, still longer to feel that I could trust them and let down my guard. Mother used to say that I was born a skeptic, and I knew that it wasn't a trait she liked. She herself was a trusting soul, sunny-natured, naturally affectionate and outgoing. Mother . . . Oh, God! I seized my glass and gulped some whisky, not appreciating the special smoothness at all—I might as well have drunk raw, cheap spirit at that moment.

"Go easy," Julian said very quietly.

I bit back a quick retort, closed my eyes and swallowed. He saw altogether too much—it was disconcerting and it was also irritating. There were no surprises between us now; he was my other self.

"Sorry," he said, making things worse.

I looked at Julian with bleak tolerance, then suddenly remembered how angelic he had been, how very thoughtful and kind, changing his plans at a moment's notice to drive up here with me, doing everything possible to ease my path, and with a smothered exclamation I put a hand on Julian's sleeve and laughed. "I'm a beast. It's just that you are too perceptive."

"I know. All my women friends tell me that I am far too understanding." He was laughing as well, and the moment of angry frustration fled from me.

In the dining room we found that we had been given a table for two close to the window. It was a balmy night, with the sky a deepening blue above, night clouds climbing slowly as the sun began to sink behind them. The sunset was swirling round the western sky in an ever-changing spectacular of orange, rose and flame. The cloud bank glittered at the edges with fierce gold and I was glad that we were in Scotland, where it stays light late into the evening, even in September. The scent of lavender and stocks drifted in through the open window, and at last a needle of a breeze sprang up and ran through the garden, whispering, waving tall shrubs, rippling through the borders and making the brightly colored dahlias sway and nod. There was something curiously menacing about the abrupt change in atmosphere and I was reminded of how quickly the weather could worsen here among mountains and on the edge of sea lochs, with the mighty Atlantic so near. Only a scattering of islands sheltered this coast from the Atlantic gales, and at this time of year wind and tide could be formidable.

"You are cold." Julian himself rose and closed the window beside us. If he had noticed that something more than a drop in temperature had made me shiver, then this time he was not going to show it. We finished our excellent steak, the plates were removed by a brisk waiter, and a laden trolley was wheeled alongside the table. Everything looked delicious and very rich, and I shook my head regretfully. Julian chose a large wedge of cheese cake, which he ate with delicate appreciation—he had the most beautiful table manners. I joined him when the cheese board appeared, and we had coffee at our table instead of in the

31

lounge. Gradually the crowded room became quieter, until only a few tables were occupied.

"Brandy?"

I shook my head. "Don't let me stop you."

"I don't want any, either. What now? A walk before going to bed?"

"What a good idea, Julian. I could do with some exercise."

In the car I had a pair of flat shoes. We do a lot of standing at sales, and comfort is everything when one has arrived at ten o'clock in the morning, only to find that Lot No. 253, the only one of interest, will not be auctioned until the afternoon; so flat shoes are always available.

While Julian went off to collect them, I waited in the hall, a square room with dark polished woodwork and beautifully arranged garden flowers. There was an enormous Chinese bowl with a green dragon squirming around the outside of it. At a guess, there was another dragon inside, but the bowl was filled with rose leaves, rosemary, lavender and herbs, which scented the air even through the drift of tobacco smoke coming from the bar.

"Miss Westwood, there is a telephone call for you." Dan Drummond himself brought the message and I frowned at him, puzzled. "You can take it there." He pointed to a telephone under a hood in one corner of the hall. "It will be quite private."

My racing mind told me that no one at all knew I was here. Julian and I had not decided where to stay until after we had left Quern Lodge. "Are you sure?" I asked, feeling —and probably looking—stupefied.

He shrugged and the light gray eyes took in my confusion. His glance was kind, speculative and on the warm side, but he simply said, "I am sure." He smiled suddenly and deep creases appeared, running from the strong nose to the full mouth. "If you didn't tell anyone you were coming to The Drums, well, there are not many hotels in the area. It wouldn't take long to trace you." He paused. "For anyone anxious enough to do so."

I could think of no one who would want to get in touch with me, but wishing I had not shown my astonishment, I nodded and made my way to the telephone. As I picked up the receiver I was aware of his following eyes, sharpened by interest.

The voice which spoke to me was not one I recognized. It was a man who said smoothly, "This is Mackenzie, Miss Westwood. I am butler to Mr. Ian MacRobert."

"Yes, Mackenzie?" The butler at Invercorrie Castle when I'd lived there had been named Stockton but he'd died years ago. I'd not met this one.

"Mr. MacRobert asks that you will visit him at the Castle before returning to London."

During the short silence which followed I was filled with astonishment and then exultation. "Very well," I said carefully, showing neither enthusiasm nor reluctance.

"It is understood that the lawyer is to be at Quern Lodge at eleven o'clock tomorrow morning. No doubt you will be lunching there, and as Mr. MacRobert rests in the afternoon, I am bidden to ask if four o'clock for tea would suit you?"

I though of Julian, anxious to be off to London as soon as possible. But what alternative time could I put forward? If Julian had to leave, I could stay another night here at The Drums if hospitality was not offered at the Castle, and doubtless I could hire a car to take me to Fort William, where I could board a train for London. "Thank you, Mackenzie. Please tell Mr. MacRobert that I will be at Invercorrie Castle at four o'clock tomorrow.

"Very good, Miss Westwood."

The soft roll of the *r*, the gentle *s* sound, was all West Highland, and music in my ear.

"Making a telephone call?" Dan Drummond had disappeared and in his place Julian was standing with my suede walking shoes in one hand. He looked as surprised as I had felt when summoned to the telephone, and made no attempt to hide his curiosity.

"The reverse." I took my shoes from Julian. "Receiving one. From my grandfather, would you believe? Or, at least, from his butler."

"That's a bit unexpected, isn't it?"

"More than a bit. Though I may as well tell you now that I was planning to go and see him before returning to London."

"Ah! I thought there was something simmering in that busy mind of yours, but that is my overactive perception working again. I must curb it." He spoke in his most languid drawl and I laughed.

"Most of the time, Julian, your perception is part of your attraction, so you'd better keep it. Some girls love it."

"Yes. But you are Caroline Westwood, V.P.P., and you resent it."

"V.P.P.?"

"Very private person." Before I could make any suitable rejoinder, he changed the subject. "If you don't particularly want to go up to your bedroom, why don't you sit on that oak settle to change your shoes, and I'll put the high-heeled ones in the car for you."

"I'll do that, thank you." Ignoring his V.P.P. crack, I sat down and changed my shoes.

As we went out I caught sight of Dan Drummond through the doorway. He was in the bar talking. The man he was talking to did not turn round, but I recognized the broad back of Robb Morrison, the tilt of his head and the set of his shoulders. P

Julian and I crossed the graveled sweep in front of the hotel and turned down a path which led to the lochside. We passed the hotel's garden wall and found ourselves by a wooden jetty with a few boats moored alongside. Out on the loch, where the water was deeper, a cabin cruiser rocked gently. She had not been there when we arrived and I wondered aloud if she belonged to one of the diners.

"Or to Drummond?" Julian mused. "I know that if I lived here, I would want to have my own boat—and that one looks just the job. Big enough to take some hard weather out at sea, small enough to handle alone if necessary."

"Can you see the name?" I peered through the fast-gathering dusk but could see only a blur where the name was painted in dark letters. There was a mooring light showing and no lights in the cabin, but the white super-structure gleamed with fresh paint and shining glass. As we watched, a gull planed in and perched on the rail. Two others joined it and I thought it probable that there was no one aboard.

"No, it's too dark to read the name." Julian gave up trying and we walked by the loch. A freshening wind was in our faces and waves rummaged on the beach, washing about in restive movement and sucking pebbles down the slope with a harsh, rattling sound. I could taste salt on my lips. The wind was coming from the west, and in front of us, as we walked, a stand of trees caught at the hurrying breeze, trapped it briefly until, shrieking, it broke free and tore away from the reaching boughs, which rattled and rustled with a melancholy sound.

I thrust a hand through Julian's arm. He was walking, as he often did, with the right hand thrust into his trouser pocket, and we fell into step companionably while I told him in more detail of my telephone call.

"Do we need to return to London tomorrow?" I finished.

"I'm afraid I do. I didn't tell you before because I didn't want to worry you, but Rosie is going to Rome early on Saturday morning, so she can't stay with the business any longer, and Mrs. Wiseman is due on Saturday to collect the Meissen, remember?"

"Oh Lord! I'd forgotten."

Rosie was a friend always willing to hold the fort when we were on buying trips, and Mrs. Wiseman a good customer who visited us whenever she came to London. I knew that she was flying back to New York on Sunday and we'd had the most awful job getting delivery of the Meissen pieces we'd bought privately for her. As very often happens, once someone has sold, this one wanted to keep the porcelain for just a few more days. A visiting relative wanted to see it, he'd said. The excuse offered in such circumstances is nearly always "a visiting relative," but we do understand the natural reluctance to part with loved family treasures and try to meet any reasonable request without quoting "business is business" to the vendor. Hence the last-minute arrangement with Mrs. Wiseman.

"I'd better come back with you," I decided. "I can come here again later. After all, I haven't seen my grandfather for twenty years, so any reunion can wait for another week or two." Hurriedly I added, "If that sounds bitter, I didn't mean it to."

Julian patted my hand and we walked in thoughtful silence for a few seconds. Then he said gently, "How old is he, Caroline?"

"Grandfather? He is seventy-eight, I think."

"And he rests every afternoon. It is a good age, my dear.

I think you should see him tomorrow, as arranged. Much better than coming back all this way again."

I knew what Julian was trying to tell me. He was saying that if I did not go to see Grandfather now, I might not have another opportunity. As I recalled the man, he was as tough as leather, but in twenty years he must have changed a good deal.

"You drive back tomorrow, then," I said, finally making up my mind. "I shall go to Invercorrie for tea, and on Saturday or Sunday I'll get a train to London from Fort William. How's that?"

"Well planned," Julian said dryly, and I knew he'd guessed that I'd already faced the minor problem of returning on my own, by train. "But how you get around in this benighted slice of the country without a car, I cannot imagine. Why don't I take the train and you keep the car?"

"You'll need the station wagon if you have to ferry any furniture around. I'll hire one up here."

"Well, at least I can take care of that for you before driving south. I'll choose something suitable and have it delivered to The Drums or to Quern Lodge, whichever you prefer."

"Julian, that would be the most tremendous help." I felt very grateful to him. It had crossed my mind that there was no way to get from Quern, or from here, to Invercorrie Castle except by car or boat, and I'd been wondering if I could prevail upon someone to take me. There might be a car at the hotel, but I did not know, and, in any case, preferred not to advertise my movements. I was glad that my grandfather wanted to see me, but I had no idea whether the meeting would end in friendship or a renewal of the twenty years' cold war. Small point, at this stage, of giving the scattered population any additional food for gossip.

We took another of those mammoth Scottish breakfasts together, with Julian working his way contentedly through fruit juice, porridge, kippers and white, floury morning rolls spread thickly with butter and marmalade or honey.

I confined myself to fruit juice, rolls and coffee, but the fresh light texture of the rolls was so delectable that I had a second, and sternly restrained myself from reaching for a third.

"Why can't we get rolls like this in London?" Julian asked.

"You can find perfect croissants in London. You can't have everything."

"I suppose you are right, but these should be advertised as a major tourist attraction."

"Especially for greedy visitors," I teased. "I don't know how you keep that slim figure. I have to work at it by abstention."

"Poor thing. I feel for you, missing these kippers."

As he spoke, his fishy plate was whisked away. Jean Jamieson was looking after our table this morning. She smiled beautifully and was very competent.

"We did not see you last night?" I queried.

"No, Miss Westwood. I was off duty for the evening."

I nodded and thanked her for helping at Quern Lodge.

"Will you be going back to London today?" Her question was merely conversational but I made some evasive remark.

When she had gone, Julian raised his well-shaped eyebrows. "Were you putting her in her place?"

"Let's say I was being discreet. I'd just as soon people didn't know I was going to Invercorrie. Do you plan to leave right after breakfast?"

"I'll drive you to Quern Lodge first." He chewed at a mouthful of roll and marmalade, swallowed it and remarked, "It won't take anyone long to find out that you're still around, will it?"

"Not if I return to The Drums tonight."

"Where else?"

"Not at Quern, anyway." The words burst from me. I could not bear the thought of staying in rooms which still, to me, echoed with raised, angry voices, the voices of my mother and myself, in everlasting argument. "But if my grandfather invited me to stay at the Castle, I think I would."

Julian's eyes were kind. "Don't hope for too much, Caroline."

A MAP OF Skerran, framed and mounted, hung at eye level in the hall of the hotel, and it showed us that even allowing for tortuous roads, it was only about thirty-five miles to Fort William, where I could hire a car.

"I'll come with you and drive myself back," I said to Julian, eager to have something to do.

He looked at his watch. "It is after nine o'clock. You would be cutting it a bit fine for getting to Quern Lodge by eleven. We don't know how long it will take to locate a car, for one thing. You'd better leave it to me."

"We can look in the telephone directory for car-hire firms." As I spoke, Mr. Drummond came into the hall from outside, and the blast of cold air which came in with him spoke of a sharp drop in temperature. I was glad of the sweater I had put on for our night drive northward and wished it was thicker.

"Did I hear you mention car-hire firms?" The lambent gray eyes were not curious, merely filled with polite inquiry.

Julian replied smoothly that he had to set off for London almost at once but I would follow later by train after a meeting with the lawyer. However, I would need a car, so we proposed to hire. "I suppose Fort William is the nearest place?"

"It is, but I have a car in the garage which I keep for anyone to use in an emergency. If that will do, you may have it, with pleasure."

It was a kind and reasonable offer, but I have a mania for independence and, besides, I could see difficulties arising if I was invited to stay overnight at Invercorrie Castle. I assumed that my grandfather had a car, and someone to drive it for him, but for a vehicle to be returned to The Drums tonight I would have to drive it back with Grandfather's car following to pick me up, an absurd complication. No, no. I wanted to be driving a car which I need not return tonight, and I would take with me my few possessions so that I was completely independent. If the visit to Grandfather proved to be a disappointment, I could then drive back to The Drums for the night, or even to Fort William, where I'd be ready to take the first available train to London.

"Caroline?" Julian drew me gently out of my reverie.

"I'm sorry. I was thinking it out. It is a kind offer, Mr. Drummond, but for various reasons it would be better for me to have a car from Fort William. And may I settle my account, please?"

"You are leaving today as well, then?" Drummond was curious now.

I nodded and said nothing.

"I hope we shall have the pleasure of seeing you both again, under happier circumstances."

He went to the desk and made out our bills himself; then to Julian he said, "It so happens I am going to Fort William for supplies. If you'd care to give me a lift, I can drive the hire-car back." He grinned. "A Scotsman always has an eye to costs—it will be cheaper for you than having them send two cars, one to take back their delivery driver."

We thanked him and it was left like that. I supposed

the lawyer would give me a lift from Quern Lodge, or Flora might drive me.

Again Julian and I walked by the loch, taking the route we had used in the half-dark of last night. The water was gray this morning and stirred into a sullen roll by the thrumming wind. There were gulls riding the waves, sheltering on this inland water from the worst of the gale, and the cabin cruiser we had admired was still there, tossing gently, the name now clearly visible. It was called *Flora* and was fairly new, but, surely, if it belonged to the Cunninghams, it would not be moored here but nearer to Quern Lodge.

"Merely named after her perhaps," said Julian when I voiced this opinion.

"Maybe. By Dan Drummond, do you suppose? Robb Morrison told me yesterday that Drummond is often at Quern Lodge."

"It seems feasible, then, but I don't suppose she is the only Flora in this area. And besides, the Flora MacDonald who helped Bonnie Prince Charlie must be a living legend in these parts."

"Yes, it could be named for the heroine herself. I don't know of another Flora living in Skerran." I frowned and sighed. "But I'm a stranger here. I would not know now."

For a moment I felt confused. I had chosen to live in London and loved it, yet a tiny part of me still reached out to Skerran. I thought of the brief talk I'd had with Robb yesterday, of the strong, tall frame and quick, intelligent eyes which saw so much. He had told me a good deal during our short conversation, reminding me of the past when it had always been Robb who kept me up-to-date with the news, sensing, perhaps, the isolation I felt. I recalled glimpsing him again in the bar last night and wondered what had brought him to The Drums. Not the whisky, I felt sure.

Julian was quiet, watching the water, leaving me to my thoughts, and silently I withdrew into deep, total concentration, wrestling with a problem I'd mulled over from time to time for a long while now. Had I chosen isolation for myself in those early years at Quern Lodge, or had it been imposed upon me? Yesterday afternoon Flora had called me a loner. Well, I had been that in the past, true enough, but for sweet charity's sake, I must no longer blame my mother for any loneliness I had endured before going to boarding school. I'd been happy enough at school and, most of the time, happy at home, even while alone. I was not a loner at heart and I ought not to allow myself to fantasize over my strange childhood in this morbid, introspective way. Grappling with the problem, I recognized that the real trouble had come later in my life and the only genuinely sad part was that I had not come to a closer understanding with my mother before it was too late. By way of atonement, perhaps I could become better friends with Flora and Cosmo. I would try.

As we turned to retrace our steps, Julian said, "You've been on a long journey, in your thoughts."

"True," I sighed. That perception of his again.

"I'm glad you've come back, for it's time to go." He put an arm around my shoulders to counterbalance the extreme lightness of his tone and we walked back to the hotel like that.

We packed our few belongings and I left my bag at the reception desk. Julian arranged to collect Dan Drummond on his way back from Quern Lodge, for he had to pass the hotel anyway. Any other roads led merely to isolated houses or gave access to plantations of pines.

There was little talking on our short journey. We kissed,

briefly, before I got out of the car, and as I watched Julian going away from me down the drive to the iron gates which always stood open, I felt a sense of desolation. He had offered to come in with me but I had refused, knowing it was time he set off on his long drive to London.

The sound of the well-tuned engine could still be heard after the car was out of sight beyond the grove, but then it died and all I could hear was the pervasive crooning of the wood pigeons and a faint sound of voices from the house. Mrs. Munro's voice, I thought, and Flora's. There was no car in the drive, so presumably the lawyer had not yet arrived. It still wanted five minutes to eleven o'clock.

Cosmo rounded the house in riding breeches and a blue sweater. "No car? I thought I heard one. Did someone give you a lift?"

"Yes, Julian did. He has gone now."

"He could have waited for you and stayed to lunch."

"I mean he has really gone, back to London." I smiled at the handsome youth, so slim, blond and upright. The hair on his upper lip was soft but not downy. Cosmo Cunningham was not a boy but already a man. He did not smile back but said abruptly, "You'd better come in."

I gritted my teeth. Soon I would return to London, to my own life there, which was full of interest and free from ghosts of the past. There was this final ordeal of discussing my mother's affairs, then a visit to Invercorrie Castle, and southward again. Today I would be friendly with everyone, even my peevish half brother.

Flora led us to a smallish study at the side of the house where armchairs had been arranged informally and, at a small desk, a tall-backed chair was ready for the lawyer. "I have no idea whether he will have a lot of papers or not," Flora said somewhat helplessly. "Will he want more space?"

Her indecision made her seem more youthful and human and I said gently, "Don't worry. He will tell you if he needs anything else."

"Yes, I suppose so. You don't remember when your father died, I suppose?"

My resolve to be peaceable and friendly fled. "Naturally not. I was only two."

"So young? I must have known, of course, but one forgets. It wasn't talked about much, as I remember." She opened an onyx box of cigarettes and offered it, taking a cigarette herself, then passing the box to Cosmo when I refused. "I don't smoke often, but . . ." Cosmo snapped a slim lighter until the flame sprang to life, held it to her cigarette and she drew in smoke and exhaled slowly. "I hate the thought of what is to come. Yesterday I was sure the funeral would be the worst ordeal, but I was wrong. Today's legal business will make Mother's death seem even more final."

She was right, and my irritation with her dispersed. I felt sick at heart myself, and for Flora, who lived at home, it was worse. She would have to come to terms with an empty chair, an empty room in the house, silence in place of Mother's lilting voice. I looked at Cosmo and saw stark despair on the boy's face. His jaw was working and under the fair skin blood flowed and then ebbed, leaving his face utterly drained of color. I had not imagined he would be so emotional and wished that the lawyer would come so that some kind of distraction could be provided, if only temporarily.

As if in answer to prayer, the doorbell rang and Mrs. Munro announced Mr. Sanders, a tall, spare man with smoothly brushed white hair, a clipped gray mustache, still dark in places, and thin, bony hands in a state of constant movement. He shook hands with me when Flora introduced us, and I had a swift impression of a handful of cold bones exerting minimal pressure and quickly withdrawing. The thin fingers moved from tie to pocket, touching a protruding handkerchief, reaching to an inside pocket to withdraw a pen and unzipping a slim briefcase. Then, with an effort, squaring his shoulders, he murmured something trite about his "sad duty" and sat down in the chair Flora indicated. He drew some papers out of the briefcase and this small action seemed to calm him. I had no impression of shiftiness, merely of a man under strain. In fact, the fine, well-shaped mouth and clear gray eyes conveyed an honesty and integrity which were pleasant. But the eyes searched mine in some puzzlement, as if he were looking for something which he did not find.

Mrs. Munro brought coffee, which I think we all needed, and then Mr. Sanders read the will. It was very brief. Quern Lodge and the entire contents except for one item and a few bequests to staff, together with all her money, my mother left equally divided between Flora and Cosmo. The one item was mine and my mother described it as "the silver leopard normally kept in my bureau, which was given to my elder daughter, Caroline Westwood, by her grandfather, Ian MacRobert."

Flora looked astonished. "Is that all?" she said when the short will had been read.

"Yes, that is all."

Cosmo said nothing. He was staring down at his fists, clenched in his lap until the knuckles showed white. The muscles along his jaw were knotted. Slowly the hands opened and relaxed.

I also said nothing, but if my half brother and sister expected me to be disappointed or angry, they were totally wrong. I had expected nothing from my mother, and was surprised only by the restoration to me of the silver leopard, a heavy ornament which I had loved as a child and which I had naughtily seized and thrown at my grandfather when he shouted at Mother, telling her that if she left Invercorrie to marry—how well I remembered his words—"that buffoon who has bought Quern Lodge and wants your money to make it habitable," then she need not return. He had added that he would gladly keep me with him—an offer that brought an indignant reply from Mother—but when he went on furiously to say that if we went, it was for good, I think that Mother did not believe him. Certainly I did not. At the age of seven I had heard threats uttered in anger, not often but sometimes. I knew that people forgave and relented, that clouds of anger broke up and dispersed and the sun shone again, often more brightly than before. What I did not know was that Grandfather Ian MacRobert had a pride so fierce and powerful that any dictum uttered by him was as irreversible as an act of Parliament.

For days there had been tension and minor quarrels, then a cold silence which persisted, blanketing my small world, in the same way that sea mist sometimes shrouded the Castle for days at a time. Finally there was the shouting match which ended in hurled abuse from both quarters and ceased only when I picked up and threw the leopard, as if by breaking my favorite ornament I could also break the hatred and tension. I aimed it at my grandfather, but by great good fortune it missed and merely dented some oak paneling before falling onto a thick carpet, totally undamaged.

After a moment of fraught silence, my mother said "Caroline!" in a horrified, strangled tone. I could see her now, with one slender brown hand clutching her throat, the other outstretched before me, as if to still my anger.

Grandfather laughed, but it was a bitter sound, not at all like his usual rich chuckle. "Don't blame the child,

Margaret. We have driven her to it. Here, Caroline . . ."
He stooped, picked up the leopard and lobbed it gently in
my direction, knowing I would be able to catch it without
difficulty—my aim might not be very good but my coordina-
tion was excellent. "Keep it," he said, and to my childish
heart this brought joy. He had given me the most precious
present possible, the thing I loved more than any of my
dolls, thereby telling me that all would be well again now.

How wrong I was. Those were the last words he had said
to me. That day we packed and left Invercorrie Castle.
Mother married Angus Cunningham a few weeks later,
and although she telephoned the Castle many times during
the next year or two, Grandfather would never speak to her.
I could remember seeing her turn away from the telephone,
first flushed and with tears in her eyes, then pale with anger
and finally—when she was big with child—with awful
finality, the light in her eyes extinguished, so that their
brilliant blue was clouded and opaque.

After that I learned that talking about the Castle brought
her pain, mention of my grandfather caused bitter comment, and I fell silent on both subjects, hugging to myself
scenes and memories of my early childhood. I looked upon
them as if they were something which had happened to
another child but which I had been able to watch, so that
they remained forever imprinted on my mind with the ut-
most clarity.

"Miss Westwood." Mr. Sanders was speaking to me with
a calm dignity which removed any embarrassment. "The
leopard is yours; therefore, technically, reference to it in
the will is merely a directive. If you wish to contest this
will, you may appoint a legal adviser. Perhaps you already
have a lawyer conversant with Scots law?"

"Yes, I do." I thought of the rotund, brisk little Mr.
Ross who acted for me when required, which was not often.

Two pairs of blue eyes fixed themselves on me, wide, expectant and wary. "But I have no wish to contest the will."

I could almost feel the relaxation of tension in the room, not from Mr. Sanders, who showed no emotion whatever, but from Flora and Cosmo, who were, I thought, tremendously relieved but also slightly puzzled.

"My father left money for me," I explained. "I inherited that when I was twenty-one and am perfectly satisfied." Indeed, I was satisfied. It had been used, along with an equal sum contributed by Julian, when Julian and I started our business and had launched us, but our capital was repaid and the business was keeping us both quite comfortably. Yes, I was satisfied but I would have liked a small memento from my mother, something of her own.

"You are expecting to get the Castle, I suppose?" Flora's voice was cool and controlled but her shallow breathing seemed uneven.

I was astonished. "The Castle? Invercorrie Castle? It is most unlikely," I said dryly. "My grandfather . . ."

"*Our* grandfather," Cosmo put in swiftly.

After a moment's pause I went on, "Yes, you are quite right. Our grandfather. I was about to say that we have not spoken for twenty years, so I hardly think that I am likely to inherit the Castle, or anything else, from him."

I was thoroughly embarrassed. Because I had hugged the memory of Grandfather MacRobert to me for so many years, and because I doubted if Flora and Cosmo had ever even met him, I had adopted a habit of thinking of him as *my* grandfather and no relation of theirs, but he was Mother's father and their grandfather as well as mine. I now wondered if I was wrong to assume that my half brother and sister had not met him. Since I left home a rapprochement might have taken place, but I would not ask about that in front of this dry lawyer from Edinburgh.

Cosmo said thoughtfully, "Invercorrie would make a wonderful hotel for about four months in the summer. Tourists would go mad over it. Garages with rooms over could be built around the courtyard."

"Turn it into a kind of motel, do you mean?"

He missed my sarcasm. "Yes. Or something much grander. One would have to make it tremendously expensive, of course, to keep up the right standard."

The mention of standard brought to my mind a different kind of standard, a torn and stained silken banner which hung on one wall of the great hall in Invercorrie, the device scarcely recognizable, the bloodstains rusty and dark. It had been carried across the breadth of Scotland with Bonnie Prince Charlie's party after the battle of Culloden, a bloody and treacherous fight which lasted for only half an hour but which changed the history of Scotland. After the Prince's embarkation at the silver sands of Morar, north of Skerran, the flag had been brought by a Cluny, most trusted of the Prince's companions, and left at the Castle for safekeeping. Whether the then occupant had permission to keep it for always was not recorded, but it had hung in the great hall ever since, for over two hundred years now, and I disliked the thought of its quiet resting place being turned into a hotel. Tourists were neither gullible nor trusting—they would think the banner a fake, put there for their benefit.

Flora saw my distaste and murmured something about luncheon, but Mr. Sanders said that first we ought to bring the silver leopard from the bureau and I could take it away with me.

"There is no silver leopard," Cosmo said abruptly.

"What do you mean?" Mr. Sanders' fingers were moving again.

"What I say, sir. It disappeared a few months after Father was drowned. You remember, Flora. Mother was in quite a state about it. Questioned the servants, and a maid left."

Flora nodded. "It is true, Mr. Sanders. It all happened just as Cosmo says."

The lawyer remained silent for a moment, then he said, "You won't mind if I have a word with the housekeeper?"

"You are not doubting our word?" Flora was coldly angry.

"No. No. Not at all. But she may have some additional information or a theory of her own. I remember having formed a good opinion of her at the time of your father's death. A sensible woman."

"Indeed, she is." Flora moved to the bell and pressed it.

I tried to remember a resident maid and failed. Apart from a man who doubled as groom and gardener, the house was run, so far as I knew, by Mrs. Munro with the help of two "dailies" who cycled from village or croft.

"Was the loss of the silver leopard reported to the police?" I asked.

Before either Flora or Cosmo could answer, Mrs. Munro knocked quietly and entered the room. Mr. Sanders glanced at me noncommittally but I received the unmistakable impression that he would prefer it if I kept silent and allowed him to do any questioning.

"Mr. Sanders would like to talk to you, Mrs. Munro." Flora turned to the lawyer. "Shall we leave?"

"There is no need. Mrs. Munro, do you remember a certain silver leopard which was kept, apparently, in a cupboard in the late Mrs. Cunningham's bureau?"

"The one which disappeared, yes."

"Disappeared." He repeated the word thoughtfully. "At the time, did no one think it had been stolen?"

"Only a maid, a young island girl who had just started working here. She thought she was being wrongfully accused, there was no pacifying her, and she left."

"When did this happen? Do you remember?"

"About eighteen months ago. March or April."

At the end of March last year I had been here in the house, briefly for Easter, so I spoke up. "It must have been April, surely?"

"What makes you say that, Miss Westwood?"

"I was here at the end of March and there was no resident maid and no mention of the silver leopard, so obviously it had not been taken then. Or it had not been missed," I added.

"Quite." Mr. Sanders frowned, looking down at his thin hands, which were lacing themselves together as if of their own volition. "Have you any theories about the ornament's disappearance, Mrs. Munro? Did Mrs. Cunningham have any theories at the time?"

"At first we thought it had been mislaid—put in a different place by Mrs. Cunningham herself, but then she . . ."

"Yes?"

"She did say . . ." Mrs. Munro paused, her thin olive face flushing with distress. "I don't like to repeat the words of the dead, words uttered in anger, forby, and the lady not here to be able to correct me if I'm wrong."

"But she did say something, and you feel you have recalled it accurately?"

"I think so."

"Then what is it?"

"She said, 'As nothing else has gone, I must assume someone in this house has taken the leopard for a specific reason.' "

"How many people knew where it was, Mrs. Munro? Can you tell me that?"

"It was no secret that it was in the bureau. When the other silver was cleaned, that leopard was cleaned, too. Not that it ever needed more than a rub, it being kept in the dark and always dry. It's the mists hereabouts that tarnish the silver."

"Yes, I see. Thank you, Mrs. Munro."

The stiff back retreated, head high, dark bun of hair as smooth as a rubber ball.

"You can add nothing to that?" Mr. Sanders addressed Flora when the door had closed. She shook her head silently. "Miss Westwood, I shall have to give this some thought. Inquiries will have to be made and I'll do what I can. May I suggest I write to you about it? If the ornament cannot be found, perhaps some reparation may be made, from the estate."

"No!" The word burst from me.

"Are you trying to tell me that you do not want me to make inquiries? For, if so, I would have to advise you, as your family lawyer, that the matter ought to be investigated more fully. You are entitled to receive your inheritance, small though it is."

I wanted to shout at him, to tell him that he was not *my* lawyer, but I knew that my exaggerated emotion was due to the strain of the past two days, a strain which was beginning to jangle my nerves. I forced myself to be calm. "It is a pity that the leopard has gone," I said quietly, "but I know that my mother would have made all possible investigation at the time when the loss was discovered, so I can see no point in reopening old wounds now. Please. I'd just rather . . . forget it."

The lawyer pursed his thin lips in disapproval. Flora looked troubled and Cosmo interested, as if he had not expected me to react in this way and wondered why I was being so forbearing. I could have told him, for the answer was simple enough. There had been a welter of bitter argument in this house in the past, with myself instigating it. I wanted no more.

"Don't you want to know what happened to the leopard?" Cosmo asked. "Aren't you the least bit curious?"

"Are we likely to find out, so long after the event?" I felt suddenly weary. "And does it matter?"

"Perhaps you know where it is." Cosmo's bright eyes were full of malice.

"Just what do you mean by that?"

"Nothing you need to take exception to. After all, it is yours." He paused. "And you were here just before we discovered it was missing."

I began to see a resemblance between Cosmo and his late, detestable father. "As you say, it is mine," I snapped. "Therefore, if I had wanted it, I would have asked my mother to hand it over to me. I certainly would not have helped myself to it and thrown suspicion onto others."

Testily the lawyer clicked his tongue. "This kind of argument serves no useful purpose. Was the thing valuable?"

"Not particularly."

"It was beautiful. I liked it, too." Flora spoke softly, regretfully. "Caroline, you said that you didn't want reparation, but you would like to have something of Mother's as a memento, wouldn't you? Please, come upstairs with me now and choose a piece of jewelry. Nothing is very valuable, but there are some pretty brooches and rings and a bracelet or two."

The lawyer exuded approval and I tried to put from me a feather of suspicion which curled at the back of my mind. Flora had never been particularly generous where I was concerned and this warm concern was out of character. And yet, how did I know the adult Flora? She might have changed. She, too, might be anxious to forget the antagonism which had existed between us.

"Thank you," I said stiffly, "you are very kind."

I followed Flora upstairs and into Mother's bedroom. How well I remembered the big windows at the front of the house with views of the birchwood to the left and, down the driveway and through the wrought-iron gates, a glimpse of the loch, gray now, and chopped with white. Beyond the loch the mountains were dark and forbidding, the purple of the heather dimmed without sunshine, green bracken brushed with the first brown smudge of decay. One cold night had touched the landscape with the unmistakable threat of winter.

"Here. Choose whatever you would like to have." Flora was opening two drawers, each with a lining of velvet on which rested small pieces of jewelry. From a larger drawer she took leather boxes and opened them. A gold chain and pendant, a pearl necklace, a watch. I glanced at them, and away. "Her engagement ring, the one she had from my father," I said hesitantly. "It was a sapphire, I remember. Would it be all right if I had that?"

Flora frowned, her finely plucked eyebrows drawing together above the blue eyes. "A sapphire? I never remember her wearing a ring like that."

"Well, she wouldn't perhaps."

"No, of course. I see what you mean. Well, let's look for it, though I'm bound to say that I have never seen a sapphire ring."

"You've looked through the jewelry?"

After a moment's hesitation Flora nodded. "Perhaps Mummy sold it after . . . your father died."

I knew Margaret Westwood Cunningham better than Flora did. She would never have sold the engagement ring given to her by my father. Her marriage to him had been one of great happiness, founded on love. Suddenly I wanted to be finished with this charade. "Never mind," I said quickly. "If you come across the sapphire ring later, in

55

some other place, perhaps you will let me have it. Meanwhile, I'd like this, if you are not specially fond of it?"

I had chosen a small silver brooch, a circlet of ivy leaves, that I had seen my mother wearing often at Invercorrie.

"But that isn't worth *anything*." Flora looked astonished.

"It is to me."

She laughed, an abrupt, hollow sound. "Oh, no! Do you think I am going to let you go back to that lawyer with a Victorian brooch of no value whatever, which you claim as suitable reparation for a silver ornament worth a great deal more? Try again!"

I felt myself flushing. "If you imagine I chose something of little value in order to strike an attitude of some sort, you are quite mistaken."

And yet I could see her point of view. My choice had nothing to do with the lawyer's opinion, it merely satisfied my own wish to avoid anything which belonged solely to the Cunningham period of my mother's life. I could remember the ivy-leaved brooch from Invercorrie days. Though I suppose Mother must have had other trinkets there, the engagement ring was the only other thing I could positively recall beyond any doubt. She had seldom worn jewelry except in the evening.

Flora was looking at me with her blue eyes snapping. My reply had not satisfied her and she said, in sharp exasperation, "I don't know whether to believe you or not. I never do. Here, take these—you can't object to accepting a string of pearls."

She snapped a tan leather box shut and handed it to me. The pearls were a single string, resting on a pale blue velvet pad, and I'd thought them pretty. Unhappy at having shattered our brief period of rapport, I took the box and stiffly murmured my thanks. Flora walked out of the room and down the wide curving staircase. I followed her, passing a stained-glass window and the great wheel of ancient weapons. To my surprise, I felt a pang of regret that this would be my final visit to Quern Lodge. It was, after all, a lovely place and had been my home. But I quickly dismissed my feeling as sentimentality. There was nothing here for me now.

Mr. Sanders was pleased with the gift, or choice, or whatever it was, of pearls, and seemed to be prepared to forget the leopard, since I was so insistent that I wanted no further inquiries made. We lunched on cold chicken with delicious salads and brown rolls, followed by a lemon pudding, and we drank a golden German wine. As Mr. Sanders prepared to leave, I asked if he would give me a lift back to The Drums. He agreed at once, but Flora, with a soft exclamation of disappointment, pressed me to stay for another half hour and have some coffee. "I can run you down to The Drums," she added. She had returned to her former gentle manner, and though I did not want to prolong this visit, there was plenty of time before I need set out for Invercorrie Castle. It was difficult to refuse Flora's offer without appearing to be extremely churlish, and so I accepted. Privately I thought that she did not want me to be alone with the lawyer, but as I had nothing to say to Mr. Sanders, she had little to worry about.

Cosmo said goodbye to us after the lawyer had gone, explaining that he had work to do in the stables. Our leave-taking was formal but pleasant enough. Mrs. Munro brought fresh coffee to the large drawing room, piled more logs on the fire and withdrew, unobtrusive and quiet, as always. Settling back after pouring coffee, Flora said conversationally, "I am so glad you are having the pearls. I hope you will often wear them. They were an anniversary present from my father."

I looked at her sharply. I was not mistaken, the bland

57

tone of voice belied a malicious gleam in her eyes. This, then, was why she had wanted me to stay after the lawyer's departure. She knew with absolute certainty that I had hated her father and would wear nothing which he had given Mother. She had deliberately selected an anniversary present to give to me, knowing I would later refuse it. She had gambled, moreover, on my handing it back to her. Well, I would not hand it back and her gamble had failed, but I would not take it out of this house, either.

"Indeed? How interesting." My poise recovered, my voice level, I set my cup aside and rose. Strolling to the bell, I pushed it, ignored Flora's snappish "What are you doing?" and waited on my feet with my back to the fire until Mrs. Munro came in.

Reaching into my handbag, I said, "Mrs. Munro, I want you to have something which belonged to my mother, to remember her by. I shall send a letter to you by Mr. Sanders to go with the gift, but please accept this now."

She glanced uncertainly from me to Flora, then opened the leather box which I held out to her. "Your mother's pearls! Oh, they're beautiful. Thank you, Miss Caroline. I shall treasure them." Her sallow face was pink, the stern composed expression quite softened as she looked at me with a gratitude I did not deserve, considering the motive for my gift. There even seemed to be tears in her eyes. Mrs. Munro left the room without looking at Flora, which was fortunate, for, under her tan, Flora was white with rage, and to me she hissed, "You bitch!"

I raised my eyebrows. "Why? For giving Mrs. Munro a small memento?"

Laughing at my beautiful half sister's angry expression, I got up to leave.

"You'll have to walk. I'll not drive you!"

I made no reply to this parting shot other than to smile.

I walked out of the house and down the drive, breathing deeply of the clean, damp air, and feeling the most enormous sense of relief because I need never enter Quern Lodge again and was leaving now without any regret. I grieved only for my mother.

# 4

THE TWO-MILE walk from the
gates of Quern Lodge to The Drums made my left leg
ache a little but it was the kind of exercise I needed to
strengthen the muscles, and by the time I reached the
graveled courtyard I felt calm and refreshed. A thin, misty
drizzle was clearing and watery sunshine glinted fitfully,
spotlighting small areas of mountainside, fingering wood
and water, moving restlessly, glowing and fading again.
The worst part of my visit to Scotland was over. At least
I hoped so, for I wanted my reunion with Grandfather
to be peaceable, whether it was loving or not. Neither he
nor I could give affection to order, I fancied, and after a
gap of twenty years we might both find that there was no
warmth of feeling left between us.

Dan Drummond had gone out, I was told, but he had
left the keys at the desk, together with a message saying
that the car could be returned to Fort William at any
time, and that although my room at The Drums had been
let, there were others. If I wished to come back that night,
they would be pleased to accommodate me.

"You'll find your suitcase in the car, Miss Westwood."
The receptionist smiled.

I found not only the case but a parcel which had "From
Julian" scrawled on the outside of heather-sprigged wrap-

ping paper. I opened it and saw a very thick, high-necked white sweater, which I held to my face in delight, loving the soft feel of the wool. How thoughtful he was. I pictured him going into one of the tourist shops in Fort William to choose it and giving a description of my size. I rewrapped the sweater loosely and put the parcel on the back seat.

When I set off for the Castle in the hired blue Ford, it was with a slightly queasy feeling in my stomach, for I realized that I wanted more than a peaceful meeting, after all. I wanted to like my grandfather and for him to like me.

I sped along by the loch, past the entrance to Quern Lodge, and followed a rough road which turned north and then west over a moor and between acres of pinewood, to emerge eventually on a rocky spur, where I parked. Below me snaked the small, clear River Branta, which tumbled into a loch of the same name, and there at last, on its own high rock, jutting out where Branta met the great sea loch, I could see the mass of Invercorrie Castle itself. As I watched, the sun came out from behind a bank of heavy gray cloud, flooding the scene with light and warming the cold gray stone of the Castle. I hoped it was a good omen. As I was early, I sat there for a quarter of an hour, drinking in the scene.

The Castle had been built to withstand attack from wind, weather and armored men: the stone walls nine feet thick; the only approach from the landward side a narrow causeway leading to double doors of immense height which I knew to be solid oak. They filled a stone archway and were usually operated, unless things had changed, by an electrical mechanism, the modern equivalent of clansmen of the past who would have lived within the walls and run to do their chief's bidding, opening and closing the heavy doors manually whenever it was required of them.

Invercorrie's resemblance to a figure eight was clearly visible from up here, for one had almost a bird's-eye view. The Castle itself rose stark, with a battlemented wall and four round towers, like a child's fort. A second causeway had been laid over jagged rocks, and this linked the Castle to a walled garden, on the landward side of which there were buildings, originally stables and storerooms, which had been converted to servants' quarters. From up here, part of the garden could be seen, with lawn and flower beds looking like a patterned carpet.

The walls protected flowers and plants from salt and wind, but from sea level the edifice seemed merely part of the Castle, an extension of Invercorrie. Heaven alone knew how many carts of soil must have been hauled from the mainland centuries earlier over the first causeway, through that great arched doorway to an inner courtyard and out again through a similar door to cross the narrower causeway and enter the walled garden. Certainly my grandfather had added truckloads of fresh loam before planting the quantities of shrubs and plants which he loved. I wondered if the climbing roses were still as glorious as they remained in my memory. As a child, I had gathered basketfuls of petals, along with rosemary, lavender and herbs, for my mother to make potpourri. I could smell the tangy scent now. The garden was sheltered, safe and, in my memory, always warm, with honeyed light pouring over it. How unhappy I had been at leaving.

Except on a calm day, no boat would approach the scattering of razor-edged rocks which pierced the water by the garden causeway. As I watched, I could see foam creaming over glistening ridges of stone and falling back into a trough of boiling sea. Sea lochs are in no way similar to landlocked waters; they are great arms of the sea, reaching far into the land, often from five to ten miles wide and subject to all the perils of storms at sea. Invercorrie, when built centuries ago, was nearly impregnable and enviably safe.

At exactly ten minutes to four the great doors swung slowly open, and I knew that they had been opened in readiness for my arrival. This preparation, too, I remembered from my childhood. Ten minutes before anyone was due, a servant opened the gates and waited in a small lodge room for the visitor to cross the causeway. Once inside, the gates would be closed again.

I reached for the ignition key, preparing to start the engine, and noticed that my fingers were trembling. It was absurd to be so nervous. Either the afternoon would be a success or it would not. A reconciliation would be pleasant, and if one took place, I would keep in touch with my grandfather by letter, but I thought I had no desire to live in the Highlands again.

The engine sprang to life under my touch and at the same moment I became aware of a flash of light over to my right. It had come from some scrubby trees, mostly hawthorn, scoured and sculpted by the wind into distorted, huddled shapes, bending away from the sea towards the ground to escape the most savage of the winter gales. While I watched, twin points of light glittered once more and vanished. There was no mistaking the flash of sunlight on a pair of binoculars, and with a shiver I wondered who was sufficiently interested in Invercorrie to watch the Castle from such a vantage point. The undergrowth was backed by dark acres of the Forestry Commission's pines, so there was no way of knowing whether the watcher had emerged from the wood before or after my arrival. I wondered whether he or she had known I was there. The track was banked on either side of me at this point, but if I could see light on binoculars, then sun on the metal and glass

63

of my car would be a hundred times more obvious and the watcher must have seen me. I would have given a great deal to get out of the car and walk towards that clump of trees, but I was expected at Invercorrie, where unpunctuality was a crime. Besides, I was afraid. A gamekeeper would not mind showing himself, binoculars and all, so whoever was in the bushes wanted to hide, and watch, unidentified. I speculated uneasily about the motive but no one knew I was bound for Invercorrie. It was probably a tourist, a bird watcher.

As I bumped over the rough road, winding downwards in second gear and making a good deal of noise in the process, I turned once to search the bushes, the track above me where I had been parked, and the trees behind, my eyes fixing on every dark shadow. I saw no one.

Moments later I entered the courtyard to Invercorrie Castle in my car, a Lilliputian visitor to a Brobdingnagian world. A young man, whom I took to be a gardener detailed to watch for me, emerged from the small lodge while the gates were still closing. The mechanism worked as if by magic, making a prisoner of me, for I had never operated those gates.

"Will you come this way, Miss Westwood?"

I had a swift impression of size, of tousled dark hair, dark eyes and a sulky mouth. The jeans and T-shirt were clean, the hands rough, callused and earth-stained. Yes, a gardener. He had opened the car door for me and stood holding it, erect, respectful yet not—what was the word I wanted—disinterested. He knew about me, not merely that I was expected, but that I was Ian MacRobert's granddaughter. I shook off a momentary feeling of surprise. Every servant here would know who I was and all about the early quarrel between my mother and grandfather. The stale, old scandals would have been revived and retold, recalled to mind by the death of my mother, enlarged upon and embroidered. I felt as if I were about to be put under a microscope. For a moment my eyes met those of the gardener and I had an elusive will-o'-the-wisp feeling of having seen him before, but he was too young to have been working at the Castle for long.

Coolly, without speaking, I got out of the car. The courtyard had not changed except that the bay trees flanking the stone arched doorway had grown larger. There were roses, hydrangeas and geraniums in containers on all sides, softening the grim, old walls and making the yard fragrant with scent, noisy with bees. The door opened and I could see a man I took to be the butler, Mackenzie, waiting for me—a tall, well-built man with short gray hair, pale eyes and a tight, prim mouth. He opened the door wider as I approached and came out onto the first of four steps which curved round the door in shallow semicircles of pleasant yellowish stone, worn hollow by centuries of use. There was a mounting block near the door and iron scrapers in the form of wild cats snarling.

The butler bowed deferentially and said, "Good afternoon, Miss Westwood." Then, with quiet authority, he added, "Would you let me have your car keys, please? We park cars on the gravel at the side of the courtyard. The master is very particular about oil stains on the stone flags."

I could not remember any gravel in the courtyard, and as I handed over the keys I glanced over my shoulder. Sure enough, there was a strip of gravel at the far end, and the gardener came forward to take the keys from Mackenzie, clearly having expected this, and lingered, waiting for the order to move my car. I turned to follow the butler inside, plunging into the dimness of the paneled hall with a feeling of nervous dread as the moment approached when I would face my grandfather again.

The sight and smell of dark wood and good wax polish lavishly applied were exactly as I remembered them. For a castle, Invercorrie was not particularly large, but in my memory this hall had been vast and lofty and now I saw that memory had not lied. It was two stories high and a gallery at upper-floor level ran round three sides. Off the gallery, doorways led to several rooms. On the paneling there hung the inevitable weapons and antlers, mandatory adjuncts to a Scottish castle, but here they were relieved by some good oil paintings and even a tapestry, all grays and browns, a battle scene with horses and knights in armor, threadbare in places but expertly repaired and immensely valuable, I thought.

The butler's footsteps remained soundless, while mine clicked lightly on occasional polished wood surfaces between islands of Oriental rugs, gold and brown, glowing even in the subdued light which filtered from narrow stained-glass windows on either side of the front door, above which hung the stained, silken banner from Culloden.

After showing me into the empty drawing room of Invercorrie Castle, Mackenzie withdrew. Immediately I was overcome by a powerful resurgence of childhood impressions. The room had changed little, and I walked straight into the west-facing windowed tower, where I remembered playing as a child, imagining myself to be at sea in the prow of a high vessel. One of the Castle's four round towers jutted from a corner of this large, square room, and from Grandfather's bedroom above it, right into the water. The windows were a recent substitute for arrow slits, making the tower a room on its own, filled with light. Instead of sitting down I stood and eagerly looked out at the contrasting views.

To my left there was the forbidding sight of castle walls growing out of rock, and below, water breaking into white foam, clawing at the stone and falling back. Ahead I could see miles of sea, dotted in the western distance with islands, and to my right, sea again and the stone causeway which spanned turbulent water and sharp rocks to reach the walled garden set on its own level outcrop. There were glimpses of hills and woods beyond the sea-girt mass, and for an instant I remembered with uneasiness that unknown eyes had watched me while I was parked over there on the hillside track. Then I shook off the absurd fancy. No one could have been watching *me*, for no one knew I had planned to come to Invercorrie except Julian, and he would be well on his way to London by now. Tenderness surged through me at the recollection of his kindness.

The footsteps, when they came, were not at all the ones I remembered. Those had been firm and strong; these were soft, shuffling and punctuated by the tap of a rubber-tipped walking stick. Twenty years had turned me from a child into a woman, but those same years had sent Grandfather scurrying along the final downhill path. At seventy-eight, he looked his years, frail in body though indomitable in spirit.

The spare body was shrunken, so that he was shorter than I, and I'd remembered a big man—misremembered, for obviously he had never been tall. The skin of his face had an unhealthy tinge and over the cheekbones there were no wrinkles; the skin was polished and transparent, as thin and fine as tissue paper. Saddest of all was the way in which brilliant light had vanished from the intensely blue eyes which my mother and all her children had inherited. He submitted to my scrutiny and I to his, and finally he said dryly, "Well, child, we've both changed. I trust you will not throw anything at me this time."

My throat constricted. The only thing I wanted to throw was myself. I wanted to run and cradle him in my strong young arms, to be close to him quickly, without words, as if, by avoiding apologies and explanations, by cutting through formal greetings, we might arrive at immediate, basic human contact and reestablish the rapport we had once known. And yet as a child I had been in awe of Ian MacRobert. He had been formidable and strict, but I had never doubted his love, which was why his long silence had hurt so much. My gradual awakening to the realization that he was not going to get in touch with me, or forgive us for leaving, had been my first experience of adult implacability.

What a pity, I was to think later, that I did not throw myself at him that afternoon. In Scotland one is early indoctrinated against outward show of emotion, but there are times when nothing else will serve, when the avoidance of it perpetuates misunderstanding. I hesitated, guilt flooding into me so that I stood rooted and stiff. Then, with what I'd intended to be a friendly smile but knew was merely a polite one, I said, "Hello, Grandfather. I shall not throw anything at you. I have changed that much, at least. I have a little more self-control."

"So I see. I suppose I should be glad of it!" He shuffled into the tower bay, moving with frail persistence, lowered himself slowly into a high-backed armchair and looked up at me, nodding slowly to himself as if what he saw had confirmed his expectation. I hoped I pleased him, but there was no way of knowing from the expression on his face. It was austere, unyielding, arrogantly aristocratic, and there flashed into my mind a realization of the revulsion with which he must have viewed the sight of his only child, his beloved daughter, throwing herself away on the worthless Angus Cunningham. Grandfather must have been outraged, and for that I could not blame him.

Tea arrived at once, and I noted that the Crown Derby

service, with its rich colors of blue, gold and rust, was still used. Grandfather asked me to pour, which I did, handling the silver pot with a strange sensation, remembering how my mother had presided in this very place, sitting perhaps in this same buttoned Victorian chair with soft down cushions at her back, and pouring tea for the man who now sat opposite me.

Sadly, I had no memory at all of Mother pouring for my own father, and Angus Cunningham had scorned tea, staying out on the moors or sailing until six o'clock, when he would come in, loudly boisterous, to pour one enormous drink immediately, before retiring upstairs to bathe and change. Then he would come down and begin drinking in earnest until eight o'clock dinner, becoming first affectionate, then aggressive and finally, the worst of all, maudlin. In my early years at Quern Lodge I'd been protected from the full cycle, seeing only the early stages before having supper and going to bed before the adult dinner hour. I had resented my banishment, wanting to share Mother with my stepfather, feeling shut out of her life to a greater extent than I had been at the Castle. Now, of course, I understood it all much better and was sorry for my mother, saddled with such a husband and a rebellious and difficult daughter as well.

I must have allowed a wry smile to cross my features, for Grandfather said, "What is amusing you?" as he offered, with a blue-veined hand, tiny scones spread with butter.

"I was thinking what a difficult child I must have been for my mother to deal with." In the act of raising the scone to my mouth, I paused and laid it on my plate again, deciding to be honest about my feelings. I owed Grandfather that much. "I missed the Castle dreadfully, you see. And I missed you. I was very lonely."

"Lonely?" He looked startled. "But there was young Morrison at Ardnacol House, and before you could turn round, a half brother and sister to play with. Here you had no one at all. Your memory is playing tricks with you, my dear girl. You were lonelier here, isolated and cut off from other young people. Possibly we didn't do enough to gather children here at the Castle for you to play with."

I wanted to point out that Robb was eight years older than I and Flora eight years younger—impossible gaps in childhood—also, I would have liked to add that there is a loneliness of the spirit which does not stem from being alone, but even to myself that sounded pompous, so I kept silent, and after a moment Grandfather went on testily, "Really, you know, there weren't any children around at the time—still aren't, come to that. Half the young people get married straight out of school and go to live in towns, while the other half don't get married at all, or at least leave it far too late. If they remain here in the country, they don't do much to populate it."

Lightly, I said, "I don't fit into either category—I live in London, but I am not married."

"Why not?" He barked the question.

"I beg your pardon?"

"I asked why you are not married. You had a young fellow with you when you came up, I understand."

I lifted my eyebrows. "You are well informed in spite of being a recluse."

"Who says I am a recluse?"

"Aren't you?"

It was like a repetition of conversations he'd had with my mother. They had gone on like this many times, with Grandfather barking questions and Mother giving oblique answers until at last an explosion came. Usually Mother simply rebelled and we would go away for a few days, to Edinburgh or Inverness, or even abroad, and then we would return to comparative but short-lived peace before the cycle started again. For the first time I saw that my mother's marriage to Angus Cunningham might have been partly an escape from Ian MacRobert. In her place, I thought, I would have tried to find a job where I could keep my child with me, but that was not Mother's style. Country-house living had been her background and she would not easily adapt to anything else. Although my father farmed, it had been with the assistance of a factor and my mother had not been a typical farmer's wife at all. I doubted if she had even so much as gathered up a basket of eggs.

I looked at Ian MacRobert and frowned. I had told him of my loneliness in childhood and that I had missed his friendship and love. He cared nothing for that. He dismissed my frankness and said that my memory was playing tricks. Perhaps he was right, for in my recollection there had been a bond of understanding between us, but now I saw a selfish old man, frail and unwell enough to bring a stirring of pity, such as one would feel for a similar figure seen in a hotel or walking in the streets. I felt pity for a stranger, but beyond that, nothing, for he was in truth a stranger to me and I could not think of him as Grandfather.

"I feel a draft. Ring the bell." He twitched moodily in his chair and waved a bony white finger in the general direction of a green silk bell-rope which he could have reached with little effort. Silently I rose and pulled it, half expecting to hear a bell, but in that stone-walled edifice sounds did not penetrate from room to room. After perhaps half a minute, thirty seconds of silence between us, the door opened after a discreet knock and Mackenzie advanced.

"Close the window, Mackenzie."

"Certainly, sir." He closed the window and withdrew as quietly as he had entered.

I was filled with amazement. I supposed there were still

71

a few houses in England where servants were summoned to close windows or put more coal on the fire, as had once been commonplace, but there could not be many. In royal houses or ducal palaces, perhaps it was still usual, but here, with me sitting beside the man and perfectly well able to close a window, it seemed absolutely ridiculous and I did not know whether to be cross or to burst out laughing.

"Now, will you have another cup of tea?" The tone was polite, even charming. Grandfather's equilibrium was restored, and after refusing more tea for myself, I poured a cup for him.

"You haven't told me about the man who came with you."

"No, I haven't." I spoke mildly, without expression.

"I see. None of my business, is that it? Well, I suppose that means it's serious—a serious relationship, that's what they call it these days, isn't it? Oh, I do read the papers, even if I am a recluse."

I could have shaken him but took refuge in irony. "A meaningful relationship is what they call it, actually. But ours isn't that kind of relationship."

"He came with you to your mother's funeral." The old man's voice had cracked just a shade on the word "funeral." He had felt this more than he was prepared to admit openly, I thought.

"Yes, he did. It was kind of him, for he came at very short notice simply because he thought I ought not to drive up alone. I didn't hear about Mother's death, you see, until the day before the funeral."

"And that was Flora's doing, no doubt. A true daughter of her father." He fairly spat the words, so, in justice, I explained that I had been away, attending sales, when Flora first tried to get in touch. But he only grunted, and with a sudden, jerky movement, leaned sideways and himself tugged at the bell-rope. I rose to take my leave, but irritably, with a stabbing finger, he indicated that I should sit down again, and when Mackenzie came in, he gestured to him to take away the tea things. "And bring that piece of silver, will you?"

"Yes, sir."

I wondered if Mackenzie ever refused to do anything he was asked. He was a cold, humorless stick of a man but a well-trained servant. I preferred the homelier Stockton of my youth.

Clouds were bowling up out of the west in great surging swells, hiding the sun, darkening the sea, chilling what had been a sunny corner, and I could see by the distant gray rods which slanted down into the water that they were bringing rain. My spirits sank. This visit had not been a success, nothing had come of it—no reconciliation, merely a sense of anticlimax. The bond that never was, that was the truth of it. An imaginary bond, forged in the mind of a lonely and fanciful child.

Mackenzie brought the piece of silver on a tray which he held in two hands reverentially, and I gazed at it in astonishment. It was the silver leopard. I recognized the loping prowl, with leg muscles shown by a master silversmith, the spots indicated by tiny indentations, the eyes silvered over, the mouth open and snarling. A narrow chased collar round the neck made a wild creature into a dangerous-looking pet.

"Recognize it, do you?" Grandfather MacRobert chuckled, his blue eyes watching me.

"I threw it at you," I said and watched him turn it this way and that in his frail hands. "Not this one," he said, half to himself, "not this one. There are two."

I was surprised. Only one had been on display when I had lived here. At least, that was what I thought, but as a child I was not allowed into every part of the Castle.

73

"The one I gave you is missing, I understand."

Mackenzie coughed, a short, dry sound. "Sir, Mr. Morrison is here."

"Is he? Well, show him in, show him in. And put this back where it belongs." He put the leopard down gently on the outstretched tray without allowing me to touch it.

Suddenly there were a great many questions I wanted to ask and there was no time. Mr. Morrison could only mean Robb and I wondered what he was doing at Invercorrie Castle. I also wanted to know how my grandfather had known that my leopard was missing.

If, as my mother half suspected, it had been taken by someone living in Quern Lodge, my grandfather might have recovered it. If so, perhaps there was only one leopard, the one Mackenzie was taking away. Grandfather was welcome to it if he wanted it so much. My childish preoccupation with the silver leopard had dwindled over the years. Because I handled so many beautiful things in my chosen profession and had a full life of my own, inanimate objects meant less to me now, but I would have liked to examine it more closely.

"Well, Robb, she came, you see. I was right. I said she would."

"I'm glad." Robb was wearing a creamy-white Arran-knit pullover and dark-brown slacks. He came forward and bent to shake the old man by the hand. Then he straightened and looked at me. There was immense depth of feeling in those gray eyes—interest, sympathy, kindness and all the warmth I had found there as a child. In addition, there was something else, a bright flicker of such passionate intensity that I could not look away from it until a grunt from Grandfather distracted us and the grip of eye and mind broke.

"Sit down, sit down, both of you."

I turned, to see a momentary smile of satisfaction before

74

it faded into one of innocuous bland charm. Oh, I was beginning to hate the old man, sitting there, manipulating servants, friends and relatives. He might be weak in body now but he was relentlessly strong in will.

"Did you have a bet on my visit?" I just managed not to sneer.

"We did, and I've won!" Grandfather's triumph was obvious, while Robb looked amused and not discomfited at all.

I'd had enough. I got to my feet and said briskly, "I must go."

"When Robb Morrison has just this moment arrived? Surely not."

Robb himself said nothing and I felt color creeping into my cheeks. "I don't wish to appear rude, but there is going to be a storm and I must be on my way."

Grandfather scowled, annoyed at being thwarted, I thought, but indifferent to my presence. I could go or stay, for all he cared. I wondered why Robb was here and whether he came often.

There came a rattle of windowpane, a roar of wind and a sound like machine-gun fire, as rain drove against the windows with tremendous force, streaming down the glass and blotting out the view.

"The storm is already here," Robb said dryly. "And that white suit is hardly the job for this weather."

"I have warm things in the car." It was a slight exaggeration but I thought with gratitude of the present of a thick sweater from Julian.

"Come, we'll move away from the window and you'll take a glass of something warming before you set out."

Grandfather struggled to his feet, pulled the bell-rope himself once more and led the way to the enormous fireplace in the main part of the room where a few logs smoldered. "Kick it into life, Robb," he said, and when Mackenzie appeared, no doubt expecting to have to deal with the fire, it was already blazing. Impassively he accepted the order to bring whisky and returned so quickly with a crystal decanter, jug of water and three large glasses that he must have had it waiting outside the door. It was smooth malt whisky and the water softness itself. I remembered that the Castle had its own well. How different whisky tasted when drunk this way. The men, of course, took theirs neat, but slowly, savoring the liquid, respecting its quality.

"You can have a bed for the night." Grandfather spoke suddenly out of a silence broken only by the crackling of the fire. Whatever had brought Robb here, it was not to be disclosed to me, it seemed.

The invitation was one I had hoped for, but uttered in this grudging and reluctant tone it repelled me. "Thank you, no."

The old man did not try to make me change my mind, but Robb looked angry. I thought he was about to protest, so I kicked a highly polished brogue which was stretched out on the rug near my foot. He looked sharply at me, and I gave the smallest negative shake of my head. Grandfather did not notice this exchange, but neither did he bring himself to repeat the invitation or demur at my refusal. He did ask, with sharp suspicion, "Are you staying overnight at Quern Lodge?"

"No."

He nodded in some satisfaction and showed no further curiosity, but little effort was required for him to guess where I would be going. No one would drive any further than the nearest hotel in this weather, and the nearest hotel was The Drums.

The gale whistled and thudded at the windows, rain tumbled down the wide chimney and hissed in the fire, and

76

I wished with all my heart that I had not come to the Castle. It had been a sad, disillusioning visit, only adding to the misery of bereavement. A happy reunion with my grandfather would not have brought my mother back, but it might at least have given some comfort and warmed a corner of Skerran for me.

I finished my whisky and rose. Robb did the same and said, "I'll drive you."

"No!" Grandfather's reaction was instantaneous and we both looked at him in surprise, Robb that he should object, I because of the vehemence. I did not want Robb Morrison to interrupt any plans he might have in order to drive me to The Drums, for I was accustomed to driving myself in all weathers and was not in the least nervous, but I did think that I should be the one to refuse his offer, and not my grandfather.

"It isn't at all necessary," I said stiffly.

"Maybe not, but I am coming," Robb said smoothly and with the kind of determination which is difficult to gainsay. Besides, he was not looking at me, only at the old man sitting back in a chair which looked too large for him.

Grandfather's expression of annoyance gave way to one of petulance, the petulance of the old. "All right, all right," he said, "please yourself."

"I shall be back in an hour or so," Robb said in crisp reassurance.

With sadness I said goodbye, taking that thin hand in mine and, on an impulse, bending to touch my lips to a cold, papery cheek. I felt a tenseness in the jaw, but he said nothing other than "Goodbye," and when we left the room he was gazing into the fire as if he did not want to see us go or had forgotten our presence at once. I did not know which.

# 5

"IF YOU would prefer to come in my car, I can have yours returned to the hotel later. I take it you are going back to The Drums?"

On the gravel strip, alongside the hired blue Ford, was Robb's own handsome Jaguar, sleek and powerful, a better car altogether for tackling bad roads in a storm.

"Yes, I'll go back there for tonight, and I'd rather take my own car. I wish you wouldn't drive me." In my response I could hear an echo of Grandfather and I laughed sheepishly. "Oh dear, I didn't mean to be ungracious."

Robb's smile illumined his bony face. "The atmosphere in there is catching." He put a hand under my elbow and we stood for a moment watching the rain bouncing up off the flagstones, forming into puddles in worn hollows, making the gravel glisten where the cars were parked.

We had let ourselves out of the Castle without summoning Mackenzie, walking across the magnificent hall quietly, like conspirators, and Robb had closed the door gently behind us. The stone portico gave protection from the worst of the rain, but the wind was swirling round the courtyard in gusts and I shivered.

"Wait here. I'll bring the car." Robb released my arm and started down the steps.

"There's no need." I was so elated at being outside the

confines of the Castle that I wanted to run, to sprint across the short distance which separated us from our transport, but I had forgotten my disability. I'd walked from Quern Lodge to the hotel this afternoon, then driven up here and sat still for too long. The weakness in my left knee suddenly asserted itself and I stumbled and would have fallen if Robb had not turned to catch me. He picked me up and stood me on my feet at the top of the steps. "All right?"

I nodded, and without wasting time he ran to the car and got in. The keys must have been in the ignition, for he started her up at once, backed around and came for the steps, where he leaped out to help me, proffering an arm and opening the nearside door.

"How gallant!" I decided to turn it into a joke, but I was mortified that my weakness had shown. Most of the time now I was able to walk without limping.

"I am always gallant when rescuing ladies from castles, if it happens to be raining." He grinned down at me, but behind the lightness in his manner there was concern, and he stowed me very carefully into the car.

When Robb got in beside me, I said, trying just once more, "You know, I can perfectly well drive myself back to The Drums, and how are you going to get back here?"

"That's simple enough. I'll borrow the spare car which Dan Drummond keeps around. He'll send for it later."

"If you're sure . . ." I knew that I was glad of his company, but it did seem to be putting him to a needless amount of trouble.

"I'm sure. Now, stop trying to get rid of me, will you?"

We stopped in the ancient gateway and he disappeared into the lodge, leaving a heavy arched door open. I could see clean flagstones, one chair made of beechwood and, mounted on a wall, some metal boxes which evidently contained the mechanism for the great gate. It opened slowly and Robb drove us out and over the causeway to the muddy mainland road.

"Aren't you going to close it?" I asked.

"No need. I've set it so that it will close itself."

"You seem to know a lot about Invercorrie Castle."

"I love the place, so I am interested in it, and I play chess with the old man occasionally."

"Is that what you came here for today?"

If Robb heard me, he gave no reply. The roadway was a torrent of water and liquid mud; he was concentrating on putting the car at a one-in-three gradient in the highest gear possible and controlling slip and skid with remarkable expertise. I was glad he had come.

"Where is that warm clothing you were talking about?" he asked, when we turned into the final bend and reached the top of the hill.

"I have a pullover here." Reaching over to the back seat, I stripped the paper off Julian's gift and began to struggle out of my jacket. Robb stopped the car to help me, easing the pale jacket off my shoulders and helping me to pull the thick sweater over my head. There was not much room in the car, and when my head emerged from the tight wool neck, his brown face was close to mine, the dark slaty eyes looking at me intently. For a moment I stared back, mesmerized, my mind tumbling back to the days when I'd been so sure that I loved this man. He drew back, leaning against the door at his side of the car to look at me with a detached and critical glance. The spell was broken.

"What is the matter with your leg?" he asked abruptly. "You've injured it in some way. When did that happen?"

"A few weeks ago. A car accident."

"Were you driving?"

"No. Julian was driving, but it wasn't his fault. A truck hit us on my side." I gave Robb brief details, and he touched my hand as it lay on my lap, saying briefly, "Bad luck," before wiping the windshield and starting the car again.

I peered out and saw dripping trees, sodden turf, dark, wet rocks at the roadside and pools of water. The sea was a gray blur, the Castle a shapeless dark mass below us.

Lightly I said, "I suppose you weren't up here when I stopped the car on my way to the Castle?"

"No. Why?" Robb snatched a quick glance at me. I was not looking at him but I could see the turn of his head from a corner of my eye.

"Someone was over there, near the trees." I waved a vague hand.

"A man?"

"I don't know. To be honest, I only saw two points of light, from the lenses of binoculars, I imagine."

"Remind me to take extreme exception to your original question." Robb sounded as if he would, too. "With or without binoculars, I do not go around watching people in cars."

Put that way, the idea was totally ridiculous and I burst out laughing. "Oh, Robb, I know that and I don't really believe this person was watching me anyway. I suppose I just happened along."

"There isn't anything to watch from here, except Invercorrie."

"And birds. Or ships at sea."

Robb grunted. The car bounced slowly in and out of a pothole and rolled onto a better surface between Forestry Commission pines which were whipping about in the gale. Robb accelerated.

The combined noise of car engine and wind was intensified among the trees, for our road was acting as a funnel, with the wind forcing its way along behind us. We could have used sails. The rain and wind were unpleasant but the storm seemed in no way dangerous, even in the wind. Yet a moment later we both saw a pine tree to our left beginning to fall, incredibly slowly, across the track.

If I had been driving, I know I would have stamped on the brake, hoping to stop the car before I reached that ominous crashing tree and, of course, on a muddy surface I'd have gone into a skid. Robb was more experienced, wiser, quicker. He put his foot down hard on the throttle and we shot forwards, swinging from side to side on the mud but getting through before the tree, impeded by other branches, fell across the road. I had the hideous feeling that we had narrowly escaped death.

Robb stopped the car and I heard myself giving a choking kind of sound as I put my face down into wet palms. But for the driver's quick reaction, certainly we might both have been badly injured. This little car was not built to withstand much impact, and we'd avoided it by such a short distance. The rear window was dark now, with bushy fronds of pine needles almost touching, and branches at all the wrong angles. On three sides now, we were in a dark green world. It was like being under water.

"Wait here. Don't get out of the car." Robb's voice was forceful and I felt icy damp air blowing in as he opened his door and ran off, round the front of the car and into the darkness under the trees on our left. I pulled myself together, rolled down my window and could hear him crashing through the undergrowth. The rain on my face revived me. I listened, straining to hear any sound. Apart from Robb and the storm, nothing was making any noise. No birds were singing, no small creature rustled, and as Robb stopped, there was only the soughing of the wind and dripping of rain, the brushing together of branches and a creaking sound from the fallen tree. The scent of pine needles filled the damp air.

At last I heard Robb returning, and he emerged, with dead brown pine needles and bits of bark clinging to his hair and his cream pullover. His hair was wet, one elbow was smeared with green from the trunk of a tree and his face was grim. He got into the car at once and closed the door, staring ahead through the windshield, which was running with water.

"Did you hear or see anyone?" Robb asked at last.

Still puzzled, I replied, "Only you, crashing around. What did you expect to find?"

"What I did find, I suppose. But I hoped I might catch a glimpse of the murdering swine who planned that little experiment." He jerked his head backwards.

Slowly I rolled up the window at my side. The cold fresh air was bracing, but suddenly I thought I would prefer to have the car closed. I even pushed down the button which locked the door, and after a moment Robb did the same at his side. I began to pick pine needles off his pullover, dropping them on the floor in an untidy fashion and flicking ineffectually at damp wool. My mind was busy.

"Do you mean," I asked at last, carefully making my voice calm and detached, "are you trying to tell me that someone deliberately felled that tree?"

Robb looked at me then. "Which way is the wind blowing, Caroline?"

I saw his point. The tree was lying at right angles to the prevailing wind. It had not blown down.

"Was it meant to fall *now*?"

"Not much doubt about it. The trunk had been sawed almost through, a V-shaped cut, and a retaining chain is still looped around the trunk. The other end of that chain was attached to a tractor which is standing in a small clearing. One upwards blow with a heavy hammer and the ring at the end of the chain comes off the tractor's towing hook.

There is a beautiful, fresh, shiny scratch mark to prove what happened. Once released, the almost-felled tree would inevitably fall. If the other trees had not been so close, it would have fallen more quickly. That slow topple was what saved us."

I swallowed. "It couldn't be coincidental?"

Robb's voice was dry. "I didn't hear anyone shouting 'Timber!' No, Caroline, I don't think it was coincidental."

"Or done merely to frighten?"

He sighed. "Maybe. Who would want to frighten you?"

I shook my head. I'd been aware of hostility at Quern Lodge and from my grandfather, but this was more than brooding Highland resentment.

"Have you any enemies, Robb?"

"I suppose so. I haven't gone through life in a blameless vacuum, but this, Caroline Westwood, is aimed at you. We are in your blue hired car. Who knew about it? Your white sweater—I happen to be wearing a sweater which is almost white. Through a misted windshield, wiped clear only at the driver's side, it would be enough. Here you come, driving along, suspecting nothing, and—wham!"

"It isn't exactly scientific," I objected. "It might have missed altogether."

"It did."

"Yes." I sighed. "But I would have braked hard, Robb. I knew that, even while you were racing through, so if I had been driving, I might have been killed."

"You might. More likely you would have been hurt, and I imagine it is quite certain that you would have been frightened?"

"I was frightened anyway." I touched his arm in gratitude for having got me out of a situation which I didn't even like to think about.

"Frightened enough to leave here at once?" He started the car without waiting for an answer and added, "When I say 'here,' I mean Skerran, of course. I imagine that is the main object of the exercise, since obviously the perpetrator ran away and hid without waiting to see the result."

"Maybe he only ran away when he saw *you* get out of the car?"

Robb shook his head. "I would have heard him."

"He's a bungling fool, whoever he is." I spoke with contempt. "Robb, I was hoping I might be invited to stay at Invercorrie for the night. I have my bag with me in readiness and I really hoped that Grandfather and I . . . might get to know each other again. I used to be very fond of him. But his invitation was so grudging that I didn't feel like accepting it, so I came away. Don't you see, Robb, it is the merest chance that I should pass this way this evening."

"The way it was braced, the tree could have been released tomorrow morning in the same way."

"Oh, I see." It crossed my mind that Robb's reasoning was so relentless that he might have been trying to add to my fears, and a shiver ran over me.

"Cold?" he asked, with almost too much concern.

"No. I'm all right."

"Who sent the gift-wrapped white sweater?"

"Julian," I replied reluctantly.

"Ah. He knew you were going to hire a car?"

"He hired it for me, in Fort William on his way south."

"And has he arrived home safely?"

"How would I know that, Robb? He left this morning, that's all I know."

My words hung in the air between us, both of us recognizing that I could not know for certain that Julian had left, but since I knew my partner well, I hadn't the slightest doubt he would have returned to London as planned.

"Dan Drummond knew about the car, and the sweater, too, I imagine."

"Did he indeed?" Robb's voice had sharpened and was full of interest.

"To say nothing of the hotel staff and almost anyone else in these parts, including yourself." I snapped at him, thinking that here again was an instance of local gossip flying around on wings.

"Don't look for enemies where none exist, Caroline. You have enough without that, it seems."

"But why should I have enemies? What harm have I ever done anyone up here?"

The only person I had harmed was dead. I could not think of anyone else with reason to bear me a grudge, unless the Cunningham antagonism had reached paranoiac proportions, and I did not want to believe that.

"The will was read today. At the risk of sounding like a vulture, what was in it for you, Caroline?"

Robb had not changed the subject, I knew that, and I half laughed. "That's not it, Robb. Nothing was left to me."

"I don't believe it!"

"I assure you it is true. I don't mind in the least. Why should I inherit *now*? My father left money in trust for me which I received when I was twenty-one. Naturally, Mother's money should go to Flora and Cosmo."

"You are the least covetous person I know. Anyone else in your position would expect at least a third." He sounded quite cross about it.

"Why?"

"Oh, come off it, Caroline. Everyone knew that Cunningham fleeced your mother, and as your grandfather disapproved of her second marriage, he won't have given her any money, so most of her money was your father's, too, I suppose?"

"Yes, I suppose so." I spoke slowly. I truly hadn't thought of it that way.

"Well, if you aren't being threatened on account of what your mother has left you, it must be because of what your grandfather is going to leave you."

"But that's ridiculous! You heard the old so-and-so. He wouldn't leave me five pence."

"Yes, I know the old devil," Robb said and left it at that, neither agreeing nor disagreeing with my comment on inheritance, and I wondered if he had more information than I had.

"Anyway, I haven't accepted that I'm being threatened."

Robb did not answer. He was driving at a sedate pace and now said with faint irritation, "Wipe the window at your side, will you, Caroline?" I became aware that he'd kept his own window clear, and also the windshield, with a long arm and large hand coming in front of me from time to time. I had been too absorbed in my thoughts to help, and hastily I did as I was asked. Robb Morrison was not going to be taken by surprise again.

There were no further booby traps. We emerged from the pine wood onto a stretch of open moor, a mottled carpet of brown and purple heather stabbed with outcrops of rock on either side. There were patches of green, green grass and curtains and backcloths of rain. Robb stopped the car again and rolled his window down all the way. Loch Skerran was visible before us, more sheltered than Loch Branta, so instead of lashing wildly with waves and foam and windy violence, it merely slurped around like dishpan water, with only an occasional patch of foam and here and there a scattering of pale flecks like petals on a pond—gulls taking shelter from the gale.

"There's no one about," Robb said with a tinge of disappointment in his voice as he peered out of the car, searching moor and road with his eyes.

I gave a spurt of laughter. "I am not surprised."

"You've become a real town dweller, Caroline. Wet weather doesn't keep the country Scot indoors."

"Naturally. They'd never go outside if it did."

"Come now, what about yesterday?"

Yesterday. A perfect, golden day for my mother's funeral. Today would have been more suitable, with all the land in mourning. I sighed. "Yes, well, the weather is changeable in England, too. I have to admit it."

"Anyway, I wasn't looking for people in order to have a social chat. I simply wondered if we might catch a glimpse of whoever had been playing dangerous games in the woods."

"It isn't likely they'd expose themselves on an open moor afterwards, is it?"

"Probably not."

It occurred to me that the fallen tree would make things difficult for Robb. "If you go back to Invercorrie, you'll have to use the coast road." I spoke uneasily. By the coast road I meant the longer road which followed the contours of Loch Skerran, deteriorating as it went. For part of the way it was no more than a ledge between the loch and a high cliff which was subject to frequent rock falls. The use of it was discouraged by local authority and landowners alike, and there were warning devices posted at intervals. Strangers used that road, knowing no better, but locals traveled along it only when weather conditions permitted. Scenically it was marvelous, but today the surface would be tricky.

Robb shot me a glance. "I am not proposing to leave you to your own devices so soon. Which brings me to a suggestion. Why not come back with me to Ardnacol for the night? Mrs. McWhirter, my housekeeper, will make up a bed for you in no time, and needless to say I'd be delighted to see you in the house again."

88

I hesitated, remembering the cool, lofty rooms of Ard-nacol House, the beautiful furniture and, outside, the soft lowing of cattle. Robb's herds were famous. The views from the house over rolling pasture, the silver ribbon of the Ardnacol Burn and the quiet, shallow end of Loch Branta, which boasted a sandy beach, were vivid in my memory. Except for the fact that Robb's parents were now both dead and his younger brother farming in New Zealand, little would have changed.

"Are you lonely in the house with everyone gone?" I asked, trying to think of that lovely place without the gracious woman and quiet, scholarly man who had lived there long ago, and without the younger brother who had made no impact at all upon me.

"I keep too busy to think of it, most of the time. I used to imagine that James would tire of New Zealand and come home, but he won't. He has married out there, a New Zealand girl who is one of a large family, and they have two children. He has settled. It's a good thing, I suppose. There may be more future for him and his family out there. Perhaps I should go, too."

"You couldn't!" The idea was preposterous.

"Why not? You left Skerran."

"That's different."

"Why? Why is it different, Caroline? That's something I want to know."

I drew back from the intensity of his curiosity. Some of the reasons for my departure I did not discuss with anyone. "I wanted to, I suppose."

It sounded lame, and Robb made an impatient move-ment. "Not good enough. I suppose you are trying to tell me that it is none of my business."

"No, I was not trying to say that." I gave a smothered laugh. "Poor Robb, when I was young, my business was all too often your business. I brought you all my troubles, and I'm grateful that you allowed me to, but by now, mercifully, I've learned to handle my own life."

"Fair enough. But you'll come to Ardnacol for the night? You said you had your things in the car."

"Yes, I have my case, but no, Robb, I think I shall return to The Drums."

"What if they haven't a room?"

"They'll have a room—they said so this morning. But if not, if the storm has driven more travelers to shelter than they'd expected, then I shall continue to Fort William. I must go back to London tomorrow."

"Then the sooner we get to The Drums, the more chance I shall have of seeing a little more of you this evening. Besides, there are things to do. Telephone your grandfather to say that I shan't be back tonight. Call the Forestry people, and the police."

"The police! Why should you call the police?"

He turned to look at me, his thick, dark brows lifted in surprise. "There was an attempt on your life back there, Caroline. Or had you forgotten?"

"Naturally, I hadn't forgotten, but I find it hard to believe that it was really an attempt on my life."

"Well, to frighten you, then. At the very least, a dangerous prank which might have had a tragic aftermath. It is the business of the police to look into such things, and I don't propose to leave them in ignorance of what has happened."

I stared at Robb for a silent moment. He meant what he said, yet the last thing I wanted was to have the police asking about my movements, delaying me, going to Quern Lodge, perhaps, where Flora and Cosmo, bereaved and bewildered, would have to face up to a police inquiry into something they knew nothing whatever about. It was a situation which was unlikely to make our jagged relationship any smoother. The friendship of my half brother and sister mattered little to me, but somehow I felt that it was important not to involve myself in any more trouble at Quern Lodge, so despising myself for feeling that I had to plead with Robb, I leaned a little closer to him, smiling, half apologetic, half pleading.

"Robb, we don't really know that it was intended for me. It might have been the action of some practical joker, mightn't it?"

"You don't believe that and neither do I."

I had forgotten how resolute, how unyielding, how absolutely stubborn the average Scotsman could be when confronted with opposition to what he conceived to be his duty. Keeping my voice pleasant and unemotional, I said, "You know, out here on the moor, where it is less creepy, I do believe it. There is no inheritance coming to me, and if there was, dear Robb, I know of no mad forester who would be likely to chop down trees in an attempt to stop it. A gun would be far more effective and scarcely noticed at all. Anyone taking a pot shot at game could hit me instead. As for frightening me away, distance is no barrier to inheritance, is it? I could be frightened in London."

I heard my own light, flippant tone and shivered. Robb was starting the car at the time or he would have noticed. It was a long shiver, which began at the nape of my neck and traveled like a tiny avalanche of soft snow right to the base of my spine.

Looking angry, but sounding calm, Robb drove over the moor at a good, fast pace and said, "Ponder on your final remark, Caroline. It's worthy of thought."

Robb parked the car in an inconspicuous position behind The Drums, took my bag from the back and screwed up the heather-strewn paper, which he then dropped into a handy wire trash basket. Watching his actions, I got out of the car.

It had stopped raining, the smell from the flower garden was sweet and clean, the interior of the hired car utterly anonymous—not even a box of tissues spoke of occupancy, but a few pine needles were still lodged around the ledges of the rear window, despite the heavy rain.

"Difficult to get rid of, pine needles. It reminds me of Christmas." Robb's voice was expressionless, but he took a handkerchief from his pocket and flicked around the window until they had disappeared, then scuffed his foot on the gravel behind the car. "There. Nothing left to show how close we were to tangling with a pine tree. Let's forget our . . . difference of opinion, shall we?"

I glanced back at the blue Ford—the ordinary, anonymous kind of car one met everywhere—then at Robb, who was up to something, shrugged and said, "Why not?" He took my arm and we walked around the hotel and in at the front door together. I was very aware of the strong grip of that hand on my upper arm and it stayed there until we had reached the desk, thanks to the offices of a departing stranger who politely held the door open for us.

"Miss Westwood would like a room for the night, if that's possible, Mrs. Hay."

"Of course, Mr. Morrison. Mr. Drummond said that he thought Miss Westwood might return." She smiled and reached behind her for the key. "We have a very nice room for you."

Robb frowned as he heard that Drummond half expected me, but I let it pass. My attention was quickly captured by hearing his next request, which was for a table for two for dinner. "What time would you like it, Caroline?"

I opened my mouth to say that I hadn't even thought of dining yet, let alone a dinner companion, but before I had time to say anything, Robb said, "I must go and telephone the Forestry Commission. They ought to know that a tree has blown down across the road, don't you think? It might cause an accident." He put a slight emphasis on the word "blown."

I was speechless at this chicanery, but Robb did not seem to expect a reply. What he was saying was that if I had dinner with him, he would telephone only the Forestry Commission and not the police. It would be obvious to any Forestry worker, when he reached the scene, that the tree had not fallen naturally, but he would not know that we were aware of that. Without seeing the scarred trunk and noting the direction of the wind, no one could know, and no one could know that Robb had examined the tree unless some watcher had lingered in the shadows, waiting for developments. If so, and if he expected to see me, he must have been startled to see a man leap from the car.

While Robb telephoned, I waited, half listening to grumbles from other guests about the rain and the sodden landscape.

"Just look at it!" someone exclaimed.

I looked. To me it was beautiful and I felt all bubbly inside.

Robb came back from the telephone.

"This is blackmail," I said to him.

"I know." He grinned down at me, not touching me except with his smile. It was a tangible smile, warming me, and I remembered it well. "Let's eat early, he said, I'm starving."

# 6

MY ROOM at The Drums this
time was larger, better furnished, and had its own bathroom. The wallpaper was pale lavender, sprigged with white,
and there were curtains and counterpane of matching
fabric. The paintwork and furniture were all white, and
the effect was restful and charming. A moment after I had
opened my bag there came a knock at the door and a maid
entered with a vaseful of garden flowers—pale blue
scabious, lad'slove with its feathery green foliage, pink roses
and sprigs of lavender and rosemary. With a smile and a
soft "Good evening," she placed the vase on the dressing
table, where its beauty was reflected in the mirror. As she
withdrew I wondered whether the thought behind this
gesture had come from Robb, and made a mental note to
ask him. The roses had an old-fashioned perfume, spiced
delicately by the rosemary, lavendar and lad'slove. Only
the scabious seemed to lack scent, but the heavenly color
made up for it. Garden flowers mean much more to me
than hothouse blooms, and these were deliciously fragrant.
Whoever had sent them to my room, I was grateful, and
I touched gently the velvety softness of the rose petals.

Quickly I bathed, and brushed my hair until it was
smooth. Julian always called it toffee color, and that was
about right. I wished for a brief moment that I had Flora's
spectacular blond hair, which I admired greatly. But at

least I had the same blue eyes and my brows were dark and needed no penciling to define them. I used a little gray-blue shadow and that was all I needed, apart from lipstick.

Last night I had dined here with Julian. It seemed a long time ago. Guiltily I remembered that I had fallen asleep when I came up to change and had had to be awakened by my hungry partner. Tonight was different. I looked at myself in the glass, wondering for a moment why I was hurrying, refusing to put the true answer into words, telling myself merely that I knew Julian too well to be eager, while Robb these days was unfamiliar, intriguing and still attractive. I was prepared to admit that much.

He was waiting downstairs, sitting on a dark settle. I'd thought he would pass the time with a drink, but he was looking at *Country Life*, flicking the glossy pages over without giving himself time to read anything, and I wondered what was passing through his mind to bring such a grim set to the firm lips. He smiled when he saw me and got to his feet at once, dropping the magazine onto a nearby table and coming over to take my arm and lead me towards the bar. "You look great," he said simply. "Not at all dismayed by the events of the day."

I smiled back at him. "Was it you who arranged to have the flowers sent up?"

Immediately I wished I could withdraw the question. He hesitated and a look of rueful dismay replaced the smile. Lightly enough, he said, "I only wish I had thought of it, but I didn't. Part of the Dan Drummond treatment, I expect. I'll buy you a drink instead."

"Thank you, Robb. I'm longing for one, but after my grandfather's whisky, I'd prefer a soft drink."

"If you imagine that nothing would match up to the Invercorrie whisky, Drummond's malt is really excellent."

I refrained from adding to my earlier blunder by saying

95

that I'd had some last evening with Julian, but Dan Drummond himself was in the bar and took pride in telling Robb that I had already sampled the malt.

Robb's eyebrows lifted. "I seem to be falling behind on all counts."

"Nonsense. I stayed here last night, you know. Tonight, truly, I would like a soft drink."

"Orange juice? Tonic water?"

"Orange juice, please."

It was produced in a tall tumbler, fresh and cold, with a slice of orange floating on top, and it tasted delicious.

To my surprise, Robb had the same, and laughed at my expression. "Is it so unusual for a man to have a soft drink?"

"In Scotland, yes, I think so."

"Well, perhaps," he admitted. "Let's sit down over there and study the menu."

We sat in a corner near an enormous log fire and I sighed with contentment. It was quiet. There were only a dozen or so people in the bar, for it was barely seven o'clock, and the crackling of the fire was nearly as loud as the quiet murmur of voices, full of soft s sounds and rolled r's, with observations punctuated with "Aye" instead of "Yes." There were English voices, too, and one or two transatlantic ones, but the local Scots accent predominated, and I thought how lovely and full and deep it was, a throaty, gentle sound.

Two large menus were produced, dark blue with regimental drums embossed on the front and the cross of St. Andrew above. I held it in my hands for a moment, then laid it aside and said to Robb, "You order for me. You know what's good here."

Without fuss, he skimmed through the menu and looked up. "How about fresh salmon?"

"Delicious."

We began with melon, imported from Israel, and then the salmon, huge steaks of it, with fresh vegetables, and we drank a perfect Meursault. Afterwards Robb insisted that we have a lemon soufflé, and at last, replete, we sat over coffee and Drambuie.

The conversation had been easy and uninvolved: an exchange of ideas on rural life compared with that in our choking cities, including London; a little about antiques; a little about Robb's herd; holidays we'd taken abroad. But at last we looked at each other and knew that there was more to be said. Conversation on a personal level could not be avoided after what we had been through this afternoon. Suddenly I said, "Did you telephone Invercorrie?"

"Yes, while you were upstairs. But I merely said I would not be returning tonight. And the Forestry Commission were going to send a man along at once."

"How much did you tell them?"

"Only that there was a tree across the road. But I may have been seen getting out of the car, you know. So if they come back to me with questions, I shall tell them the conclusion I came to, without attempting any explanation. I shall be mystified."

He smiled as he uttered the last sentence and the hooded eyes sparkled like a gray sea with sun on the water. He looked younger when he smiled. Perhaps I did, too, when I smiled back at him, for impulsively he put a hand across the table, palm upwards. After a moment I put mine into it and watched the strong brown fingers close. The thumb and forefinger gripped the third finger of my left hand.

"No ring," he said, speaking more slowly than usual, as if searching for words. "But you've had friends, special friends?"

"From time to time."

"We're two of a kind. We prefer our freedom."

I assumed he was right about himself, but certainly he was very wrong about me. Preference for freedom was not what had kept me single. If I married, I wanted it to be a lasting union and I had never been sure enough of anyone I'd met. The traumas of divorce were all around me in London, and I'd seen enough of them to know that I didn't want to get involved in that kind of a mess—too soul-destroying. And so I had remained single, but not in order to fall into the arms of Robb Morrison. In case he imagined that, I withdrew my hand.

"What did my grandfather have to say when you telephoned and explained that you were not coming back?"

"He was not available. Mackenzie said he would pass on the message."

"What do you make of Mackenzie?"

"An excellent servant. Cold. Correct."

"That's the impression I got. He's not at all the kind of man I'd have expected Grandfather to engage. Do you remember Stockton? A dear old boy who did his job well without any of that inhuman stiffness, and found time to play with me in his off-duty hours. I loved him."

A smile crept over Robb's face and I added, "Robb, don't be ridiculous. I am not expecting to play with the butler now, but you know what I mean. Can you imagine Mackenzie playing with a small girl?"

"Not even with a fully grown one," Robb said with conviction, and poured more coffee from the silver pot which had been left on our table. He added sugar to his coffee, I added cream to mine and listened while Robb continued: "Your grandfather was without a butler for some time after Stockton died. Butlers are a dying breed, you know, difficult to find, especially men who will stay in these remote parts. Invercorrie got along with Mrs.

Stockton doing the cooking and daily help from the village for some time, but when Mrs. Stockton decided to go and live with her sister in Ayr, your grandfather was really in trouble. Finally the Mackenzies happened along and Mrs. Mackenzie does the cooking. Apart from casual help and the gardener, they have only one maid living in, an island girl who was at Quern Lodge for a short time. Did you ever meet her?"

"No, I never did. What was she like?"

"I only saw her once or twice. Dark, I think. There was some sort of trouble, but the reason why she left Quern never did leak out. Amazing, in these parts. Anyway, whatever the cause, it didn't worry your grandfather, apparently."

"You knew the reason, didn't you, living so close?"

"No. I don't think anyone knew, outside the family."

"And not everyone inside the family. I didn't know about it myself until this morning." I picked up a spoon and made mountains and valleys of Demerara sugar. "An ornament went missing, a silver leopard, and when my mother asked about it, this girl left, though she was not suspected of taking it. My mother told Mrs. Munro that she thought someone in the house had taken it. It was something Grandfather gave to me when I was small, and doubtless he regretted the impulse later. Anyway, it's missing. Lost, stolen or strayed, take your pick."

"Are you talking about that ornament you so unsuitably used to carry about with you? The one I found you playing with once, in a jungle of bracken by the Branta?"

"Yes, that's the one." I laughed, remembering the incident. Robb had sent me home, saying that I would lose it, and I had been furious with him. I was careless of some of my possessions, but never of that, for it was the symbol of happier times for me and I loved it, though admittedly I wasn't supposed to take it outdoors.

Robb frowned. "But didn't I see Mackenzie carrying it out on a tray this afternoon, when he showed me in?"

"That was its twin. Grandfather had a pair, evidently."

"Then where is yours now? Someone must have it."

I shrugged. "Mother left word in her will that it belonged to me, but it seems to have disappeared from the bureau where she kept it, before she died. A pity."

"Is it valuable?"

"It is of sentimental value to me, and intrinsically it may be worth more than I'd suspected, judging by the one I saw today. But not truly valuable, no."

"It was an extraordinary gift for a child, if it is one of a pair."

"Extraordinary," I agreed. "I think he only gave it to me because of a whim—a kind of reluctant admiration for a child who would throw a silver leopard at the all-powerful Ian MacRobert. He must have viewed me as a battling midget!"

Then Robb Morrison said a strange thing and I wondered if he knew me better than I knew myself. After looking at me intently for a long time, he said, "You'd still do battle with any man if the cause was good enough, wouldn't you, Caroline?"

My mouth went dry, remembering battles with my stepfather, and I could not answer at once, but at least I smiled and replied that fortunately I was not often put to the test nowadays.

"Would you fight to get your leopard back?"

"Fight for an ornament? Oh, Robb, *things* are seldom worth fighting for. People and causes, yes, but I am a woman without a cause and I've learned to do without people for most of the time."

"What about an inheritance, a large inheritance—is that worth fighting for?"

My eyes met the slaty, dark hooded gaze of Robb Morrison. His full mouth twitched, the nostrils of the curved nose looked pinched, and for some reason I felt that my reply had a special significance for him. If so, I could not see what it was, and therefore I chose my words carefully, framing them into a reply which told him nothing.

"That would depend," I said with assumed indifference, "on whether I wanted it or not."

He made a quick movement of irration, leaning back in his chair away from the table, away from me. "You make it very difficult for your friends to help you, Caroline."

With sharp coldness I snapped, "Have I asked for help?"

Robb scowled at me. "You see what I mean? You're battling again, always on the defensive."

Obviously, he liked yielding, dependent women, and I remembered Flora as she had looked yesterday after the funeral, giving melting glances across the room to the watching Robb while talking and leaning near to Dan Drummond, hanging on his words. I also remembered Cosmo's obvious resentment.

Flora, beautiful and so attractive to men, would marry early, I thought, and if she married Robb, the land belonging to Quern Lodge would be merged with Ardnacol, since Quern was left equally between Flora and Cosmo. I wondered if Cosmo would object. Perhaps he would be bought out and go elsewhere.

Why it had not occurred to me before, I did not know, but it hit me now with daunting force that Ian MacRobert had only one grandson, Cosmo Cunningham, and if Cosmo were to inherit Invercorrie, I would lose my right of access to the Castle forever. In that same instant I knew that I still loved the place and that neither Cosmo nor Flora would ever have the feeling for it which I had, and a slow, burning pain welled inside me.

The conversation I'd had with Flora and Cosmo this morning came back vividly to my mind. I remembered Cosmo's airy chat about turning the Castle into a hotel, with garages built around the old stone courtyard. It would be sacrilege and I wondered if he had ever crossed the bridge and entered through the tall gate into that dreaming stone refuge, or whether he had only looked down on Invercorrie Castle from above.

While I had been tussling with my own thoughts, Robb had sat quietly, watching me. I was aware of his scrutiny, yet I felt no resentment, for his glance was quite impersonal.

"Tell me something," I said slowly. "If you were to inherit Invercorrie Castle, what would you do with it?"

"There's no question of my inheriting Invercorrie." He spoke so sharply, I was astonished.

"I know that. I only wanted to know what you would do *if* you inherited it. Or any other similar castle, for that matter. A purely hypothetical question."

"You mean if I was left the kind of dwelling which is an anachronism in this modern world?"

"Yes, if you put it that way."

"I think that is the point of your question?"

"Yes, it is."

He gave it thought, which pleased me, because the decision to dispose of any historic dwelling seemed a serious matter to me. At last, with a kind of helpless resignation, he said, "I simply don't know. The upkeep is so impossible nowadays, yet I think I'd live in it if I could afford to."

"Truly? Would you really?"

"If it were left to me and I had no other house of my own, yes, I think so. On the other hand, I am a farmer and I cannot imagine myself ever leaving Ardnacol, even for a castle."

"I can't imagine you anywhere but at Ardnacol, either," I said frankly. "But you agree that Invercorrie should be lived in?"

My persistence puzzled Robb but I was really having a conversation with myself, clarifying my thoughts, and everything he had said so far confirmed my own opinion of Invercorrie's proper function.

"It is lived in now," Robb said, shrugging, "and it seems to suit the old place. Anyway, what is the alternative?"

Thoughtfully I said, "Cosmo would turn it into a hotel, with garages and flats built around the courtyard."

"My God!"

"My reaction exactly."

"Your friend Julian, what would he do if he inherited Invercorrie Castle?"

I laughed. "What an idea!" Try as I might, I simply could not see Julian living in the remote western Highlands of Scotland for more than about a week, and only for that length of time if the weather remained good. He had liked it here yesterday, but in today's weather his worst feelings about Highland life would be confirmed. Cold, wet, inhospitable country . . . today he'd hate it. "Julian would probably turn it into an art gallery or an antique shop, and the things he had on view would all be for sale—except the banner from Culloden." My voice was light, but I was serious. I knew that Julian would do just that, and he'd revel in making the place suitable for his purpose without spoiling it. Julian had taste and a sense of history and tradition.

"He and Cosmo should get on," Robb said. "Together, they'd make a great team."

"Oh no! Julian would not spoil Invercorrie."

"He would not live in it, either."

"He might, for a short time in summer."

We both laughed.

The dining room had emptied but for us, so we rose and went into a large room running from front to back of the house, full of old-fashioned, comfortable armchairs and sofas, with soft down cushions. We sat together on a low sofa.

"How about a nightcap?"

"I could drink some more coffee."

"Let's have another Drambuie, too." Robb signaled to a hovering waiter and he brought coffee and the tiny glasses of tawny Drambuie at once. While I poured coffee, Robb returned to our earlier topic of conversation. "Do you think that Invercorrie Castle may be left to Cosmo Cunningham? Has anything ever been said about it?"

I shook my head. "I haven't the slightest idea what Grandfather will do with it. Anyway, I don't like to think of the time when . . ." My voice dried up.

"Caroline, you saw him today." Robb's hand covered mine. "He is not a well man."

"I know. Robb, I wasn't very nice to him and I feel awful about it. I meant to be kind. At one time I thought of throwing myself into his arms, but then I didn't know what he would do, and the impulse passed."

"I know what I would do. Try me sometime." Robb glanced at me sideways, soberly, with nothing flirtatious in the look. Taken by surprise, I felt myself coloring, and at that moment Dan Drummond entered the room, evidently expecting to find us there, for he came straight over, smiling a greeting, and asked about dinner and our general comfort. He was slightly brash and self-confident, and despite his handsome looks, he riled me at times with the overdone charm.

"Women usually like him," Robb said mildly after he had gone.

"You were watching my hackles rise."

"It wasn't that bad. You looked inscrutable, but faintly on the defensive. He isn't such a bad chap when you get to know him. He tries too hard, that's all."

"Tries too hard at what?"

"At everything. Being mine host, friend to the neighborhood, public benefactor, countryman, sage. No reasonable request turned down." Robb shrugged. "That sounds damned bitchy, but it's the only way I can describe the man. He works hard at trying to please people, and mostly he succeeds."

"I got the impression yesterday that Flora rather likes him?"

"If so, it's mutual, I think. He called his boat after her and, believe me, it's a very beautiful boat. Expensive too." He sounded rueful. "I'm thinking of buying it."

I remembered that Julian and I had seen the boat moored out on the loch last night, and that I had seen Robb in the bar, talking to Dan Drummond.

"Very suitable, I'm sure. Flora likes you too," I could not resist saying.

Robb Morrison's deep tan reddened before he said, "What gave you that idea?"

"I'm perceptive."

"Don't go looking for what isn't there. Come and see something which *is* there, instead."

"What is that?"

"The *Flora*. She's moored out there and the weather has improved. It's still light enough for you to have some idea of what she is like."

"Well . . ." I hesitated. I would be leaving early in the morning and suddenly I was deathly tired. The events of the past two days seemed to be swimming in upon me, smothering me with a dark tide of shock and sorrow.

"Please. I could do with another opinion," Robb said.

"Thank you. I'd like to see your boat."

"She isn't mine yet, but I want something I can put to sea in, and live aboard for a while. The islands have a fascination for me and the small boat I have limits what I can do around these uncertain coasts."

We moved towards the front door and Robb said, "Haven't you a coat with you at all?"

"No, but I shall be all right with my new sweater. I'll go and get it."

The staircase creaked as I went up to my bedroom. From the bar there came the rumble of voices punctuated by laughter. Somewhere there was a television set spurting noise. I looked at my watch and found that it was only nine-thirty—I'd thought it must be later. Tiredness left me. I put on my thick sweater, brushed my hair back and renewed my lipstick, and then I ran downstairs again to join Robb.

The rain had quite gone, with only a pool or two and the smell of damp earth to remind us of the downpour. It was still cold, with a stiff breeze, but the clouds were clearing from the west and there was still a flush in the sky together with some gilt-edged gray cumulus.

We walked to the jetty and Robb drew in a small boat and steadied it until I stepped down and sat squarely on the middle of a seat in the bow. He fixed the outboard motor, which was lying in its waterproof case in the bottom of the boat, and it roared to life at a touch. I smiled, remembering that Robb always liked to have things in working order.

"The water is icy," I said, putting a hand in to test it.

"The rain will have chilled it but it will warm up again. We shall have an Indian summer yet."

"You sound very sure."

"I am trying to persuade you to stay."

"I can't. I must go back tomorrow."

He did not answer but turned away from me to look back towards the hotel. When he looked in my direction again it was when he brought the small boat alongside the *Flora* to make her fast.

"Aboard with you." He did something deft which brought down a small aluminum ladder, easy to climb, and in a moment we were both aboard.

The *Flora*—a thirty-footer—was so beautifully built and so well appointed that I could not imagine why Robb would hesitate for an instant about buying her, unless the price was too high—but Morrison of Ardnacol could not be hard up. The galley was perfect, with equipment looking as if it had never been used; the saloon had dark-blue cushions narrowly piped with white, blue and white curtains and soft lighting. Robb switched on the wall lights at once, and in the warm intimate glow we examined everything together, I exclaiming like a child at the marvelously intricate yet simple way in which everything fitted into its rightful place.

"Oh, Robb, she's so lovely!" I turned impulsively to congratulate him. "Of course you must have her. You couldn't possibly resist."

He smiled at my enthusiasm. "I have nearly made up my mind, I suppose, but it is always nice to have another opinion. I wish you'd stay and come out in her tomorrow."

"I'm sorry, Robb, I can't." The words came out more sharply than I'd intended. I was afraid of involvement with Robb Morrison, or anyone else in Skerran.

Our return journey to the hotel was quick, and we talked little. If Robb married Flora, then his boat would be named after his wife, which would be right and proper. The thought depressed me.

We parted near the staircase. "How will you get home?" I asked.

"I see Cosmo in the bar. He would give me a lift. Or I can borrow Drummond's spare car. Are you still going back to London tomorrow?"

"I must."

"Farmers get up early. I'll come over and see you before you go."

I went upstairs, feeling as if I had lost direction. The time spent with Robb had been not so much the renewal of an old friendship as the tentative beginning of a new one, a pointless beginning, for it could proceed no further. Our paths had diverged long ago.

# 7

THE BED was comfortable but sleep did not come. Insistently, Robb's words kept returning to my mind: "Who sent the gift-wrapped white sweater?"; "Has he arrived home safely?" Robb had been talking of threats, the inheritance of Invercorrie Castle and matters of which Julian knew nothing. But there was another kind of inheritance of which Robb in turn was unaware. Julian and I were without dependents, so our lawyers had drawn up an agreement which would be subject to alteration if either of us married. As it stood, if Julian died, I would inherit his half of our business; if I died, he would inherit mine. It was a sensible agreement which spelled security for both of us. I tossed in bed, threw off the eiderdown, felt cold and drew it up about me once more in a restless state between waking and sleeping, haunted by indecision.

From outside came the occasional sound of a car door closing, voices saying goodnight, steps across a flagged yard.

Suppose, I thought, suppose Robb himself had staged that elaborate tree-felling? But he could have no motive. If Julian was not yet home, would I, could I, possibly suspect him of threatening me?

The hotel was not yet asleep. I lifted the bedside telephone and Dan Drummond's voice sounded in my ear. "Yes, Miss Westwood, what can I do for you?"

I asked for Julian Bennet's London number, and in a moment, to my intense relief, Julian himself was on the line. "Caroline, is anything the matter?" He sounded surprised.

"Nothing at all. I just wondered if you had got back safely."

"Nice of you to ring. Yes, thanks, I had a very smooth run. How was the Invercorrie visit?"

"Sticky."

"No fatted calf?"

"Not so much as a veal escallop."

"Are you very disappointed?"

"A little. I don't know what I expected, but something pleasanter, I suppose. You warned me not to expect too much, and you were right."

"Poor Caroline. And what about the lawyer? Is there much work for you to do?"

"Nothing."

"Nothing?" He emphasized the word, his voice edged with curiosity.

"I do not inherit under my mother's will, so I have no further duties."

"That's pretty rotten, isn't it?"

I was becoming tired of telling people that I saw nothing odd or sinister in being left out of the Quern bequest, so I laughed and said, "Well, that isn't quite right. I was left a silver leopard."

"The one you threw at your grandfather?"

"Did I tell you about that? Yes, the same."

"It will look nice on your mantelpiece."

"It would have, but it's missing."

"Stolen?"

"No one seems to know. I'll tell you about it when I get back. How's the weather in London?"

"Hot."

"We've had quite a storm and it's cold here now. Oh, Julian, I almost forgot to thank you for the present. Your lovely thick white sweater has already been worn. I don't know what I would have done without it."

"Then I'm glad I thought of it. Is the car adequate?"

"It's fine. I'll be back tomorrow night, Julian."

"I'd invite you to dinner, but it's my quarterly date with Amanda."

"Good luck." I hung up, laughing. Amanda was an actress, neurotic and usually "resting," but Julian adored her—when they were apart. When they met, they quarreled, and for weeks afterwards, would not be on speaking terms, but then she would telephone and the whole mad relationship would begin again, if an association so brief and intermittent could be said to begin. Julian deserved better than the sultry Amanda. I once asked him why he went on seeing her.

"Heads turn in restaurants," he replied laconically.

"Ask a silly question," I'd murmured in reply and he had looked quite astonished.

"No, I mean it. You'd be surprised how many men take out girls because of the reaction from other men."

"It doesn't seem a good enough reason," I'd said feebly.

"Oh, there are other reasons."

His smile teased wickedly and I had thrown a handy cushion at him. I seemed to be good at throwing things. The habit acquired early in life had never been lost, apparently.

After talking to Julian I slept soundly and woke early, to find that it was wet again, the rain falling in steady gray sheets.

There were few people in the dining room when I went in—a couple of men who intended to go fishing and two middle-aged couples traveling together and planning on making an early start. We exchanged greetings and I ordered coffee and rolls, which came piping hot. There was no sign of Jean Jameson this morning, but Dan Drummond was around and it was he who summoned me to the telephone. "It's the Castle," he said.

Puzzled, I went to the phone. I had put any connection with Invercorrie into the past after yesterday's visit and I could think of no reason for my grandfather to get in touch with me again. My visit had meant nothing to him, he had not been particularly pleased to see me and had treated me as a stranger. I did not exactly regret the time spent there yesterday, for the visit had clarified my feelings towards Grandfather and the far-off childhood years at Invercorrie. My years there were a dream which I need no longer try to keep alive, the corner of my mind in which I had cherished memories of the Castle for so long was now a vacuum. But a vacuum is there to be filled, and as I listened to Mackenzie's dry voice on the telephone telling me that my grandfather had been taken ill, I burned and then shivered, my throat closing with fright, so that I could not speak until Mackenzie said, "Miss Westwood? Miss Westwood, are you there? Can you hear me?" Even he, that cold, unlikable man, sounded agitated, even concerned. Perhaps under the emotionless exterior of the perfect butler there lurked a man with feelings.

"Yes, I am here, Mackenzie. How ill is my grandfather? When did the attack occur? This morning, you said, but at what time?"

"Early, Miss Westwood. He rises early, and when he saw your parcel, he became very angry. It brought on this attack."

"What parcel? I sent no parcel."

There was a short silence, and when the man spoke

again, he had regained his poise and managed to convey without saying so that he did not believe me. "That may be so, Miss Westwood, but at any rate, at that point he became ill and had a slight seizure. He is now asking for you with some insistence. I have undertaken to use all possible persuasion for you to return here this morning."

"Have you sent for the doctor?"

Despair tinged a voice which suddenly lapsed into Scots as Mackenzie said, "Och, he'll not see anyone while Dr. Farr is away in Australia. I keep telling him that Dr. Staines is well enough qualified but he'll not listen. Maybe he'll heed you, Miss Westwood."

I thought of the man I had seen yesterday—shrunken, selfish and opinionated—and doubted if he would listen to anyone who opposed his own views. I bit my lip, thinking hard, trying to reconcile duty with inclination. They were irreconcilable—I wanted to return to London but I could not go without first at least visiting Invercorrie once again to see if there was anything I could do for my grandfather. If it was a wasted journey, at least I would have done my best for him. After that, it was up to Mackenzie, as it would have been if I had not been in Scotland, for I was fairly sure they would not have sent to London for me.

"I'll come," I said with no enthusiasm, and casually I added, "I heard there was a tree across the road. Has it been cleared, do you know?"

Surprise made him lapse from his formal manner. "It must have been cleared, surely. The postie would not come the coast road."

For the second time I settled with The Drums, paying my bill before going upstairs. Dan Drummond looked at me intently but said nothing, and I merely thanked him for accommodating me before saying goodbye. I was wearing the cream suit to travel in, but now I took it off and put on my trousers and white pullover. I could have done with a waterproof, for outside rain was falling with that awful persistence which belongs to mountain country, and muttering my annoyance, I folded the suit carefully and packed it.

Robb Morrison had not yet come, though he had said he would see me before I left. But it was still early and he would not expect me to be leaving so soon. After some thought I decided to leave no message. I did not want Robb feeling obliged to follow on my account and he would hear of Grandfather's illness soon enough. I left the car park and turned left, well aware that I would be observed, and any watcher was bound to surmise that I was going to Quern or Invercorrie, for I was driving in the wrong direction for Fort William and the railway to London.

In the cold light of morning I dismissed any thought of danger. Robb's reaction in the woods yesterday afternoon had been oversuspicious and I simply did not believe that anyone wanted to harm me personally. It would be nice to think that he was being protective towards me, but I thought he had become infected with the Highland love of a mystery.

Anxiety on my grandfather's account led me to drive fast. I sped by the lochside, passing the open gates to Quern Lodge, noting that smoke drifted from the chimneys in wisps to thread round the roof, not rising far, held down by the damp air. The calm surface of the loch was dotted with falling rain, ringed where the fish were rising, and on the shore I saw a lone fisherman, motionless in yellow oilskins, holding a rod. The mountains beyond the water were headless, their peaks hidden by quilts of cloud pressing close about them.

I turned across the moor and plunged into the pine woods, then slowed. Beneath my wheels there was a layer of mud, needles and husks from cones—slippery, I imagined —and I treated the surface with respect, driving more slowly. As I approached the place where the tree had fallen across the road, so narrowly missing us, I saw that it had indeed been removed and was lying at the side with branches lopped off the trunk. The tractor, however, had emerged from its clearing and was parked on the road facing in my direction. It was to one side but still blocking the way. By driving onto the bright green verge I could pass, but it looked very spongy, with water gleaming in rivulets among the tussocks of grass and moss which grew in a thick border. In England one came across signs at the roadside reading SOFT VERGES, but this part of Scotland was too remote for such niceties and perhaps too many notices would be needed in wet weather.

I stopped the car, staring at the blank, glassy face of the tractor cab. I could not see if there was a driver there or not, but there was no movement, no shadow passing behind the windshield. I rolled down my window and leaned out. Rain soaked my hair and shoulders, falling with a swishing sound and tinkling along in small streams by the side of the road. The beginning of a west wind stirred in the tops of the pines, not blowing but merely gathering the branches and shaking them gently, reassuringly, as if to say "I'll come soon and blow the clouds away and dry you." Then it died again and there was no sound except the falling rain, not even the song of a bird among the trees.

"Is there anyone there?" I called loudly and was startled at the sound of my own voice hurling itself around the tree trunks in that hushed place. No one answered. Suddenly angry, I put the heel of my hand on the car's horn and kept it there. Still no response. The tractor was abandoned, at least for the moment. Perhaps the forester had returned to wherever he lived for some hot food, a second breakfast. Frustration seized me. I could not move forwards without risking getting bogged down and I certainly could not turn the car here. I remembered a rocky outcrop, leveled off at the side of the road where it entered the woods. No doubt a passing place had been made there on purpose, and grumbling under my breath I put the little car into reverse and began to back carefully, steering a straight course which would keep me in the center of the narrow road. For the first time I thought with jumping fear that if anyone had followed me I would be nicely trapped between two vehicles, but I saw no one, and eventually I emerged after backing for nearly a mile. I was soaked and had a crick in my neck from leaning out of the car. The rear window was misted over and the rear-view mirror none too secure, tilting every now and then to show a view which had little to do with the road behind me.

Out of the shadowy trees, I sighed with relief, backed swiftly onto that hard, rocky passing place and turned the vehicle to head back along the way I had come, across the moor. There was nothing for it but to return to the lochside and proceed along the low road. It was the only alternative way to reach Invercorrie, other than by boat or on foot, so I had no choice.

I met no one on the way to the loch, saw no one on the moor, but who would be out in such weather by choice? Not even a countryman, I thought. By Loch Skerran I turned along the road which bore a sign saying UNSUITABLE FOR HEAVY VEHICLES. BEWARE ROCKFALL. My vehicle was not heavy and I trusted that the rocks would stay in their place for the short time it would take me to pass the cliff which, if memory served me, was a mile or two beyond this point.

The cliff reared up at the side of the road soon enough,

the road itself narrowing a little as it crept by. Within half a mile of here Loch Skerran, Loch Branta and the sea met in turbulent water. On stormy days perilous inroads were made on the rocky shore below. It was a sheer drop to my left, so there was no way of swerving to avoid falling rocks without taking a plunge into the loch itself. I kept on, trying not to look at the dark cliff face soaring upwards to my right. Inevitably, however, my eyes were drawn there, where sheer rock was streaming with water and patched with scree. Green ledges supported spindly trees, tenacious of life and twisting upwards in tortured shapes, struggling against the twin hazards of starvation and salt winds.

This was the kind of weather which precipitated landslip, I thought, and even as this unpleasant truth sneaked into my mind I saw a trickle of gravel ahead of me, dropping from ledge to ledge and settling at the roadside. A stone or two followed, then a clump of earth tufted with green. Mindful of Robb's quick reaction yesterday, I put my foot down hard and shot along the wet surface, fleeing towards the threat in order to win my way through. I hoped there would not be more than a trickle but I was taking no chances, and when the car skidded on a mud patch I was consumed with fear. Somehow I got it under control and sped on, with a rumbling noise growing above the sound of the car engine. I did not slow up until the cliff leveled off and curved away from the road. Then, with wet palms and shaking knees, I braked to a stop and turned to look behind me.

There was a sizable pile of rocks and gravel on the road with a cloud of dust above it in spite of the wet, but that was not what caught my attention. At the top of the cliff I caught a flash of yellow, visible for an instant and then gone, lost in gray rain and tangled shrubs. My bird watcher of the previous day, I told myself, a forestry worker or a fisherman. I was angry rather than afraid. Surely any normal, friendly stranger on top of a cliff who had seen a car narrowly escape running into a rockfall would at least have called out to the driver after the car had stopped, to see if he or she was all right. But whoever was scrambling about up there was not interested in making friendly overtures. I hoped he would get very wet indeed.

At a more sedate pace I proceeded to the Castle, rounding the corner by the seldom used southern approach to the gateway. Before me snaked the road which I had traveled yesterday, glistening with water but better surfaced than the perilous route I had been forced to use today.

The gate was open, ready for me, and this time I parked on the gravel alongside Robb's Jaguar, surprised that no one had garaged the handsome car for the night. There was no sign of the gardener this morning.

Mackenzie opened the door before I had time to ring, and his impassive expression was touched with concern. "You didn't come the forest road, Miss Westwood—I was watching for you coming down out of the wood, but you came from the coast road, did you not?"

"Yes, I did. Some fool had left a tractor on the road in the forest. I couldn't get past."

He tutted and murmured something about dangerous roads and my wet clothes, but I never take cold from a wetting and said so. Then I sneezed, and he tutted some more but agreed to take me to my grandfather at once.

"I hope you have managed to keep him in bed?" I asked as we made our way upstairs.

"Yes, I have. No persuasion was needed, Miss Westwood, which makes me know he feels bad. He's not one for staying in bed."

We walked along the gallery to my grandfather's bedroom above the drawing room, and it was exactly as I remembered it from my childhood. Memories flooded back as I glanced briefly about me and had a swift impression of ivory-backed brushes with silver initials placed neatly on the old-fashioned mahogany dressing table. There was an enormous wardrobe in which I had hidden as a child sometimes, pouncing out on a man who had pretended to be startled, sharing the joke with the small girl who could not possibly be me, surely, any more than the tiny white figure lying in the enormous bed could be the bluff, hearty man I remembered. The tower section at one corner of the large room had been made into a study, and today an atmosphere of chill was brought right indoors by tall windows streaming with water and looking out on a tossing sea.

Most of the islands were blotted out by mist and rain. I wished passionately that the weather would clear, letting sun into this dreary sickroom.

"Mackenzie, why have you not lighted a fire?" I was shocked.

"The master would not have it, Miss Westwood."

The master opened his eyes and looked at me in silence, his expression utterly unreadable.

"Well, I am not going to sit in a cold room in wet clothes, Mackenzie, so if the master wishes me to remain, there will have to be a fire immediately." I spoke with authority, briskly but kindly, and he turned and left the room. A few moments later the young gardener entered quietly and began to lay and light a fire in the big stone fireplace.

"What are you doing here, Hamish? You've no right to be in my room." Grandfather was petulant rather than angry, and after saying "I'm sorry, sir," the boy continued doggedly to make the fire, and in no time smoke was curling up the chimney and flames licking at the dry wood he had brought. He left a large basket of logs in the hearth and departed quietly. I was thankful that the chimney was wide and tall so that the fire drew without smoking, although that fireplace had not been used for months, presumably. Grandfather hated central heating. He'd succumbed to having it installed in the public rooms and some of the bedrooms during my mother's residence, but refused to have any radiators in his own rooms. In winter he would consent to having a fire, but many a summer day in Skerran would be as cold as winter and Invercorrie was almost an island. I wondered how he survived.

When Hamish left the room, my grandfather subsided on the bed again, grumbling to himself but calm. He seemed to have forgotten having asked for me. "Well, Caroline," he said, "you have come back. There was no need. I shall be well enough again in a day or two. I have had these attacks before."

"No doubt," I said, affecting a detachment I did not feel. "But I could hardly set off for London knowing you had suffered some kind of sudden illness. What kind is it, by the way? What does Dr. Farr say about your health these days?"

"Dr. Farr is in Australia." He spoke as if the doctor's holiday had been taken out of personal pique against him.

"And you hadn't had one of your attacks before he went?"

"I didn't say that." He sighed and moved restlessly, his blue-veined hands plucking at the bedcovers. "He said it was a touch of heart trouble and gave me enough pills to stock a chemist's shop."

"Are you taking them?"

His blue eyes met mine in a challenging stare and I said, "No, you are not, of course."

"I take the small white ones when I need them."

"Well, that's something, I suppose." I knew about small

white pills—amyl nitrite, was it? Something to dilate the arteries, anyway. I had an elderly friend in London who needed them and carried them with her always, in a tiny enameled box. I sighed. London seemed a long way from here.

"You haven't seen Dr. Staines? I'm told he is very good."

"No, I have not seen Dr. Staines. He has long black hair and a long black beard and makes his rounds in blue jeans." My grandfather uttered a snort of contempt which nearly choked him, began coughing and went scarlet in the face, but mercifully he got himself under control almost at once. Perhaps some of his outrage was assumed, and with a little persuasion he might be willing to see Dr. Staines, but I thought it wiser to leave the subject for the moment.

"That boy, Hamish. Have I seen him before somewhere?"

"If you are staying, you may as well sit down." Irritably, Grandfather waved a pajama-clad arm towards an exceedingly comfortable-looking chair near the fire, but I drew a high-backed chair near to the bed and sat in that, where I could see him better. I would have liked to make some sarcastic comment on the warmth of his welcome, but I bit it back and waited with eyebrows raised for a reply to my question.

At last, tired of fixing me with an aggressive stare, he dropped his head back on the pile of white pillows and said, "You will have seen him at Quern Lodge, no doubt. Mrs. Munro's son, Hamish."

"Of course—I remember now, but I haven't seen him for years. He went to agricultural college, didn't he?"

"Horticultural college, yes, but he wasn't up to it, didn't finish the course. He takes care of the gardens here now."

"A maid left Quern and came here too, I believe?"

"Who told you that?"

"Robb."

"H'm. So you've been discussing my affairs with Robb. Well, we needed help after Mrs. Stockton went to live with her sister. Stockton died, you know."

"Yes, I heard about Stockton. You must have missed him."

For once the old man forgot his cold manner and said simply, "Yes, I missed him. He'd been with me a long time, knew my ways. Mackenzie is well enough, though. I'm fortunate, I suppose."

I thought that he was, indeed, fortunate but I knew that servants did not compensate for a family, so when he said, looking at the ceiling, "If I'm not better by tomorrow, maybe I'll see Dr. Staines," I knew that he wanted me to stay overnight, though nothing would have made him ask me in so many words.

I thought about it. This was Saturday. I supposed I could stay until tomorrow, and no doubt a summons to Invercorrie Castle would bring the new young doctor out on a Sunday, or late tonight, for that matter, if there were any more attacks.

"Would you like me to stay over until tomorrow?" I asked, and received the peevish reply: "Please yourself, Caroline, please yourself."

He may have caught sight of my enraged and mutinous face, for I glimpsed a brief return to courtesy as he added, "You will be welcome."

I was not given my old room, which was on the top floor, but a large and comfortable room near my grandfather's, overlooking the sea. From the window I could see a tower on either side of me and a necklace of small islands half hidden by rain and mist.

The young girl who had shown me in here after Mackenzie answered Grandfather's bell must surely be the island girl who had worked so briefly at Quern. In answer to my question she told me that her name was Maggie, and I learned that in addition to herself and Mrs. Mackenzie, two women came in daily from the village to help with rough work and were fetched by Hamish in a small truck used for shopping. It was little enough help for a castle and I sighed, remembering the adequate staff kept when I was small. Maggie, however, seemed happy enough and said shyly, "Mrs. Mackenzie said to tell you that this room is always kept ready."

Ready for whom? I wondered.

"I've switched on the electric blanket to be certain the bed is aired. Is there anything you would like now, Miss Westwood? Some coffee perhaps?"

Coffee was exactly what I wanted most in the world just then. I had begun shivering, but the radiators had been turned on in the room, and as I walked over to touch one of them, Maggie said, "You're awful wet, Miss Westwood. Would you not change and I'll have your things dried for you?"

So I changed into my suit, handed my wet things to Maggie and sat down by the radiator in the window to await my coffee. It came in a handsome silver pot with a cup and saucer of Staffordshire china, brown sugar and cream, and a small silver dish of homemade biscuits speckled with sugar and nuts. Grandfather lived well, it seemed, and I sipped coffee and nibbled at a biscuit, prepared to try to enjoy my brief stay at Invercorrie Castle.

Only then did I recall that Mackenzie on the telephone had said something about a parcel which had sparked off my grandfather's attack. He had not mentioned it during our meeting and neither had I.

# 8

WHEN I went downstairs, Mackenzie emerged from a small room off the hallway which I remembered as being Stockton's sanctum in the old days, and bowed. "The master's sleeping, Miss Westwood. Would you like me to send for the doctor?"

"We'll see how Mr. MacRobert is when he awakens. He has agreed to call in the doctor tomorrow if there is no improvement, so it may be better to wait awhile." Seeing the worried frown on the man's forehead, I added kindly, "Don't worry, Mackenzie. I'll take the responsibility."

The frown cleared at once and I said, "You mentioned a parcel, Mackenzie. What was in it?"

Before he could reply, there came the sound of a car engine. The vehicle stopped, then started up again and departed. A moment later the bell rang. "That will be Mr. Morrison for his car," Mackenzie said. "He telephoned, so I opened the gates for him." With a measured, unhurried tread which nevertheless took him quickly to the front door, Mackenzie opened it.

"Good morning, Mackenzie. I would like to see Miss Westwood if she's available."

Mackenzie glanced at me over his shoulder, and to save him the problem of prevarication, I moved into view and said, "Good morning, Robb."

"Good morning." He smiled at me as he came in. "My grieve drove me over to fetch the car and I saw yours standing there. What brought you back?"

"Would you like some coffee?" I asked, without answering his question, and when Robb accepted, Mackenzie led the way to a charming room with chintz and rosewood where the radiators were on and a fire burning. He had now realized that I was an effete southerner and liked warmth on a wet, cold day.

Robb was wearing a checked tweed jacket over a yellow sweater, and his cavalry twill slacks were darkly splashed with the rain, which seemed never to have stopped for an instant.

"Whew, it's hot in here." He peeled off the jacket and slung it over the arm of a chair. "You don't mind?"

"Not at all." I smiled. "I'm afraid I shall be setting everyone by the ears, asking for heat."

Robb looked astonished. "Does that mean you are staying here?"

"Yes, I am. At least until tomorrow."

"Well, I'm damned! Your esteemed grandfather must have more appeal than I have."

"Naturally. He's a blood relation."

"H'm. Well, whatever the reason, I'm glad you came back."

Mackenzie himself brought the coffee and more of the little sugared biscuits. I poured for both of us and passed a cup to Robb while he held out the dish of biscuits for me. I shook my head. "This is my second cup of morning coffee—my third, to be exact—and I sampled those earlier. I can scarcely resist them, they are so delicious, but I'm not hungry." Then, abruptly, I asked him, "Did you know I was here before you saw the car out there?"

"No, but I thought you might be. I promised to come

and say goodbye, if you remember, but when I got to the hotel, I was told that you had gone, but not in the Fort William direction. I didn't think, somehow, that you would be at Quern, and there is nowhere else. Where is the old boy? As you are staying, I assume you have seen him?"

I told Robb then about Grandfather's illness. "He's in bed but I have seen him. We talked for a little while and I arranged to stay overnight. He has half agreed to see the doctor tomorrow if he isn't better."

Robb looked angry. "It's ridiculous, his refusing to see the associate. Staines is young but just as highly qualified as Dr. Farr."

"He has long black hair and a long black beard and goes visiting in blue jeans."

Robb laughed. "So that's it. Well, if your grandfather has agreed to see him tomorrow if necessary, that relieves you of some of the responsibility, though doubtless, when the time comes, he'll say it isn't necessary. I suppose you wouldn't have dinner with me tonight?"

"I couldn't possibly go out."

"You could invite me here."

"When I am only staying for one night? No, I couldn't, Robb, I'm sorry."

He sighed, looking frustrated.

"Did you come through the wood this morning?" I tried to keep my voice casual, but I must have failed because Robb's response was a sharp "Why? Why do you ask?"

"I just wondered."

"Don't fence with me, Caroline. I haven't much time to spare this morning."

"Sorry. Idle curiosity. Truly, Robb. When I tried to come through the wood, there was a tractor blocking the road and no one about, that's all."

"What did you do?"

"What could I do? I hung about and shouted for a while and then came by the loch road."

"In this weather?" Robb's amazed expression registered his opinion of such foolishness.

"As you see, I arrived safely."

He stared at me for a moment and I stared back. I was not going to tell him what had happened on the road, least of all that I had caught sight of someone up on top of the cliff. He would want to tell the police and make all kinds of a fuss.

"I wonder if your partner got back to London safely," Robb murmured and his gray eyes, bright with curiosity, sought mine.

"Yes, he did. I telephoned last night and spoke to him."

"Did you now?" He looked almost disappointed, and I wondered why on earth he had cast poor Julian in the role of villain. Because of the total absence of any other candidate, I supposed. I decided in my own mind that there were no villains at all. A series of small, unpleasant incidents added together and stirred with imagination could always be magnified into something nasty.

"More coffee?" I offered.

Robb glanced at his watch—a flat, square gold affair with a worn black leather strap—and frowned. "No, I'm sorry. I can't stay any longer. I have a sick cow at the farm and I'm expecting the vet. I'll be in touch, Caroline, before you leave. I'll ring you tonight, or something. You will send for me if you need help?"

"Thank you, but there is help here. I shall be all right so long as my grandfather continues to improve. In fact, we are both very well looked after. This is all rather different from my London flat, which is minute and cluttered."

We were standing now, and Robb looked down at me, still frowning. "You should consider a permanent exchange.

I'm sure your grandfather would be delighted to have you back."

"He turned us out once, my mother and me. Had you forgotten that, Robb?"

"No, I hadn't forgotten, nor have you, I see. Or forgiven him, it seems. Isn't it possible that you heard only one side of that story, Caroline? And isn't your memory too long?"

"Certainly, I heard only one side of the story. I was seven, remember." My voice had become harsh, like my thoughts. "Grandfather gave me no chance to hear his side of it. He simply . . ." I choked, groping for words which would not come because I felt baffled even now when I thought of what my then-beloved grandfather had done to a seven-year-old. To be so hostile to his daughter and to extend his hatred to a *child*. "He turned us out and I haven't forgiven him. I can't ever forgive him. You don't know what it led to, for me . . ."

I broke off, control deserting me. I had almost said too much and I turned in panic to run out of the room, across that great paneled hall and up the long staircase. Behind me I heard Robb coming after me to the foot of the stairs, calling "Caroline! Caroline, come back," but I took no notice. I flew into my room and flung myself down on the bed in a paroxysm of rage and frustration such as I had not felt for a long time. I did not cry. I have always found it so hard to cry. That time by the loch, with Julian, had been the only occasion in years when I had been able to let go, and how healing it had been. Now I wished I could weep more often, but some wounds never heal completely. They skin over, then break out again, suppurating, making one feel unclean. For a long time I lay on the bed, dry-eyed and with my head aching. Hammers beat behind my eyes and all manner of black thoughts crowded in upon me: Cosmo's watchful demeanor, Flora's sudden flash of hatred over my mother's jewelry, a felled tree, stones falling from a clifftop in a long, slow rattle, and above all, my own loneliness. There was no one with whom I could be totally frank, not even Julian.

I got up at last, washed at the basin, touched up my face and brushed my hair. Still heavy-hearted, I walked to the window. Angry water dashed itself to pieces on the rocks below, but the clouds were higher in the sky, breaking up and fleeing eastward before the wind in long gray streamers. Gulls wheeled and dipped or rode the waves. I believed the sun might shine later. I hoped it would, for I longed to see the walled garden where I had spent so many childhood hours and where, in my memory, the sun was always shining. If the rain continued to fall, today's visit to the garden would be spoiled and the memory tarnished. I searched the sky for some sign of fair weather, and like a beneficence it came. While I watched, clouds parted, and hesitantly and then with sudden glory a rainbow arched across the sky and at last the sun broke through, washing the water with glittering shafts of light.

"Come in," I called absently in answer to a knock on the door and Maggie entered.

"I came to tell you that luncheon is ready, Miss Westwood." Her kind face was filled with concern. She had not yet learned to mask her feelings, and I thought wearily that my outburst would have been discussed in the kitchen.

I went to the dining room without appetite and took my place all alone at the long mahogany table. Mackenzie was standing by the sideboard. He spooned broth from a tureen and put it before me, thick and steaming. I stared at it without seeing the traditional ingredients of carrot, turnip, peas, barley and fragments of lamb.

"Mackenzie . . ." I said, intending to ask him to remove the broth.

"Yes, Miss Westwood?"

"Nothing."

"Is there something you would prefer to the broth?"

"No. No, certainly not. The broth looks very good." I spooned a little into my mouth and found that it was indeed very good. Scotch broth as it should be, nearly thick enough to stand a spoon in and exactly right for the cold day. The rain had stopped, but the sun was struggling against the moisture which lay all around.

"I hope my grandfather is taking lunch?"

"A little beef tea and an omelette—a light diet."

"The same would have done for me, Mackenzie."

He looked shocked, removed the broth and brought in a dish of cutlets. I fell silent and did my best with them, but I am not accustomed to hearty meals in the middle of the day and my appetite had fled. I refused dessert and cheese but agreed to coffee in the small room where I'd entertained Robb that morning. It, too, was filled with memories of agitation. I picked up a copy of *The Scottish Field* and flipped over the pages to soothe my anxious thoughts.

When Mackenzie brought the coffee, he put it on a low table and poured for me. "Is there anything else, Miss Westwood?"

"Yes, there is. You still have not told me about the parcel I am supposed to have sent, and which apparently upset my grandfather. I sent no parcel, Mackenzie, and I want to know what was in it. I don't care to question my grandfather directly today, so perhaps you will tell me about it?" I lifted the small coffee cup and took a sip, watching him over the rim. There was nothing in his demeanor which was other than perfectly correct. He stood almost at attention, his arms straight down at his sides, head slightly bent, eyes resting on mine in polite response.

"I quite understand about your not wanting to trouble

Mr. MacRobert, Miss Westwood. In the circumstances, I see no reason why I should not tell you." He paused. "The item in the parcel was a silver leopard."

I was in the act of sipping coffee again, but I stopped and then slowly set the cup down in its saucer. "A what, Mackenzie?"

"A silver leopard, Miss Westwood."

"Like the one which you brought to show me yesterday?"

"Exactly, yes."

I took a deep breath, holding that impassive gaze with mine. "Mackenzie, did you know that a silver leopard belonging to me had gone missing at Quern Lodge?"

After a moment's hesitation he replied, "Yes, I did."

It occurred to me that nothing that happened at Quern remained secret from those at Invercorrie. But Mackenzie was still speaking. "Miss Westwood, we all know why Maggie left Quern Lodge, and my wife and I, we know her parents on the island. Maggie is an honest girl with the fear of God in her. She would not steal."

"As I understand it, she was not even suspected of stealing, so why did she leave? It made her look guilty, Mackenzie, but all the same, she was not suspected. No one seems to have the slightest idea of when that leopard went missing, anyway, never mind who took it."

"Quite so, Miss Westwood. It was all most unfortunate, but it is better for Maggie to be working here."

His face had closed into its usual composure. I knew he would say no more on that subject, so I tried another tack. "My grandfather spoke of a pair of leopards, Mackenzie, so it looks as if the one in the parcel is mine. Unless the one you brought to the drawing room yesterday has disappeared?"

"No, Miss Westwood. It cannot have disappeared."

"You seem very sure." I began to sip my coffee again.

"It is kept in a safe. The master and I have the only keys."

"Mr. MacRobert might have removed it himself?"

"For what purpose?"

"I do not know. But I suggest you check the safe now, Mackenzie."

"I never go to the safe without instructions."

"I have just given you instructions."

"I mean, instructions from the master, Miss Westwood."

"Mackenzie, I am here at the master's request, because of his illness, and I shall remain only so long as I am able to be useful and to take my grandfather's place when necessary. I cannot do that without your help and I shall not stay without your cooperation. At the same time, I give you my word that I shall not expect you to do anything which would be disloyal to your employer. Now, Mackenzie, will you please use your key and check whether the leopard you brought yesterday for me to see is still in its place."

He appeared to think over what I had said for a moment, then he bowed. "I will look," he said and made his way to the door, where he hesitated and turned. "If you please, Miss Westwood, it would be more satisfactory if you were to be present when I open the safe."

He was right and I agreed.

"Then perhaps when you have finished your coffee?"

"No, Mackenzie, I shall come at once."

I followed Mackenzie into the hall and out of it again, then downstairs to a corridor which led to the back of the Castle. Off this we entered a small room, noisy with the sound of the sea, for below it lay sharp rocks where the sea boiled in endless motion. The room was mostly lined with drawers and cupboards; it was a storeroom of some kind which I had never entered before. There was a side table with a lamp on it and in one wall, quite visible, there was the safe, an old-fashioned affair which would not meet with the approval of any insurance company, I thought wryly.

Mackenzie took a bunch of keys from his pocket, selected one and used it.

"Have you keys for all these cupboards and drawers, Mackenzie?" I asked, looking about me.

"No, Miss Westwood. Only for the safe. We keep spare cash in it for wages and the running of the house, so I need access for that purpose. The master keeps most of his silver collection in the drawers, and for those he has the only keys."

I nodded and watched him as he swung open the thick steel door and reached into the dark interior. It was not a large safe and he produced the leopard at once, wrapped in several sheets of black tissue paper. He unwrapped it and handed it to me in silence. I examined it more closely than I had been able to do when my grandfather had shown it to me without allowing me to touch it, and with more knowledge than I'd had when, as a child, I'd played with its twin.

I nodded my thanks and handed it back to Mackenzie. He wrapped it up and put it back in place before locking up the safe again.

"And the one from the parcel, Mackenzie?"

"The master kept it in his room, Miss Westwood. He put it into a drawer in his dressing table."

"I wonder why he didn't mention it this morning."

"He was not well."

"No." I shivered. The arrival of that parcel had upset him sufficiently for his health to be affected. At the very least, it had been an unpleasant practical joke; at the most, a dangerous one.

I went to the window and stared down at the incessant movement of water, creaming foam and green waves, stabbed by black razors. There was a level shelf of rock, half submerged, and I remember grownups swimming from there on calm days when I was small. Although I could swim well, I was not allowed to bathe there but was always taken to a sandy shore on one of the lochs or to a small island which we called Seal Island.

"You are cold, Miss Westwood. Come back to the morning room, if you please, and I shall bring you some fresh coffee."

"Thank you." I went through the door he held open for me. "My grandfather will be resting by now, I suppose?"

"Yes. It is usual for him, after luncheon. He asked that you should take tea in his room with him today at four o'clock. I hope that will be agreeable to you?"

"Perfectly, Mackenzie."

Fresh coffee was brought and I put the wretched silver leopards out of my mind for the time being. I could do nothing until I had seen my grandfather, but if he was not too ill to be questioned, I intended to discuss the return of the leopard with him this afternoon.

Outside the sun was shining fitfully, with a warmth reminiscent of the day I'd arrived in Skerran. I remembered that Robb had been sure of an Indian summer and hoped he was right. I glanced at my watch and found that it was not yet three o'clock. There was time for me to visit the garden.

There was no one about when I left the morning room, not even Mackenzie, and the paneled door of his small room remained shut. I opened the heavy front door, closed it behind me and stood on the steps, taking deep breaths of damp, salty air. There were watery noises everywhere as the rain collected and ran off pitched roofs high above, along ancient lead gutters and down the long, long pipes which carried it underground. A few drops pattered onto the flagstones and ran into hollows, but even as I watched, the final sunny sprinkle ceased. It was like April rain now, suddenly scattering, quickly ceasing and leaving the air fresh and surprisingly warm. I walked down those curved, shallow steps and around the corner of the Castle on the landward side, where a flagged roadway about eight feet wide skirted the building. To my right, beyond the boundary wall, I could see the low hills of Skerran rising, with the zigzag roadway climbing up through scrub and scree to the pine woods, and I was glad that I did not have to face driving up there this afternoon. I would have to take that road again tomorrow, but I refused to contemplate my return journey for the moment. This afternoon I was going to see the garden, the sun was shining for me and the last of the heavy, rain-laden cloud was flying inland before the west wind.

I crossed the causeway, where the noise of the sea was pierced only by the shriek of sea birds. The archway to the garden and stable block was no longer gated as it had been when I was a child, and when I got to the arch I saw that iron hinges were still in place but had not been used for a long time. There had been a stout wooden gate, I remembered, but it might have been there only because of the presence of a small child. With no children at the Castle, gates were not needed here.

The stable block was on my right, converted to a row of small houses with, at the far end, storerooms and garages. One door stood open because the interior was being decorated. Pots of paint stood in a neat row on the floor and a wall had been knocked down, so that, by unashamedly looking through the doorway, I could see right through the house and through a window on the far side to the same view I'd seen while crossing the causeway, except that from here I could see more of the approach road. From inside the house, I imagined, it would be possible to see the shore of the loch, with water lapping on the stony beach, and by looking along to the right, even the approach to the Castle gateway would be visible. It was a splendid outlook for whoever was to occupy the cottage. At present it was empty and the smell of new wood and paint hung thick about the doorway.

I glanced along the row and thought how lovely the tubs and flower beds looked, filled with bright marigolds, stocks and forget-me-nots. There were climbing roses, too, their soaked petals filling the air with scent.

The flagged roadway on which I was walking led to the garages, but opposite the cottages there was a strip of lawn with a few benches for sitting out on, and beyond the lawn, a yew hedge, dense and dark, with an archway cut through it at the center. That was what I remembered best, the archway and the breath-taking view of the gardens from it. Unconsciously hurrying, hoping I would not be disappointed in that view, I went through the arch.

I was not disappointed. The lawns were as close-clipped and velvety as I remembered; espaliered apples, pears and plums still heavy with fruit clung to the sheltering walls, the spreading beech tree was reaching further than ever and flower beds were bright with blossoms, loud with bees. Beyond, there was a large kitchen garden and I strolled across the lawn, meaning to glance at the vegetables before sitting down on one of the painted iron benches. My feet were silent on the lawn, and before I had gone far, I heard voices. They came, I thought, from a stone-built toolhouse, half hidden by shrubs.

A masculine voice, blurred with love, was murmuring, "Don't worry, my darling. No one will ever know. No one."

"Are you sure? Are you sure?" The girl's voice fell out in a hurried tumble of anxiety.

"I'm sure. I promise you, I'm sure."

A smothered exclamation was echoed low and followed by an eloquent silence, but I had recognized the voices. I hurried away across the lawn, my leg hurting a little as I made haste, and went out through the gateway to the clamorous causeway. There was no one about, so I stood and watched the sea for a few minutes, resting my leg. Then I made my way back indoors and to the morning room, where I picked up a magazine and began to leaf through it. I took in nothing of what I saw on the glossy paper. My thoughts were more interesting than the pages I turned. I was wondering how many people knew that Maggie and Hamish were meeting out there in the garden and what it was that no one would ever know.

# 9

MY GRANDFATHER'S color had improved. He seemed calmer and his hands had stopped their ceaseless plucking and lay quietly on the coverlet. I thought the rest had done him good, and said so. He did not trouble to reply but looked at me with a sardonic gleam in his faded blue eyes, as if asking me to spare him the niceties. I stared back, and it was he who looked away first. Impatiently I thought how childish we were being, and almost said so, but then Mackenzie brought in the tea tray and set it on a small table. He would have poured, but Grandfather said irritably, "Leave us, Mackenzie," and the man left the room on silent feet, without moving a muscle in his face.

We drank tea and ate scones and fingers of shortbread. I mentioned my visit to the garden and complimented my grandfather on its appearance. "Hamish evidently knows how to look after it."

"Yes, the boy enjoys his work, so it shows. He has green fingers, it seems. Everything grows for him. I thought he would not stay here for long, too quiet for him, I imagined, but he has been here for a while now."

"How long?"

"Six months or so, I think. Mackenzie would be able to tell you, if you are especially interested. Are you?" He fixed me with a look of surprise.

I shrugged. "Not especially." But I was interested. Six months or so. That meant he had started to work at Invercorrie around the time my leopard had first been missed. The timing of his arrival here might be significant, but if so, at the moment I could not think why. I knew why he did not leave Invercorrie. Where Maggie was, Hamish would stay. The voices I had heard outside were those of two young people deeply, passionately in love, and I felt a momentary twinge of envy. They were so young. How good life could be if one loved simply and suitably, the right person at the right time. For me the timing had always been wrong, and my brief love affairs had been unsatisfactory, unsettling experiences which left me drained and disappointed.

We finished tea, and Grandfather said, as if he had been waiting for the moment, "Have a look at this." From under the eiderdown, he produced, like a conjurer, a small parcel.

Inside the brown paper there was a box made of rough, thick cardboard with metaled corners for added strength, and inside the box, in plenty of white cotton wool, there was a silver leopard. I took it out, and laying the wrappings aside and examining the animal in detail, felt the familiar excitement of handling perfect workmanship. I hadn't held "my" leopard for ten years or more but I knew that this was mine. There was a small roughened place under the neck. My forefinger had rested there when I used to carry this little beauty about with me as if it was a toy. When I felt the rough place, the years dropped away again and my personality began splitting, so that I could look on that child and see not only loneliness but perverseness, too, and I wondered what Robb had really thought about me. I must have been an odd little creature. Robb's comments about my long and unforgiving memory were no doubt justified, but he didn't know the whole story, either.

Knowing that there were two leopards made me recognize

them now for what they were: the handles of a two-handled cup, late eighteenth-century or early nineteenth-century, I fancied—George III, probably. The date and initials of the silversmith would be on the original piece, not on the handles which had been most skillfully adapted for ornaments. I went over to the tower window for good daylight and looked more closely. My eyeglass was in the handbag which I had left in my bedroom, but I did not need it for this. There were faint marks on the base of the paws where they had been filled, silver-soldered and smoothed over after being separated from the cup. Indentations had then been made, to delineate the pads. It was a beautiful conversion, and the vessel itself, I thought, had probably been damaged long ago and sold for melting down, or discarded. It would have been thin by comparison with the sturdy handles. I thought of the period, the war of American Independence, the Napoleonic wars. A handsome silver cup of good workmanship might have been carried in the box of some general, lost in the field and damaged. Making up a romantic past for unrecognizable fragments was one of my diversions; delving into the history of some authenticated antique was quite a different matter, to be treated seriously and researched thoroughly, a fascinating but time-consuming part of my profession, where I had to have facts and could not indulge in fanciful ideas.

"Well?" My grandfather, driven beyond endurance by my long silence, was craning round to see what I was doing. I walked back to the bed thoughtfully, but smiling a little. I thought I was being put to the test.

"I wish I could have seen the original cup," I remarked.

"Eh? What's that?"

"The two leopards formed the handles like this." I held the animal vertically, head and forepaws upwards, so that the curved slender body, held like a handle, was in the position, roughly, of a rampant lion. The feet and tail would have been joined to the original cup.

A slow smile crept over the old man's face, stretching the fine skin, and his eyebrows rose. "I thought you were playing at shop, just keeping an antique business because it was fashionable. I see I was mistaken."

"Didn't your spies tell you that I had trained at Sotheby's?"

"Oh, yes, they did. But I wasn't to know how much work you put in, was I?"

"I would not have been allowed to stay there if I had not worked very hard, and the same goes for Julian."

"Julian?"

I nodded. "Julian Bennet, the man who came up with me to Scotland. My business partner."

He looked at me for a long time, something kindling in his eyes which might have been pleasure. "So that's what he is, a business partner?"

"Yes."

"Nothing else?"

"Nothing else." I changed the subject. "This parcel has not come through the post."

Grandfather looked startled. "I didn't say it had."

"Mackenzie told me . . ." I broke off and reached for the brown paper, turning it over. No postmark, merely GRANDFATHER written in capital letters with a black felt-tipped pen. A very anonymous hand indeed.

"What did Mackenzie tell you?"

I replied slowly, "What Mackenzie said was that you had been taken ill when you received my parcel. Then, when I asked him about . . . something else . . . he said that the postie had got through to the Castle this morning, so I suppose I assumed that the postman had brought the parcel."

The ironic gleam was back. "You were always good at jumping to conclusions, Caroline."

"Yes, well, I've certainly come to the conclusion that this is the leopard you gave me, and I wish I could guess the identity of whoever brought it here. We might then know who had taken it from my mother's bureau. Is Robb Morrison your only visitor?"

"Are you casting him in the role of petty thief, Caroline?"

"No, I am not, which is why I asked if he was your only visitor."

"Not quite. He is my most regular one, but his uncle comes, too, for he is my lawyer as well as your mother's. You met him yesterday, I believe?"

"Mr. Sanders?" I stared. "He is Robb's uncle?"

"His mother's brother. Not a well man, but he is getting old. We are both getting old, I suppose." Fretfully my grandfather moved in bed, pulled up the clothes around him. "Get back to the leopard. You didn't return it to me yesterday? It was found in a dark corner on a chest in the main hall."

"When was it found?"

"This morning, early."

"And you thought I put it there? You thought it might have been there since yesterday afternoon, is that it?" I was hot with anger, for I would not have used such an underhand method of returning the leopard, and if it had been in my possession, I would not have returned it, anyway. It was rightfully mine and I valued it. I said so now to my grandfather and added, "Fortunately, I can prove that I did not leave it there. Mackenzie was with me from the moment he opened the front door until he had conducted me to the drawing room, and I am sure he would have known if I had sneaked back to the hall alone before you joined me. In any case, I hadn't time. And when I left, if you remember, Robb was with me and he can vouch that I left nothing behind."

My grandfather sighed and seemed depressed as he commented, "That's satisfactory, then. But it means that Sanders may be right when he says that someone at Quern probably took your leopard out of petty spite. What a family they are, what a family."

I wanted to remind him that they were as much his family as I was, but thought better of it on account of his health. "Has Mr. Sanders been to see you since yesterday's reading of the will?"

"He came before, in the morning, for half an hour or so. He visits socially when he is in the neighborhood, and on business when I want him to come. It happens seldom enough these days. After the reading of the will, he stopped at the hotel and telephoned to let me know what had happened."

"And he thought the leopard was taken out of spite? Then why should the thief return it to you?"

"Caroline, you are not a child now. There could be only one reason. To make me think ill of you." His voice strengthened harshly. "To keep the rift between us open. To make sure I would not want to get in touch with you again."

His face had become mottled and I put a hand on his. "Grandfather, you have talked long enough. You should rest." I wanted to ask him questions but I was afraid, when I looked at him, of prolonging this interview.

"I'll tell you this first. I wrote to your mother, before she was taken ill, and asked her to come and see me. She refused. After the way I'd treated you both, she said, she did not want to come. Yet all that I told her about Angus Cunningham she learned was true. She learned it to her cost. And with him dead, our quarrel could have been healed." One hand lifted and dropped down in a gesture of defeat. Then he roused himself again. "But I wrote a second time to say that I would be writing to you, Caroline, to see if you felt any more charitably disposed towards me." He turned his head to look at me. "Would you have replied?"

"I would have replied."

"Then I wish to God I had done it at once. A few days afterwards, your mother was taken ill and I thought you would be coming to Scotland, so I waited, planning to telephone you at Quern Lodge. I knew her illness was serious, Caroline, but I never for one moment dreamed that it was critical and that she would die."

His head turned away from me on the pillow, and with pity for both of us and for my poor mother, too, I watched as a tear came from under the tightly closed eyelids and crept down a crease in his cheek. My proud, arrogant grandfather was crying for a daughter he had not spoken to for over twenty years. I bent and kissed the damp cheek gently, but he gave no sign that he had noticed my action other than convulsively clutching the sheet. I went over to the window and looked out, seeing nothing but his torment and mine. I gave him time to recover. When I went back to the bed, alarmed at the long silence, he had dropped asleep with the suddenness of the very young and the very old. I crept out of the room and went downstairs again.

There was no one about. The fire in the morning room was a pile of gray ashes in the grate, so I went to the drawing room and found that it had been made ready for me. There were flowers everywhere, and I wondered if Maggie had brought them in when she came back from the garden and her meeting with Hamish. Someone had arranged them in artless, natural beauty, without stiffness or particular expertise, in urns and vases. Their scent was strong, for the flowers were still damp and touched with silver from the day's rain.

My watch told me that it was twenty minutes past five. Julian would be at home, preparing for his evening out with the delectable Amanda and imagining, if he spared a thought for me, that by now I would be back in London. I decided to let him know what had happened, and looked about me but could see no telephone, so I rang the bell for Mackenzie. In moments he had brought an ivory-colored instrument and plugged it in near the fireplace. The cable was very long and would have gone anywhere in the enormous room, even into the tower, but I chose to have it near the wood fire, and Mackenzie placed it on a small table and withdrew in his customary near-silence.

As soon as Julian heard my voice, he said accusingly, "You're still in Scotland. I thought you were coming back today?"

"I intended to return today, really I did, Julian." I told him what had happened this morning and of my grandfather's condition.

"So now what?" he asked.

"Goodness knows. It depends on how he is. He has at least promised to see a doctor tomorrow if it is necessary, but he's as stubborn as ever. He will probably refuse when it comes to the bit."

"Which would leave you free to return, I'd say. But Sunday travel is pretty awful, isn't it? Slow trains and all that?"

"There may not be a train at all on Sunday from Fort William." I saw a loophole and slipped through it. "Shall we say Monday, Julian? Could you manage on your own until Tuesday morning?"

"Sure, I can manage. Have you told the old boy about your missing leopard?"

"It has turned up here at the Castle."

145

"It has *what*? How did it get there? You're not trying to say that your grandfather pinched it?"

Like a fool, I told Julian of the leopard's anonymous return and Grandfather's interpretation of it. At the other end of the line there was silence, bristling with suspicion and speculation. "What do you make of it?" Julian asked at last.

"I can't make anything of it, but my grandfather thinks it is an attempt to keep the rift between us wide open."

"An offensive action, then. He could be right. And the implication of that is clear enough, isn't it, Caroline? Someone wants you cut out of your grandfather's will."

"I suppose so," I said slowly and reluctantly. I hadn't wanted to face it, but Julian was a great one for facing facts and he wouldn't let me go on living in my woolly dream world now. I knew that.

"Perhaps you should have a word with the young Cunninghams. Or, better still, the lawyer."

"The lawyer, I find, is Robb Morrison's uncle, and he's my grandfather's lawyer, too."

After another long silence, I said, "Julian?"

"I'm still here, trying to think what to make of it all. This lawyer, is he discreet, do you think?"

"I haven't any idea. Everyone seems to be linked with everyone else in some way. I am the only outsider. But I shouldn't think there's anything wrong with Mr. Sanders. He seemed most correct and rather concerned for me, really."

"How about his nephew, your friend, Robb? Whose side is he on?"

"Mine, I think." I laughed. "He's even mildly suspicious of our accident in Park Lane." A moment's idle chatter about Robb had betrayed me into amused recollection of his attitude towards Julian and I cursed myself, for I had no intention of telling Julian about the tree episode.

"Has he driven down Park Lane recently? It's a race-track. Accidents happen every day, unfortunately. Not that I don't blame myself for it."

"You shouldn't, Julian. We've been into all that. It wasn't your fault."

"Caroline, this leopard business. It's very odd. If there's no train until Monday, would it be better if you went back to The Drums?"

"Oh, no. Invercorrie is like a fortress, and apart from the servants, there is only Grandfather and me here. Don't worry. I'll call you tomorrow."

"Do that. But not too early, please."

"I wouldn't dream of calling early. Have fun with Amanda."

"Thank you. I'll give her your love, shall I?"

"Don't bother," I said and hung up.

A telephone call to Fort William let me know that there was, indeed, no daytime train on a Sunday, so I would have to spend at least two nights at Invercorrie. I hoped that would not be outstaying my welcome.

When I had replaced the receiver, the silence was absolute. Outside the wind had moderated and the sea moved silently under a ruffled white coverlet. Far out I could see tall triangles of blue, rust and red, as weekend sailors took their craft through the channels which crisscrossed between the islands. I had sailed a little and envied them their freedom, hearing in imagination the slap and thrum of the wind in the sails, the high singing of ropes, and feeling on my face the salt spray quickly drying in the breeze.

On Saturdays dinner was a cold meal, Mackenzie had told me, and normally served in the dining room at eight o'clock. Unless my grandfather was awake and wanted my company, I could not stay indoors for another two and a half hours while the sun was shining. I went upstairs to have a look, and when I opened the bedroom door, I found that he had scarcely stirred. He lay peacefully sleeping, with no sign of distress on his face, and I was glad that he was comfortable.

I made my way down the wide staircase into the paneled hall and passed beneath the famous standard which hung in limp folds. I felt sad that this castle was not one of those which had remained in one family. Originally built for a daughter of the Maclean clan, it passed from that family centuries ago and had changed hands several times since. My grandfather bought it from a friend of his, a Lowland Scot, but both men loved it well and preserved the atmosphere of historic dignity while making it comfortable to live in, in spite of ancient stone walls. The faded glory of the standard, undisturbed by changes of ownership, caught the light as I looked up at it and the stylized rowan tree and wildcat were discernible. The wild power of the lithe embroidered animal, sinister and threatening, reminded me of the silver leopards.

"Miss Westwood, telephone for you. It is Mr. Morrison."

Mackenzie had emerged from his small room and was walking to the drawing-room door, opening it for me.

"Thank you, Mackenzie. My grandfather is sleeping, so after I have taken the call, I shall go out for a walk for half an hour or so. Will you open the main gate, Mackenzie, and leave it open for me until I return, please?"

"Very well, Miss Westwood." His agreement was reluctant, his expression unhappy. I knew that he disapproved of my leaving the Castle just now, but I was restless. A walk along the shore of Loch Branta would be very enjoyable.

Robb asked first about Grandfather and was relieved when I told him that the old man seemed better, but embarrassment tinged his voice when he told me the real reason for his telephone call. "I don't know how I could possibly have forgotten, Caroline, but I have a small package for you. Your mother gave it to me a long time ago, to hand on to you after her death. The eventuality seemed so remote at the time that I locked it in a drawer which I never use, and simply forgot about it. I am most awfully sorry."

I was so astonished that I did not know what to say, and I murmured feebly, "That's all right."

"I can bring it over whenever you want. Tonight or tomorrow morning."

My mind was filled with curiosity and something more, a longing to know if there was a letter for me from my mother, some message from beyond the grave. But if the package had been given to Robb a long time ago, there could be nothing recent enough to give me comfort over our later differences of opinion. The memory of my own behavior towards Mother was beginning to trouble me. How arrogant I had been, suggesting that she should leave her husband, the father of two of her children. I had known she was not happy and I'd meant well, but I should not have interfered. I was the only person not connected in any way with Angus Cunningham and I had good reason to be biased against him, but I should have pretended, perhaps, that I noticed nothing wrong. And my attitude to Grandfather, according to Robb, was cruelly unforgiving. The recollection of the scene I had made this morning filled me with shame still and I was not keen to see Robb again today. I would be too guarded, too anxious about exposing my feelings of pain and guilt to be natural with him.

"How about tomorrow, Robb? In the morning? Or do you go to church?"

"Sometimes, but not tomorrow. I'd like to come over, and perhaps I may be able to see Mr. MacRobert if he is well enough."

"At around twelve? I'm not planning to go back to London until Monday."

"Good, then I shall see you tomorrow morning. Caroline, how are you filling your time? It must be dreary for you."

"I have walked round the garden and now I plan to spend half an hour on the shore of Loch Branta while Grandfather is asleep."

"What about your leg?"

"It's all right and better when exercised."

"That's a pretty rough beach. You take care."

"I will. Thanks, Robb."

Poor man. He still felt the need to admonish me, but I thought it was more a hangover from the past than concern caused by yesterday's little adventure in the woods. Like a parent, Robb could not believe that I had grown up. The thought pursued me out of the castle door, across the court-yard and through the great double doors which Mackenzie had opened. Of Mackenzie himself there was no sign, and as I turned to look back at the Castle, I thought how forbidding were the stone walls from here, how little the Castle looked lived in. But for the tubs of flowers and my little hired car, one would have imagined the place deserted. The drawing-room fire had died down and there was not even a thread of smoke from the chimneys.

A slope of large, smooth blocks of stone led down to the shore of Loch Branta, laid there, no doubt, to facilitate the carting of seaweed used as fertilizer on the crofts of long ago. It was a convenient approach to the water, and further along by a small wooden jetty and a spit of sand, two rowing boats were drawn up on the beach. One of them belonged to the Castle and the name INVERCORRIE was painted on the side, but it looked seldom used and in need of attention. The other boat was in process of renovation and had recently been painted pale blue and white. It awaited another coat, I imagined, for there were no markings on bow or stern.

I rounded a small rocky point and there, before me, stretched the long bay which I remembered so well. It was not sandy—one had to go right up to Ardnacol for good sand—but there were rock pools and drifts of pebbles, white, umber and pink, smoothed by endless tumbling in the sea. Large rocks lay heaped at the back of the shore, and above them were grassy banks bright with gorse and thrift. Small shrubs climbed upward in a haphazard way. It could not be called a cliff; this coast was gentler than the one on the other side of Skerran which I had driven along this morning. There was nothing awesome about the heights above me, softened by shrub and distant pine, green with grass, warmly hollowed and approachable only by sea or on foot. There was no road nearer than the one through the woods, more than a mile from here and curving away from this shore.

I stood listening. It was so quiet, so peaceful. A curlew cried mournfully over the moor; waves rolled onto the shore, broke among the pebbles with a scattering rush and receded; gulls wheeled soundlessly, cruising beyond the waves, seeking food, diving suddenly to bring up a fish and gulp it down before resuming the silent search.

London seemed far away when I stood with closed eyes, listening to the sea, and I wondered what it would be like to live here in Skerran again, accepted, belonging. But since childhood I had not belonged. From hostility and unhappiness I had fled, and the bitter recollection, like a conjurer's black wand, seemed to summon the forces of evil with a loud crack of doom and the devil himself. My lids flew open. What was it, the sound which was like a shot and yet not like a shot? I looked about me, but there was no one at all on the beach as far along as I could see. The tumbled bank, then, must hide someone, for something had hit the beach near me. I felt watching eyes and wanted to turn and run but I would not allow myself to retreat with such lack of dignity. Slowly, deliberately, I turned my back on the sea and stared upwards at tussock, bush and rock. Nothing stirred. I saw no one, but fear gripped me, and with quickened breath I began to walk back towards the Castle. Above the point which I had rounded in my walk I could see the upper part of the great, solid Castle and knew it to be my refuge. My steps crunched on the beach—measured, deliberate, unhastening—and then it came again, the crack. This time I saw a spurt of shingle rise before me, less than a meter away, but I had heard no shot, only a singing whine and the sound of impact. Another crack and the missile hit a rock this time, so that I knew it for what it was—a pebble flying from a catapult and hitting a selected target just before me. It might be a child playing dangerous games, but I thought not. A stone like that, with deadly aim, could kill if it hit the temple or throat, and I was left in no doubt that whoever was firing from the bank could hit me if he chose. A moment later a stone landed just behind me. Still I refused to quicken my pace, so the next shot came closer, sending up stinging grit, which caught me in the back of the legs.

A sob escaped me, the sound of panic. I hurried my pace a little, only a little, but another flicking stone made me take to my heels, hating myself for retreating in panic-stricken disorder, spiritless and riddled with cowardice. The vilest part of the whole scene was that there came no human sound, neither shout nor laughter. No one jeered or cheered.

The malevolent silence was hateful, and I stumbled as I looked over my shoulder, still searching for an attacker. The strain proved too much for damaged muscles. My knee twisted in an agonizing pain and I gave a muffled cry and stood, clutching it. Now, I thought, now he has me. He will choose his moment, take careful aim and hit me on the neck, the temple, the eye. Quickly I looked out to sea. Anything but the eye, for loss of sight has always seemed to me the greatest deprivation of all. The moments lengthened and nothing happened; the only sounds were my own breath rasping in my throat, and the sea and the curlew's plaintive call. My attacker had tired of the game, I thought, for there could be no other explanation for the sudden cessation of hostility at a time when I presented such an easy target. There would be no sorrow that I had stumbled and hurt my weak knee, no pity for this stranger in Skerran.

Round the point there came a boat with two aboard, a man rowing, a girl lying back in the stern, trailing one hand in the water. A peaceful summer scene, exquisite in its normalcy, and instantly I understood why the attack had ceased. From that small, quietly moving boat it would be seen, and no one wielding a catapult against a defenseless human being wanted witnesses.

As I passed the wooden jetty I noticed that the newly painted boat had gone from the beach, and gave thanks for my unwitting rescuer, an unknown oarsman in a nameless craft. I went on my way, limping badly, moving slowly, but all the time drawing nearer to safety, to Invercorrie.

# IO

WHEN I limped through the gates and into the courtyard, I was astonished to see two cars parked near to mine and Mackenzie gesticulating at the front door to a knot of people dressed in holiday clothes.

"This is a private residence," he said, his usual calm fractured by indignation, his *r*'s rolling fearsomely as he made shooing gestures. Two middle-aged couples moved away at once, looking abashed, but a younger couple with three children were incredulous. "Is it no' open to the public?" they asked, persisting.

Mackenzie caught sight of me and of my limp and his attitude of distraction intensified, so that I felt more concerned for him than I did for myself. "Miss Westwood, you have hurt yourself," he said, not knowing whether to hurry towards me or defend the door against intruders with his slender body.

"It's nothing," I said calmly enough. Now that I had regained the safety of these walls, the pain eased miraculously, and I knew that with cold compresses and rest, the knee would quickly improve. I'd had bouts of this since my accident and had been told that it was only to be expected.

To the huddle of visitors I said, "I'm sorry, but as you have been told, Invercorrie Castle is a private residence, at no time open to the public."

At that, they moved away, but the young man threw me a parting shot. "Why d'you no' put a PRIVATE notice outside the gate?"

"Do you have one outside your gate?" I asked pleasantly enough, and after shooting me a disagreeable look, he returned to his car, hustled his family in and drove away, spurting gravel over the flags.

I looked at Mackenzie and we exchanged rueful glances. "Does this often happen?" I asked.

"Och, it's worse at weekends, but this is why we always keep the gates closed."

"I never knew that," I said wonderingly.

"They don't believe me, half the time, when I say they can't come in. Excuse me, Miss Westwood, I'd better close the gates and then I'll help you indoors. You've twisted your ankle, maybe?"

"My knee. I was in an accident a few weeks ago." I perched with the weight on one leg while Mackenzie hurried past me to the lodge and closed the gates. "How does the mechanism work?" I asked when he came back. "You'd better show me sometime so that I can do it for myself."

"There's no need for you to do it, Miss Westwood," he said firmly, his sense of propriety returning to him. "But it's easy enough. There's a lever in a box. You just pull it down for the gates to open and push it up for them to close, but when you go out in a car, you can set it for them to close automatically with a time switch. Now, would you take my arm, or would it be better for you to lean on my shoulder? That Hamish has disappeared, but it's Saturday and he's not supposed to work on Saturday afternoons. It's just that I could have been doing with him to get rid of those people. The master gets angry when he sees intruders inside the walls."

"It's my fault, Mackenzie. I asked you to leave the gates open for me and I could see you didn't like it, but I couldn't think why. I'll put a hand on your shoulder, I think."

But before I could do so, we heard the hard slap-slap of bare feet running on the flags, and Hamish came round the corner of the Castle from the direction of the causeway, out of breath and wearing only brief black swimming trunks. His near-naked body was muscled and deeply tanned. When he saw Mackenzie, he checked, looking warily at the old man, who gazed at him with an outraged expression on his face.

Quickly I said, "Hamish, I am glad to see you. I'm sure my weight is too much for Mackenzie. Come and give me your arm."

"What are you doing"—Mackenzie stopped, utterly at a loss for words—"dressed like that?" he finished, abandoning the middle section of whatever he wanted to say.

"I've been swimming," Hamish muttered and shot an apprehensive glance at me. Instantly I recalled the rowing boat with the man and the girl in it, both dark. Hamish and Maggie, of course, but I had no idea how Hamish had got back into the Castle from the sea without coming through the gate. "I saw Miss Westwood limping on the beach, and I came back as quick as I could to help."

"Thank you, Hamish. That was very thoughtful of you." My thanks put a stop to Mackenzie's remonstrance.

Hamish had indeed been swimming, and since rowing, I thought, for the arm on which I rested my hand was covered with fine, dark hair which was wet. His whole body gleamed with water, and the hair on his head dripped clean salt water which ran down his neck and between his shoulder blades. He had swum from the boat, I thought, and wondered if Maggie was rowing now by herself, waiting for him to swim back to her.

We must have made a strange picture, the three of us,

making our way across the courtyard and up the curved steps. "Will you manage now?" Hamish sounded anxious but he glanced down at himself, the prospect of crossing the threshold into the great hall of the Castle in his wet and unclothed state clearly more than he could envisage.

"I shall manage very well." I smiled and nodded my thanks, keeping my arm still on Mackenzie's and entering the Castle. There, I sighed, for although I knew that the acute pain would soon subside, it was a nuisance, a setback. Also, it made me feel more vulnerable to attack. Until now I had tried to persuade myself that a few isolated incidents, acts more mischievous than dangerous, did not add up to the kind of threat hinted at by Robb and Julian. Now I knew that I must come to terms with the knowledge that someone was conducting a private vendetta against me. Robb and Julian thought it had to do with inheritance, and unlikely as it seemed, I could think of no other reason —unless my presence in the area was so obnoxious to someone that it provided sufficient provocation in itself.

Mackenzie led me to a high-backed chair in the hall and brought a stool, worked in faded petit point, for my leg. "I'll fetch Mrs. Mackenzie," he said and hurried away.

I thought how odd it was that up to now I had never set eyes on Mrs. Mackenzie. She proved to be a bustling little body with round, rosy cheeks and a mass of curly white hair, but her mouth was set in tight folds, as Mackenzie's had been when we first met. I thought with some bitterness that I had a good deal of prejudice to overcome. But I was beginning to succeed with this woman's husband and I could succeed with her also, if I tried. Far from wanting to return to London, I now wanted to stay for long enough to identify my attacker and expose him. Or her, I added silently, remembering Flora's malevolent expression when we had parted at Quern Lodge.

"It is strange that we haven't met before, Mrs. Mackenzie." I smiled at her.

"I was cooking at the time when you arrived, Miss Westwood. I hope Maggie attended to you properly?"

"Yes, indeed. She seems a capable girl, and thoughtful."

"She is that. You are hurt, though. What may I do to help you?"

"Perhaps Maggie could bring me a bowl of cold water and a clean cloth to bind around by knee. If you happen to have such a thing as a crepe bandage, that would help."

"Maggie is out, Miss Westwood. I will bring them myself."

I had known, I reflected dryly, that Maggie was out, but had I needed confirmation, there it was.

"Do you wish to attend to your knee here or in your room, Miss Westwood?"

"Here. It will be easier to get upstairs to my room after I have the support of the bandage." As the woman was leaving I added a question. "Is Mr. MacRobert still asleep?"

"I believe so. Mackenzie has gone to the master's room now to see that he is comfortable." She hesitated, then said softly, "We look after him well, Miss Westwood."

"I am sure that you do."

While she was away, I reflected that there was no one else to look after the old man, no blood relation living in the Castle, and I was sorry, but then I reminded myself that he had brought loneliness on himself—and on others. A stubborn nature is a curse, I thought passionately, knowing that I had one myself, inherited, no doubt, from the old man upstairs who might well be hovering only a few steps from death. Of those who took part in the drama of long ago, two protagonists were already dead, my mother and Angus Cunningham. Only my grandfather remained— the oldest, the toughest and the most tenacious. Life was a topsy-turvy business. I did not think I had been of any importance in that long-ago feud. Then I was merely a pawn, but now, it seemed, I had become something more.

Mrs. Mackenzie brought the bowl of cold water and a cloth for bathing, as well as a clean crepe bandage. When I had attended to my knee, I found that I could walk better in spite of the thickness of a cold compress and bandage. I mounted the stairs slowly to my room, washed and freshened up to be ready for dinner, and went to see my grandfather. He was awake, propped up on many pillows encased in fresh linen, and he looked frail.

"Come in, Caroline. You have hurt your leg, I hear."

"My knee, yes. It is nothing much."

"The servants are looking after you properly? I intend to dine downstairs with you."

Gently I said, "Why don't I have a tray up here with you? Mackenzie mentioned that it was a cold meal on Saturday nights."

"That's so. To give the servants some time off." An ironic smile twisted his lips and reached his eyes. "We preserve that illusion that we still have servants, not merely the Mackenzies and one girl, plus women from the village on weekday mornings."

"And Hamish."

"Outdoors only."

"But you're lucky, Grandfather. That is quite a staff for nowadays."

"A staff for the times we live in, perhaps, but not for Invercorrie, which deserves more." He became petulant again. "Your mother should have stayed on here, cared for the Castle and kept you with us. Then I could have left the place to her and to her children, with an easy mind, instead of not knowing what to do for the best."

"Where do you keep your heart pills, Grandfather?"

He stared at me with a baleful eye. "We were talking about Invercorrie."

"We were. And I have a few things to say to you about it which you may not like."

Most people with chronic complaints keep medicines in a bedside cupboard. My grandfather was no exception. I bent down with difficulty, for I had strapped my left knee tightly and I had to thrust it sideways and lean on the bedside while I pulled open the small door of the mahogany cupboard and pushed aside the cord dangling from the bedside phone. The medicines were there, unwrapped and arranged tidily, no doubt by Mackenzie. I lifted out the brown glass bottles one by one until I found one containing small white pills and labeled Trinitrin. That would be it. I thought of my elderly friend in London and hoped my grandfather's condition was much the same as hers. I was furious with the stubborn old man but I wished him no harm. "These are the ones, aren't they, for emergencies?" I held them where he could read the label.

"I don't need them." He wouldn't even answer my question.

"When you have heard what I have to say, you may need them, so I'd rather you took one before I started." I shook one pill out onto the palm of my hand, reached for the water carafe, uncovered it and poured a glass of water.

With a flash of delicious irony which must have been an echo of his younger days, he said, "In the best detective tradition, this is where you either give me an almighty shock and withhold the pill or give me the pill, having poisoned the water. Which is it to be, Caroline?"

In an attempt to match his tone, I said, "How do I know which to do, when I haven't heard the contents of your will?" My palm was steady, the white pill lay upon it and I held the glass where he could reach it.

After a moment's hesitation, he laughed in such a way that I thought he was enjoying the situation, took a swallow of water before handing the glass back to me, and placed the pill under his tongue. "You'd need to lace water with whisky to get me to take more than a sip, and in any case, it is not needed with these pills."

"I didn't know. But your Invercorrie water is like wine. You've said so to me many a time."

"A long time ago."

"Yes." The pill had no noticeable effect upon him, but I knew it would give instant help to his circulation and therefore his heart.

"Which brings me to what I wanted to say. It is time you faced facts, Grandfather. My mother left here when I was seven years old, twenty years ago. Why say now that she should have stayed—so that you would know what to do with your possessions? She left your house, and I left with her, and it is all in the past. I make no claim on Invercorrie. Put it out of your mind, Grandfather, and make your decisions as if we had never lived here. If my father hadn't died, we never would have lived here."

"But for the death of your father, I would not be in any difficulty. You'd have had brothers and sisters, no doubt, and the inheritance would be clear."

Steadily I said, "But I do have a brother and sister— or at least a half brother and sister."

"You're not suggesting that I leave Invercorrie to Angus Cunningham's children?"

"They have as much right to Invercorrie as I have. An equal right. The same mother, your daughter; a different father, that's all. Have you ever even met them?"

"No, I have not. And by all accounts, your own meetings have not been occasions for fraternal love, merely for duty."

"That's true."

"Then why are you trying to persuade me to act in their favor?"

"I'm not doing that! Oh, Grandfather, I am only trying to get you to face facts, asking you to look at things as they are instead of living in the past, mulling over your disappointments, wallowing in bitterness. At least see Flora and Cosmo, you owe them that much."

As I spoke I wondered why I was doing this. I disliked Flora intensely, Cosmo almost as much, and I did not think they would love Invercorrie. Perhaps it was I who owed them something and was weighted down by a debt I felt I ought to pay.

"Well, thank you for giving me a lesson in family obligations." Grandfather hitched himself up higher in the bed, looking steadily at me. Silently he pointed to a chair and I drew it up a little closer and sat down, my bandaged knee sticking out awkwardly in front of me. "Now I'll give you a lesson, and there's no pill to help it over. Property brings obligations, too. It must be looked after, and if the owner dies he must try to ensure that it will be cared for, if not by his family, then by someone else. I bought Invercorrie because I loved it, and I still love it. I sold off unprofitable land and invested in pictures and some silver so that there would be something to sell later, to provide for the upkeep of the Castle. The income from stocks and shares is useless these days; desirable objects are the currency of our times." He smiled slowly. "You have found that out for yourself. Maybe some of your interest was inherited from me. Did you ever think about that?"

I had thought about it, and said so. He looked pleased.

"We're agreed, are we, Caroline, that ownership brings obligations?"

"Yes."

"Would you agree that an owner should have integrity

and determination and not run away when the going gets hard?"

"Certainly."

"Then we have some more facts to face, haven't we, Caroline? You never liked your stepfather, did you?"

"No." The word came out as little more than a whisper. I disliked even talking about Angus Cunningham.

"You thought perhaps that I should have had you here to stay, kept you away from him as much as possible, while you were a child?"

I felt my brow wrinkle as I tried to remember exactly how I had felt then. "I don't think so. I think I just wanted to be able to come here, to feel that you wanted me here."

"I wanted you, Caroline. I wanted you very much." He sighed. "But we are trying to face facts. Your mother and I had a serious quarrel. Would it have helped for me to have you here? When could you have come, when you were so small you would have had to be brought here? Every second Sunday? For part of the school holidays? Remember, I was totally estranged from your mother. I shall never understand why she married Angus Cunningham, never. Would it have helped matters if I'd given you a refuge to run to, here at Invercorrie? Wouldn't you have used it too often, instead of staying at home and learning how to make the best of things?"

"I might. Instead I used the moor as a refuge, and the beach near Ardnacol. I had a solitary childhood, Grandfather. I'd have liked your company sometimes."

"By all accounts, you had Robb Morrison to befriend you."

"By all accounts, yes. Robb must have been sick of me, but he was kind. I have been realizing, more and more, that you knew what was going on most of the time. Who brought you such regular information, Grandfather?"

"Various people. The Stocktons heard a good deal in the village. Gossip, mostly. Mrs. Munro, from time to time. Sanders, sometimes."

The lawyer. Yes, he would know what was going on in Quern Lodge, and in Grandfather's mind, but I doubt if he knew the kind of man my stepfather had been. Mrs. Munro would know. If Grandfather had any accurate information as to Angus Cunningham's wild ways, it would be from my mother's housekeeper.

"Mrs. Munro," I said softly.

"She was a reliable informant. She told me you were given to running away when things got too tough for you. Over the moor to the loch, later to London."

I was startled. I had not thought of my going to London as running away. One has to have a career, and the kind that I wanted was best pursued in London. "I don't agree about London."

"Maybe not, maybe not. But on your mother's birthday, the night that your stepfather died, you ran away, did you not?"

It was as if cold water had been flung over me from a height and I gasped and shivered, not knowing how to react, what to do, how I should answer. Finally I said, "I did not run away. I was there on the boat, and afterwards. I stayed until after the inquiry."

"You pushed your stepfather that night, and he fell. It was not mentioned at the inquiry, but you were seen, Caroline. Yet you have never spoken of it. Why?"

The events of that hideous night flooded over me like a black tide and locked my tongue. I stood up and stared at my grandfather. His thin face, with those penetrating, pained, anxious eyes, swooped towards me and receded. It was like a nightmare, like the Day of Judgment, standing there, having to answer his questions. But I did not have

164

to answer. I had only to keep quiet, as I had taught myself to keep quiet during the twenty-three months since the death of my stepfather, a horrible death, truly in the midst of life, of rejoicing on my mother's birthday. I hated to think of it and would not speak of it.

"Tell me about it, Caroline. Tell me *all* about it."

"There is nothing to tell."

"You're running away *again!*" His voice gathered strength and lashed me.

"No." It seemed to be all that I could say. I took three steps backwards. His face was accusing, shocked, angry. I turned and limped from his room, hurrying as fast as I could go.

# II

I WAS wild with frustration
once more, but tearless as usual, and this time, instead of
lying on the bed, I paced the room slowly and carefully,
exercising the muscles, before sitting in a chair near the
window and putting my leg up on a stool.

The accusation made by my grandfather—that I had
pushed my stepfather that night—shocked me immeasur-
ably, for I'd imagined that he would know nothing of that
birthday party. Robb's aggression of the morning had been
upsetting, but I had thought it concerned only his own
opinion that I ought to come back here to live. Now I
wondered who had seen me on that fateful night, for
someone certainly had. I supposed it might have been
Robb himself. He had been there, like almost everyone
else who lived around.

It had been quite a party, on my stepfather's usual lavish
scale, Mother's birthday an excuse for extra extravagance.
Her lovely face floated before me, the dreaming face of a
woman who lived intensely in the present and gave little
heed to the future. A face which could be full of determination—willful and yet yielding. What a mixture she had
been. I took a deep breath. I, too, was a mixture, my natures
perpetually at war with each other. My romantic love for
the Highlands quarreled with absorption in my job in

London, my business, the thrill of searching for beautiful things. Desirable objects were the currency of our times, Grandfather had said, but to me they were more than that.

Forcing myself to be calm, I turned my thoughts back to the birthday party. I'd gone forward briefly to get away from the crowd and be quiet for a few minutes, but Angus Cunningham followed and put his arms round me from behind in a way which was far from fatherly. All my loathing had risen in one bitter, engulfing tide, but because my mother was aboard, and many of our friends, I fought in silence, not wanting them to know of his beastliness. For Mother, it would have been the ultimate in mortification if this scene became public. I struggled and pushed. He was a strong man, and my efforts would have been useless but for the fact that he was already half drunk and off balance, and I crazy-strong with hatred.

I finally pushed him off and he stumbled and fell, but not overboard. Dear God, not overboard. I was hazy about the rest of the evening, but I had seen him later, swaying and staring at me, and yet . . . and yet . . . I wished I could remember clearly. The earlier part of that night remained with me like a recurring nightmare. What happened afterwards was jumbled up and elusive, as if a curtain had fallen over something my mind did not want to remember. I could not tell Grandfather more than he knew already, and I wondered who had told him about that night. The pain I had seen in his eyes was wounding me also. It would have been better for both of us, I thought, if I had not come here.

For a few moments I added Robb's probing to my grandfather's questions and wondered if they had decided together on a campaign and joined forces against me. But if so, I could not imagine why. Robb had said I ought to consider coming back here to live; Grandfather had accused me of running away. So perhaps they both wanted me to stay and fight the hidden menace. A feeling of persecution still hung over me, but I believed that I was not threatened here in the Castle. I brooded on that for a while and became, of course, doubtful.

It was seven o'clock by my watch and the sun was brilliant in the western sky, this morning's storm forgotten, the rain-washed air clear. There were still yachts cruising about between the small islands. It had been among those offshore islands that Angus Cunningham had met his death. I thrust the memory from me and decided that action, my sore knee notwithstanding, was the best cure for self-pity.

My trousers and old sweater, dried and neatly pressed, had been returned to my room—by Mrs. Mackenzie, presumably, since Maggie was off duty. I changed into them and went to knock on the door of Grandfather's room.

"Well, my dear, are you feeling better?" He was completely calm, his anger gone, and he laid the book he was reading face down on the bed. Vasari's *Lives*, I noticed.

I smiled doubtfully. "I ought to be asking you that question."

"Well, the answer would be yes."

"I'm glad. Grandfather, would you excuse me if I don't dine with you? It's not that I don't want to spend time with you—I'll come and see you later—but I couldn't eat anything tonight, so I'll leave you to have dinner on your own, if you don't mind."

After a moment's silence he said, "I don't mind. I am accustomed to taking meals on my own. But why can't you take food tonight?"

I half laughed. "I have eaten so much today. A huge breakfast, morning coffee with biscuits, broth and cutlets for lunch, food again with tea—there are limits to my capacity."

"There shouldn't be, at your age."

"I am not so young."

"Twenty-seven."

"Yes." Twenty-seven was not young, I thought, but I supposed that viewed from the age of seventy-eight, it seemed so.

"Well, you are old enough to know your own mind. You are upset, naturally, and I am sorry about that, for nothing plays havoc with the digestion more quickly. If you want something later, you have only to ask for it. Mackenzie will bring it to you. It's a pity you can't go for a brisk walk, with that leg. Nothing better for bringing back an appetite."

I smiled. "Brisk I may not be, but I am going to manage a walk round the garden again."

"So that is why you are dressed for action. Good, good. I shall see you later, then, Caroline." He picked up his book and prepared to read, meeting with total equanimity, apparently, the prospect of dining alone. As he had said, he was used to it.

The great hall was shadowed, for it had no west window. I crossed it, hearing my own limping footsteps where the polished floor was not covered by rugs, and I let myself out of the front door. There was no sign of Mackenzie, who would be busy, no doubt, helping to prepare the trays. I considered summoning him to say I would not want any dinner, but decided that my grandfather would deal with that.

A slight breeze had sprung up and it was cool over the causeway. I walked slowly, in no hurry, and took deep breaths of the salt-laden air, loving it. The peace of the place enfolded me so that I would have been able to forget the episode of the catapult on the beach but for Hamish's alarmed reaction and his inexplicable appearance inside the purlieus of the Castle. I was on my way to the garden to investigate that now. Also, though an attack by catapult spoke of nothing more than small boys playing dangerous pranks, the aim had been deadly accurate, and there were the other incidents—the falling tree, a landslip on the coast road and the return of the silver leopard to my grandfather to make him think ill of me, as he put it.

The last ploy had failed, I believed, and the attacks were puzzling somehow. They were not near misses, they were deliberate misses. The tree and landslip might have misfired, but the hand behind the catapult today had been sure and steady, scoring direct hits, but not on my person. I had received warning after warning, telling me I was not wanted here, but as I had no intention of being driven away, the persecutor would have to take more serious action sooner or later. At least I was beginning to recognize that danger existed, and the knowledge was an armor in itself. Here in the Castle I was safe enough, but outside I would be very careful indeed where I went, and walks along the beach by myself were out. I would drive, and lock myself in the car. The thought nagged me that if I drove, there were only two routes I could take. One led through the forest, the other along the bad surface under that overhanging cliff, the way I had come this morning. Something about that had been nagging unpleasantly at the back of my mind. Now I recalled what it was. I had caught sight of a flash of yellow at the top of the cliff, and Robb, when he called later, had been wearing a yellow sweater. I shivered. But there had been a fisherman by the loch earlier, an unrecognizable figure wearing yellow oilskins in the heavy rain. Impatiently I dismissed both events from my mind. If my persecutor succeeded in making me suspect everyone, he would succeed in frightening me into bad judgment and I would fall prey to the perils of my own imagination. I had enough trouble without that.

The shadow of the great beech tree lay on the lawn and

a pair of wood pigeons made gentle, loving noises high in its branches. The door of the cottage where I had seen paint pots earlier was closed and no sound of voices came from the stone toolhouse in the shrubs. Sparrows, robins, blackbirds and thrushes hopped on the grass, pecking at invisible tidbits, and when I went through the yew hedge into the kitchen garden, a cloud of birds rose, screeching at being disturbed. A blackbird, orange beak wide with alarm, rushed close by me to perch on a stone wall and scold me with an angry chip-chip-chip, displeased at having been disturbed while he supped on enormous cultivated blackberries. I could not blame him and reached out to pick a few berries for myself, staining my fingers in the process and doubtless my mouth, too. The taste of the rich juice brought back poignant childhood memories. My mother had liked to gather fruit herself, for preserving.

The blackbird fell silent, gazing down at me, tilting its head sideways and looking at me with a bright, round eye, seeming to recognize that, after all, I meant it no harm. When I began to walk round the garden, he returned to his feast, rustling among long, thorny branches and leaves which were already turning crimson.

The crops were good and there were few weeds, but I would not find what I sought among the vegetables. I searched the wall but there was no gate or doorway on the sea side, and when I came back to the archway, I told myself that I had known there was no way down from there. I could remember the rockface as seen from the sea, and it was sheer and dangerous, with no flight of steps for access. The water here was seldom calm enough for small boats to approach the rocks, but today it would have been possible.

I sat on one of the benches in the flower garden for a while, watching the birds, which were so tame that after a while they hopped close to my feet. My thoughts were drifting, but I had in no way forgotten the object of my visit when footsteps on the lawn made me turn. It was Hamish, as I had known it would be.

"Do you live in one of the cottages, Hamish?"

He nodded. "What happened on the beach today, Miss Westwood? Did you have a fall, or what?" The urgency in his voice tensed his whole body.

He had seen something from the boat, I thought.

"I stumbled, hurrying."

The boy frowned, his dark brows meeting above the round black eyes, so like his mother's. He stared at me, trying to assess my answer, I supposed, in the light of whatever he had seen.

"Were you and Maggie swimming from a boat?" I asked, smiling, I hoped disarmingly.

"You saw us?"

"Not exactly. I put two and two together, when you came running. How did you get from the boat to the Castle? That's what I don't understand."

"I climbed the rock over here." He waved a vague hand in the direction of the far wall.

I felt a spurt of anger at being taken for a fool. "I don't believe you, Hamish. I know what the rock is like over there."

He scowled and went sulky again.

"It must have been dangerous for Maggie, having to control the boat near the rocks while you went into the water."

"She wasn't near the rocks. I'd not let her take the boat near the rocks, Miss Westwood, even when it's calm."

"You took the boat from the beach. I'd seen it there earlier."

"Yes. I'm allowed to. I'm doing it up in my spare time."

"Is it yours?"

"No, it belongs to the Castle, but who else is going to use it?"

Who, indeed. "I'm not objecting, Hamish. I am only wondering why you came from this direction and not through the gate, after I had"—I paused—" hurt my leg."

"This was the quickest way from where we were."

"And you thought I might be followed to the Castle gateway. That's it, isn't it, Hamish?"

"Who would be following you?"

I sighed. "I thought *you* might know that."

"No. I don't."

"Well, you might have suspicions, then."

He was silent.

"You still haven't told me how you got into the Castle grounds, Hamish."

"I do some mountaineering. I know how to use ropes," he said at last, after deep thought.

"Maggie, too?"

He missed the irony and said, "Aye."

"But why use ropes to the Castle? You may come and go as you please in your free time, surely?"

"We like to swim. I manage to have a swim sometimes when I . . . when I should be gardening. On a hot day, just for a few minutes, it does nae harm." He was warming to his subject and I looked at his earnest young face, filled with a mixture of relief and satisfaction at his own ingenious explanation, oblivious of the fact that I did not believe a word of it.

"A rope," I said contemplatively. With grappling irons, it was just possible, I supposed, if put in place from above.

"Do you want to see it?" he asked, suddenly bold.

"No, thank you." I shrugged. If he was offering to show me a rope, he would have one to show. Immediately I wished I had asked to see it. If he had used a rope as described, one end of it would still be wet, but I would not belabor the subject any more.

"Where is Maggie now, Hamish?"

His whole face cleared and brightened. "She's getting dressed up. We're going to the dancing over at Invera-corachie."

"What about you? Aren't you going to dress up?" He was wearing grimy jeans and a washed-out T-shirt, streaked with blue paint.

He looked down at himself. "Och. I'd better go. It's only cords and a clean shirt for me—nothing fancy, you know—but the girls like to dress up."

I laughed, liking the boy even if he was not being entirely open with me. "I'm sure you'll have a good time, anyway. Enjoy yourselves."

"Thanks, Miss Westwood."

I got up and moved across the lawn, trying hard not to limp and succeeding pretty well. I did not want Hamish to think I was much incapacitated, but whether that was out of pride or fear, I scarcely knew. I hated the thought of someone pelting me with stones from a catapult and, by such simple means, reducing me to terror and flight. Yet it had happened. I also hated the thought of being underpowered, so to speak, if I had to start running again, and I took my walk back to the causeway at a steady, careful pace, strolling and enjoying the cool evening.

As I went through the gateway and out onto the cause-way itself, the wind caught at my hair and blew it across my eyes. I pushed it back and saw someone standing at the Castle end of the causeway, looking down at the rocks below. It was Robb, and after a moment he caught sight of me, moved away from the parapet and came towards me. I was so astonished at seeing him there that I faltered and put a hand on the stone balustrade to steady myself.

"Robb, what a surprise!"

And what a feeble greeting, I thought to myself angrily. Where has your wit gone, Caroline Westwood, the ready quip, the joky remark which would show this man that you have fully recovered from your tantrum of the morning and attached no importance to his interfering remarks.

He was near to me, his eyes steady and inquiring on mine. "I know you don't expect me until tomorrow morning, but your grandfather telephoned a short while ago and invited me to eat with him. It appears you're not hungry."

Grandfather did not invite Robb over just to eat up my dinner, I thought, but did not say so. Aloud I said merely, "How good of you to come at such short notice."

"I always come when your grandfather wants help. Someone has to."

"I'm glad you're available," I responded tartly.

"Come, Caroline, let's not quarrel again. I shouldn't have spoken to you as I did this morning. I had no right."

Somewhat mollified, I shrugged and smiled. "That's all right. I don't want to quarrel, either. There have been enough quarrels around here."

He did not reply to that, but took my elbow and turned me so that we were both looking out to sea, the freshening breeze blowing our hair back from our faces. I glanced at Robb's profile, the curved nose, prominent bones above the eyes, strong jaw, and wondered what he was thinking about. His next remark steered me away from Invercorrie's problems for the moment.

"How about that view, Caroline? There's nothing like that in Hyde Park."

"Nothing," I agreed, "but the park has other joys."

"The Serpentine?"

"The Albert Memorial."

"A monstrosity. With my apologies to Sir George Gilbert Scott."

"Knightsbridge Barracks, then." My mouth twitched in a smile.

"Another monstrosity. Different, I'll grant you."

"Well, the horses in the Row, you can't dislike the horses."

"There is also the traffic all the way round and even through the park, making the air full of the scent of city. *Eau de trafic*."

"You're a countryman, Robb."

"Through and through," he agreed.

I thought it must be nice to be so sure, so solidly implanted in one's own place.

"Have you seen Grandfather since you arrived?"

"Briefly. He asked me to make sure you were all right. I gather you had a difference of opinion."

"I believe I have had a difference of opinion, as you call it, with almost everyone I know during these past two days. It must be me."

"Everyone?" He was taken aback.

"Mrs. Munro may have escaped. And Maggie."

"What about Julian?"

"Why are you so interested in Julian? You always drag him into the conversation."

"Do I?" He picked up my hand and examined it as he had done when we dined together at The Drums, but this time he was looking not at a bare ring finger but at purple marks. "You have been stealing blackberries. Look at those stains!"

"I expect my mouth is just as bad." I tilted my head to show him, and I swear I was not being coquettish. What is more, Robb knew me too well to imagine I was being provocative; people don't change that much after the age of eighteen. So what happened next shocked me. Robb's arm came round my waist like a steel bar and swept me round against him. Then he bent his head and kissed my mouth most expertly. It was a long, hard kiss, and dizzily I thought that since the last Christmas party kiss he had given me, heaven alone knew how many years ago, Robb Morrison had certainly had a lot of practice. I wanted to say so, to be flippant and woman-of-the-worldish, but I found, when he lifted his face, that I was clinging to the front of his tweed jacket with one hand and the other had somehow reached the back of his neck where the hair sprang roughly under my fingers. I could not think of anything to say. Robb's arm stayed where it was, around my waist, pressing me against him, and a hand came up to touch my cheek and hair before sliding under my chin to lift it. He waited a moment, looking at me, his eyes searching my face, asking questions I did not know how to answer. Then a slow smile began at his lips, spread to his eyes, and he bent. At that moment we both heard running footsteps, and while we didn't exactly spring apart as if guilty of some crime, the spell was broken—my hands slid from him and his arm relaxed, to hold me only lightly as we turned.

Hamish emerged from the garden gateway, carrying a flat parcel, resplendent in pale-blue cords and a dazzling white shirt, his hair neatly brushed and his face shining with eagerness. He checked when he saw us, his eyes widening a little, then he continued, quickening his pace and saying a breathy "Good evening" as he passed us.

"He is going to a dance with Maggie," I explained.

"Indeed? Lucky fellow." Robb glanced at his watch and grimaced. "I am bidden to a more sober gathering and I see that I am already late. Your grandfather will fear that I haven't found you. I'd better go back, Caroline." He spoke without any particular regret and I could have hit him, but I turned immediately and began to walk with him, forgetting my knee. Instantly, of course, it weakened and made me stumble.

"That knee of yours is worse, or have you hurt it again?" In his voice there was a mixture of anger and concern, and as his eyes flicked to my all-concealing trousers he frowned. "*Have* you hurt it again?"

"Well, you warned me about the beach," I said lightly.

We began walking back to the Castle and he tucked my hand through his arm. I expected another scolding but he only said, "Bad luck. Should you have it seen to?"

"Oh, no. It will be better in a day or so."

"Won't you change your mind and join your grandfather and me?"

"I'll join you for coffee," I compromised. "I am not hungry, Robb. Truly."

"How disappointing," he said, his eyes teasing me, and I almost changed my mind.

As we reached the flagged courtyard and turned to the great door of the Castle, which was standing open, with Mackenzie hovering inside where we could see him but he could not hear us, Robb said, "May I still come tomorrow at twelve?"

"Yes, of course. The package from my mother . . ."

"I have it here." He drew it from his pocket and handed it to me—a small, square parcel, in one of the thick palegray envelopes which matched the notepaper my mother always used. It was supplied to her by Jenners of Edinburgh and the sight of the envelope brought her back. I wondered at my own behavior, so light-hearted so soon after her death. But we had died the deaths of many partings, she and I, in recent years, slashed asunder by misunderstandings.

Robb kept my arm in his as we mounted the steps, I holding the package in my right hand and looking at it. Then in the great hall Mackenzie came forward to close the door and the two men made for the stairs. Mackenzie hesitated and looked back at me. "I'll take coffee with the gentlemen later, Mackenzie. Perhaps you will let me know when they are ready."

"Yes indeed, Miss Westwood." The sibilant s's were soft and gentle. He had accepted me.

I hesitated, not knowing whether to make for the small morning room or the drawing room. I chose the morning room, for it was nearest; and because it looked out on the courtyard I saw Hamish and Maggie emerge from a side door. The truck which Hamish used to bring staff from the village was waiting for them, polished and glittering, and before Hamish handed Maggie into it, he whipped the paper off his parcel. The expression on Maggie's face when she saw the contents made me catch my breath. The soft sweet smile, which was often there, spread gloriously as Hamish produced a stole and gently draped it around her shoulders. He wanted to kiss her but glanced up at the Castle, wary of being seen. I was too far back in the room to be visible and so I saw Maggie lift her mouth to his, saw her two hands at the back of his dark head and the pride in her face as she drew back and put those hands on the stole, arranging it as if she thought it would keep her warm for the rest of her life. Perhaps it would, for it was a tartan stole, the Munro tartan of scarlet, green and purple, and Hamish would not have given it to her unless he meant to make her a Munro. It was like an engagement ring, I thought, smiling with tenderness for them, touched by their young love. If they could keep that alive they would do well together, and I wished them well.

The truck left and I looked down at my small package,

hesitating for only a minute longer before tearing open the envelope and withdrawing a small red leather box. I knew instantly what was inside, and opened it. In a cream velvet slot, there lay my mother's sapphire engagement ring. The name of a famous Edinburgh jeweler was inscribed in the lid—Wilson and Sharp, Princes Street. There was no note, no letter of explanation. I was glad to have the ring, which I remembered so well, but how I wished she had written a letter to explain to me why she should have given it into Robb Morrison's keeping. To receive a wordless gift from her, with no message at all, flung me into a pit of despair. I snapped the box shut and was holding it tightly in my palm as Mackenzie entered.

"Miss Westwood, I have mended the fire in the drawing room for you. It is cold in here."

"Yes, it is cold." I found that I was bone-cold, shivering, but I managed to summon a smile for Mackenzie. "Thank you. I had better wash and change, I think, but then I shall go to the drawing room until the coffee is served."

Like an automaton I washed, did my face and hair, and changed into my suit. How sick I was of suit *and* trousers and jersey. I wished I had brought a dress or, better still, a long skirt such as Maggie had been wearing when she went out with Hamish. Still, the day after tomorrow I would be on my way south again.

As I thought of the ring my depression lifted. Mother could not have known that it would reach me so soon. She might have intended to leave a letter for me. I clung to that thought as I went down to the drawing room, passing the door of my Grandfather's bedroom and hearing a rumble of voices from within. They were discussing something in staccato phrases and were not, I thought, entirely in agreement.

Downstairs I settled in a comfortable armchair near the

fire and picked up a large *Historical Guide to the High-lands of Scotland*. The pictures were magnificent and there were many of the Skerran area. I began to read, but was interrupted when a knock came on the door and Mrs. Mackenzie entered with a silver tray bearing a crystal jug of milk, a tumbler to match and a small silver dish filled with tiny triangular sandwiches and decorated with slices of tomato and leaves of chicory and a scattering of cress. When I sighed and began to protest, she said, "I have brought this myself, for Mackenzie is busy upstairs with the gentlemen, but I bring it on the master's orders, Miss Westwood. He says you're to take something."

Laughing, defeated, I said, "Thank you, Mrs. Mackenzie. It looks very tempting."

She withdrew, looking gratified, and regretfully I laid aside the beautiful book, not wanting to mark the pages, and picked up a magazine to look at instead. I almost never ate on my own without reading, unless I had some music to listen to, and music seemed to be the one thing missing from Invercorrie. If I stayed for long, I would have to remedy that.

I took coffee later with men who were obviously at loggerheads, but we made polite conversation as we drank it, and small glasses of a whisky liqueur were poured by Mackenzie before he withdrew.

"Is there an atmosphere in here, or am I mistaken?" I asked after a silence, knowing well that I was not mistaken.

"There is a slight coolness on Robb's part, but he will come round, Caroline."

I raised my eyebrows.

Robb drained his coffee cup and said nothing. Then he sipped at his liqueur, all the time watching my grandfather, waiting for him to continue, scowling.

"You see, I have acted on your advice, my dear. I think you are right, and I ought to meet Flora and Cosmo." Grandfather made a small *moue* of distaste at even having to mention their names. "So I have invited them both to come here for luncheon tomorrow, and, of course, when I heard that Robb was coming at noon to visit you, I asked him to stay also. I intend to lunch with you all, downstairs."

"Don't you *want* to stay for lunch, Robb?" I turned my eyes on him.

"Oh, I want to stay. I wouldn't miss it for anything." He tossed back the rest of his liqueur, wasting the delicate flavor entirely, and he rose to his feet. "If you don't mind, I think I had better get back."

He looked just as he had this morning. Furious.

"The sick cow again?" I asked, which was unkind of me, but I thought Robb was behaving in a ridiculous manner.

"She is still sick, if that is what you mean." He said goodbye to Grandfather, shaking the frail old hand gently enough, and I went with him to the door, and downstairs. In the great hall where dark shadows lurked in every corner, Robb turned to me. Crossly he said, "I suppose you mean well, telling your grandfather he ought to meet Flora and Cosmo, but it will be a great strain on him. I don't like the idea at all."

"He is resilient, Robb."

"I hope you are right."

# 12

IT WAS astonishing, I thought as I went upstairs, how quickly Robb Morrison could change. All in one day he had probed unmercifully into my private affairs, telephoned like a cooing dove, kissed me and snapped my head off.

"What is the matter with Robb?" I asked my grandfather.

"He seems put out, doesn't he? The Morrisons never liked to be crossed. He's descended from the Lewis branch, you know, a mixture of Norse and Irish. Terrible."

"Grandfather, you are trying to sidetrack me."

"Perhaps I am. And I suppose it cannot be done, unless you'll agree to being sidetracked?" He looked up at me like a tired but spirited gnome and smiled.

I smiled back and said, "How about a game of backgammon before you settle down?"

He brightened up at once. "Splendid, spendid. Robb plays chess with me sometimes and Mackenzie and I play backgammon in the evening, but I don't ask him to give up his Saturday. How did you know I played?"

I nodded towards the board, which I'd noticed earlier in the day, brought it and set it up on a bed table. My grandfather was a better gambler than I. We played two games and he won both.

At eleven o'clock Mackenzie knocked softly and entered with some hot milk. He managed, like the good butler he was, not to look surprised at finding me there, but humanity overcame him and he looked astonished when Grandfather asked him for the pills in the bedside cupboard. "You'd better give me whatever I'm supposed to take at night, and then in the morning we'll decide on the daytime ones." He gave a sigh of great martyrdom. "I suppose I may as well try Dr. Farr's remedies. Would that please you, Caroline?" He shot me a piercing glance.

"Very much," I said. "And if those pills don't do you any good, we'll send for Dr. Staines and ask him to prescribe something else. I want to see you well again."

"You're a persistent girl, like your mother."

I bent and kissed his cheek. "Perhaps we both take after you." I had used the present tense for my mother as well. In that context, it seemed fitting, though I had not given it any conscious thought.

As I was leaving, Mackenzie asked if he could bring me anything, but I refused.

"Did you eat the sandwiches I ordered?" Grandfather barked, reminded of them.

"Some of them. Thank you for thinking of it."

He nodded and reached for his milk. "Horrible stuff," he muttered. "I wouldn't drink it if it wasn't from Ardnacol."

I was surprised. I'd had no idea that Robb supplied milk to the Castle.

After I'd had a bath and was in my nightdress, robe and slippers, I looked about my comfortable room with pleasure, even affection. The fire still glowed, my bed had been turned down, the electric blanket was on and there was a carafe of water covered by a glass at the bedside. There was everything I could want, except a book for bedtime reading. There were a few books on a walnut side table, between book ends, but they were Victorian novels for the most part, with a volume or two of essays. I was not in the mood for either, and was tantalized by the memory of the delectable book on Scotland which I had started to look at in the drawing room.

There was a light burning outside my room and another by the staircase, but below me the hall was in darkness and I had no idea where the switches were. I looked about me at the top of the stairs but could see none, so I decided to creep quietly down, feeling my way, and cross the hall without turning on any lights. Without summoning servants, too. I had my own ideas about being waited on, and approved of it only in moderation and at reasonable hours.

My knee behaved itself and I reached the drawing room door without difficulty. My hand was on the knob when I heard a voice inside, raised in hot refusal. "I'll do no more. I've done enough. You're playing dangerous games now and I'll not help you." After a pause the voice came again, "You're *what*? I don't believe you!" Then, after another pause, there came a tinkle of telephone bell and a crash as the receiver was slammed down. I opened the drawing-room door. Earlier I had spied on Hamish as he spread a stole round Maggie's shoulders; now I was eavesdropping on him and disliked myself for it, but I could not have expected to find Hamish Munro in the drawing room.

"What are you doing here, Hamish?" I asked sharply.

How he had changed from the happy boy I'd seen earlier. His face was pale and strained, his eyes full of apprehension as they met mine.

"I was using the telephone," he said at last.

"I realize that. Who were you talking to?"

"I can't say."

"You mean you won't say."

He did not reply.

"Do you usually use the drawing-room telephone?"

"No, Miss Westwood, but it is the only one I can get to which is private."

"I see. You had permission?"

"No. I haven't seen anyone to ask." He looked even more unhappy.

"All right, Hamish. I don't propose to take it any further."

He had troubles enough, I thought, and it was none of my business, but I wondered whether I ought to make it my business. As he was leaving the drawing room, I said, "I thought you were going to a dance?"

"We went." He smiled wryly. "You're forgetting this is a God-fearing country where the dances end at midnight on a Saturday so as not to encroach upon the Sabbath."

I had indeed forgotten. "Did you have a good time?"

His face softened and glowed. "We did that."

I nodded and he slipped out like a wraith. He was wearing sneakers.

Thoughtfully I picked up the book I had been looking at earlier and waited a few moments, flipping through it without seeing anything. I closed it and looked at the telephone. There was no directory or pad or pencil near the phone, so whatever number Hamish had called he had known by heart or carried in his pocket. It was late to make a call, so he knew the habits of whomever he had talked to. But it was useless for me to speculate. I knew nothing of Hamish Munro's life or friends, but one of his friends was becoming a nuisance, it seemed.

I read for hours, fascinated, for in that book there was a great deal about the Morrisons of North Skerran, and I learned that the family had once owned all of the northern coast of the peninsula along the shores of Loch Branta, including Invercorrie Castle itself. Robb had never mentioned this to me, which was strange, because the land had been in possession of the family for generations, right up to the seventeenth century. Apart from being landowners, the Morrisons then had been deemsters, and a search in the glossary told me that deemsters were lawmen.

Finally putting the book aside in the early hours of the morning, I puzzled over why Robb had never told me of his ancestors' ownership of Invercorrie, and wondered if he ever felt he wanted it back. I switched off my light and lay a long time in darkness while the Castle brooded about me, with ancient timbers creaking, the gusty wind whirling in off the sea, thrusting at the windowpane, crying in the chimney. Below I could hear the ceaseless swell and crash of waves on rock. It was a lovely, sad, lonely place, in need of young people who would throng the stone passages and bring the echoing rooms and stairways to life again. The gardens, sheltered and beautiful, needed children . . . I drifted into sleep and knew nothing more until Maggie, smiling, was in the room with my breakfast tray, pulling back the long, handsome curtains of purple velvet, exactly the color of thistle tops, and letting in sunshine.

As I sat up, my spirits quailed a little, remembering that today Flora and Cosmo were coming to lunch, largely at my instigation. I hoped nothing unpleasant would happen, especially as Grandfather had decided to be present. Robb, I hoped, would keep a rein on everyone, if it should be necessary. He seeemed to be the only person with real influence over Grandfather MacRobert.

As we exchanged our morning greetings, Maggie and I, I thought that she looked very happy and beautiful, her eyes soft and smiling. She was dreaming of last night and Hamish, no doubt. I hoped he would not disappoint her, and wondered who it was he had telephoned in such angry protest, saying that he would not help any more because he or she was playing dangerous games. It was a man he had been talking to, I fancied, from the tone of his voice.

I drank my orange juice, ate a boiled egg with brown wheatmeal toast and finished up with an oatcake and honey. It was all delicious, and as I drank an enormous cup of coffee, sitting up against high pillows, I felt pampered as I had not been for years. How easy it would be to slip back into this life, so far removed from the hurly-burly of auction rooms, the endless searching of junk shops in small towns for the occasional item of value at a reasonable price. Real bargains, in a world increasingly aware of the value of beautiful items from the leisured past, were now hard to find. But I loved the search for glass and silver and porcelain. Idly I wondered if I ought to have a look round the Western Highlands before returning to London. The area might yield some old Scottish furniture or a silver quaich or two. Salted porridge eaten from a silver quaich must have put heart into many a Highlander on a cold morning, but today was warm, the sun was shining, and I decided that I would gather flowers from the garden and arrange them in vases before the guests arrived.

First I called on Grandfather and found him looking remarkably well. The prospect of his luncheon party was having a rejuvenating effect and he told me he had slept well. "Were you comfortable?" he asked.

"Very." I bent and kissed his paper cheek. "And now I am going to gather flowers for the house."

"Good, good. Mackenzie will show you where everything is."

"Is your leg better, Miss Westwood?" Mackenzie spoke over his shoulder as he showed me to a narrow room, stone-walled, at a level below that of the great wall, and I replied that it was. On one side of the room there were shelves with vases of all shapes and sizes. Scissors hung on a hook near an ancient white porcelain sink with a single cold-water tap.

"This is the flower room," he explained. And from beneath the sink he produced a trug, a long, shallow basket in which to put cut flowers. "Is that everything you'll be needing, Miss Westwood?"

"Everything, thank you, Mackenzie."

"Maggie will help you with the vases when you have arranged them." He seemed pleased that there would be plenty of flowers, I thought.

"This room is like a cell, Mackenzie." I could not remember having seen it before when I had lived at the Castle.

"That's what it is, a cell. The window was once just a slit. The Invercorrie men had a short way with their enemies, I'm told. As often as not they put them in here and forgot about them until a relative came to claim the body, dead or alive. Then they yielded up the prisoner, wrapped in a plaid of his own tartan—specially obtained—filled his rescuers with good whisky and sent them on their way."

"How barbaric!" I looked about me and shivered. There was little in the room to remind one of those days, apart from a few initials faintly scratched on the wall, but it was cold, deathly cold, and outside the window the water was not far below. The causeway to the garden was higher than this window and to the right.

As I glanced out I could see at the other end of the causeway and beneath it—so as to be entirely concealed from above—a thick knotted rope. Mackenzie's eyes followed the direction of mine and he smiled a wintry smile. "Hamish Munro's private route. He thinks I do not know about it but I have known this long time. But och, he is a good boy. I do not mind if he goes for a swim occasionally, or off ashore for a wee while."

There were times when the exquisitely deliberate speech of Mackenzie the Highlander became more pronounced. I thought about what he had said. "Off ashore" there was a bank with good hiding places and small stones to fire from a catapult. And a wood with trees to fell. Well, at least Hamish had told me the truth when he'd said he had a rope, though that thick cord was not the type for mountaineering.

"I must go, Mackenzie, or I shall not have the flowers ready by twelve o'clock."

"Of course, Miss Westwood." He stood aside for me, and after I had passed him and walked into the stone passage, he said, "Would you be knowing when it was that the master invited Miss Cunningham and Mr. Cunningham to come here to lunch?"

"Last evening, I believe." I could hear Mackenzie's quiet footsteps behind me on the stone floor. "You know that Mr. Morrison is also coming?"

"Oh, yes, but Mr. Morrison has often been before." The old man was puzzled. Grandfather's invitation probably had little to do with my unasked-for opinion. By a sudden whim on his part, he had agreed to see Flora and Cosmo, but he was so prejudiced against them that it would be difficult for them to win him over. Still, they were formidably attractive. Given today's opportunity, they might do very well, and I wondered how I would feel if Grandfather decided to leave the Castle to his younger grandchildren. If he did that, Invercorrie land would be joined again to the land belonging to Quern Lodge, for the Forestry plantations did not take in the lochside. In my mind, I took speculation a step further. If Flora then married Robb Morrison, the whole of North Skerran would again be in the hands of the Morrison family. How very neat and fitting that would be. History repeating itself. I had no right to feel angry at the possibility. My place was not here in Invercorrie or any other part of Skerran.

I picked a basketful of late roses, phlox and the lovely King George V Michaelmas daisy. Then I added leafy branches, trails of blackberry, senecio leaves and berberis, and with an armful as well as a basketful, I returned to the little stone cell, with Hamish's rope hanging mute beyond the window, and I arranged the flowers and foliage in huge, tall vases. Then I decided to cut a few small roses and some lavender for a low table arrangement.

During my earlier visit to the garden I had seen no one, and still there was no one about, but the door to the cottage under repair stood wide open to a through current of air. The smell of paint wafted towards me and I glanced inside at clean white walls and paintwork in what would be a living room running from front to back. I could also see a kitchen, being painted in light blue, and I remembered the stains on Hamish's T-shirt.

I soon found the pink rosebuds I wanted, and the sprigs of scented lavender, gray and misty blue, and was turning back when I saw Hamish in the doorway of the cottage. He was dressed in cords and a clean casual shirt of light blue, and he seemed to be watching me, waiting to see, perhaps, if I would refer to last night's episode in the drawing room, but I merely smiled and said "Good morning."

I would have passed him but he called softly, "Miss Westwood."

"Yes, Hamish?"

"Would you mind not . . . not mentioning my telephone call to Maggie?"

"I have forgotten about your telephone call."

He looked startled, then smiled as he understood, and I caught once again the ghost of a likeness to someone, but I could not think who it was—not his mother, certainly. I considered telling Hamish that Mackenzie knew all about his rope route in and out of the Castle, but decided against it. One act of discretion required another, perhaps.

"Is this cottage going to be yours, Hamish?"

He went scarlet but said that it was nobody's in particular; he had merely got permission to do it up. Quickly he added, "But not on the Sabbath. I'm only doing some tidying up now, and then I'll be at the gate until the guests have arrived." He glanced at me curiously. "We don't often have visitors at the Castle, except maybe Mr. Morrison."

"So I believe. May I see over the cottage, Hamish? I have to hurry, too, but I'd like a quick look."

"Surely." He stood aside without hesitation and I went inside. The removal of a wall had made a beautiful room of the ground floor, and the kitchen was surprisingly spacious. Hamish stood by while I looked, feigning indifference, but I could feel his dark eyes boring into me and he looked pleased when I said I thought it would be beautiful when he had finished.

"Do you want to see upstairs?"

"I don't really have time, but . . . . yes, I'd like to."

If I had not gone upstairs, I might not have seen the dark and dusty Volvo station wagon parked off the road which ran down to the Castle entrance. I ran to the window. Surely, *surely* it was our car, the firm's car, with Julian at the wheel? I tried to open the small window and stood wrestling with the catch for a few seconds, pushing and muttering in irritation. The painted window had been closed too soon for the damp, salt atmosphere, and had stuck fast. As I watched in frustration and thrust in vain at the window, the car started up and moved not to the Castle entrance but past it and round the point to the rough road by Loch Skerran.

"Did you say something?" Hamish's voice came from the foot of the stairs and no doubt he had heard my exclamations.

"No, nothing. We'd better go, Hamish." I complimented him on his good workmanship, the charm of the bedrooms and the view, and if he noticed a change in my attitude, he said nothing. We parted at the next cottage, where he lived, and I went on, pausing at the causeway to search the view for any sign of the Volvo, or Julian, but all I could see was a family of picnickers near the old wooden jetty. Before I entered the house, Hamish passed me at a run, his hair neatly brushed, making for the great gateway.

I sent for Maggie to carry up the finished vases of flowers and asked her to put them where she thought best, in drawing room, dining room and hall. "This one I am doing for the dining table." Quickly I thrust soft mesh into a small pewter bowl, eighteenth-century and probably by Chamberlain. It was sacrilege and I worked very carefully, only using the receptacle because it had been employed for this purpose before and the blue and pink flowers would look exquisite against the gray sheen of the pewter. I had buffed up the bowl with the ball and heel of my thumb, and when the flowers were arranged, carried it with me to the dining room, where a round table had been laid with silver and crystal in the old-fashioned way with white damask. A dark-red tablecloth would have looked good, I thought, but I was perfectly certain that my grandfather would not own such a thing and, moreover, would dislike it intensely. Anyway, the traditional table was a delight to the eye.

There was time to run upstairs, wash my hands, tidy my hair and put on lipstick and eyeshadow before the guests were due. My last action in the bedroom was to slide Mother's sapphire engagement ring onto the third finger of my right hand. The large square stone glowed darkly. I wanted to see Flora's expression when she spotted it. She had claimed never to have seen Mother wearing a ring like this, but a sapphire was a sapphire, and she would put two and two together, I had no doubt.

Mackenzie was opening the door to Robb as I descended the great staircase, and his eyes, adjusting to the dimness inside, came straight to me. He watched in silence for a moment and then said in a composed tone, "Good morning. Your knee is better, I see."

"Almost completely recovered. These twists seem to right themselves quickly."

"I'm glad." He was still cool and followed me to the drawing room, where Mackenzie poured sherry for me and whisky for Robb before leaving us.

I tilted my chin up, smiled at Robb and lifted my glass— he lifted his but did not smile. He was frowning, his gray eyes somber.

"Oh, come on, Robb. You may be dreading the luncheon and perhaps the whole thing will be a disaster, but surely you agree that Grandfather ought to meet his other two grandchildren? It is too silly for him to behave as if they didn't exist."

"Perhaps you are right," Robb said smoothly. "Have you seen your grandfather this morning?"

"Yes, I have. He seems very bright, and I think he is looking forward to having company." I could not help thinking of my mother, wishing she had come back here earlier, bearded the old lion in his den, and perhaps made up their quarrel. My mind came back to the present. "You haven't seen Julian, I suppose?"

Robb was startled. "Julian? Your partner? Is he back here?"

I shrugged and did not answer directly, for I could not. "There are plenty of dark-blue Volvo station wagons around, I suppose."

There was time for no more because Mackenzie opened the door and announced Flora and Cosmo. I thought Flora looked pale but defiant. Cosmo had a brilliance born of excitement in his blue eyes and they whipped around the room, taking everything in, before coming to rest on Robb and me. My half brother and sister joined us in the tower section; Mackenzie poured drinks from the beautiful decanters and said that the master would be down directly.

"Does Grandfather call himself the master?" Flora looked at me with amused astonishment.

"No. That is what Mackenzie calls him. There is quite a bond between them. Grandfather is lucky."

"So, I should imagine, is Mackenzie." It was a sneer—there was no other way of describing it—and I looked at Cosmo with dislike, but he had the grace to say quickly, "Sorry. I did not mean that the way it sounded."

Flora had moved to Robb's side and was looking up at him, smiling, exuding pleasure in an exaggerated way, I thought. Behind Robb's answering smile there was steely warning and I was beginning to wish I had not arranged this. But then, my invitation had been only to Robb, for a drink. Grandfather had elevated the social occasion to a luncheon party and invited the young Cunninghams.

When Ian MacRobert came into the room, I caught my breath in admiration. Evidently he was one of those men who could summon strength and presence at will if he wanted to, despite ill health, and he displayed a veneer of well-being and alertness. He was dressed in a casual suit of good tan tweed, wore a soft silk tie, and his handmade shoes were polished to fine brilliance. I could scarcely

195

recognize the shuffling old man who had greeted me only two days before, and who had looked white and frail in his great bed yesterday. I took enormous pride in his achievement. He looked every inch the man of means who had dominated the neighborhood for decades and I was proud to be his granddaughter. Doubtless Flora and Cosmo were proud, too, but Cosmo looked startled and wary when he shook hands, while Flora was almost dismayed. Puzzled, too.

It was odd. Whatever they had expected, it was not this, and Robb and I were taken by surprise as well. Grandfather clearly enjoyed his sensational entrance. How much he owed to Mackenzie's help, I had no idea. I thought that a stiff whisky had probably been added to the morning's quota of pills, which I knew he had dutifully swallowed.

"As you see," I could not resist saying, "Grandfather is a great deal better."

He bowed to me, his smile slightly mocking, and then, with the most exquisite politeness, he talked to Flora and Cosmo in turn, giving and receiving condolences, saying how unfortunate it was they had not met in recent years, shrugging it off by saying, "One of those family disagreements, so difficult to resolve."

Except by death, I thought silently, and was angry, first with Grandfather and then with myself. For *that* would have been the answer, I thought with sudden, blazing clarity. I could have brought them together again, my mother and Grandfather, if I had insisted on going to see the old man after I'd grown up, and then persuaded *him* to see my mother. Sometimes the young do not use the power they possess, not realizing until too late that it is there, latent and poised.

"I see you do a lot of flower arranging." Flora's wide, innocent blue eyes relegated me to womanly pursuits for idle moments.

"Not a lot, but I enjoy it," I replied calmly.

"Between attending auctions, valuing silver, traveling in search of and selling antiques, I am sure Caroline enjoys flower arranging." Robb's expression was bland.

"And what do *you* do with yourself?" Grandfather asked Flora.

She allowed tears to well up, and if I sound heartless, it is because I was convinced that at that moment she was fishing for sympathy and not feeling sad for our loss. "Now I shall have to run Quern Lodge."

"Yes, but before, what did you do?"

"I ride a lot and we swim and fish."

"I'd heard that Cosmo is an exceedingly good swimmer, like Caroline." Grandfather nodded towards me, smiling. We were sitting grouped in the tower, with the sea moving in its everlasting pageant outside, talking politely, and our wariness made a sixth person in the room.

Mackenzie entered to replenish glasses and offer small savories, and he bent to murmur a word in Grandfather's ear.

"Show him in, show him in." Grandfather looked across at me—I was almost directly opposite him. "You have no objection, Caroline?"

"Objection to what?" I had no idea what he was talking about.

"To your partner joining us. He has only now arrived, it seems."

"But I did not invite him here." I felt a mixture of unease and downright annoyance inside me.

"Did you not?" Grandfather was unperturbed and unsurprised, I thought. At least Julian's arrival explained the car; I had not been mistaken about it being ours.

When Julian came in he smiled easily at me, but his face was pale, his eyes hollow and he looked completely exhausted. I introduced him to my grandfather, and Julian bent and shook hands in a way which I knew would meet with approval—just the right mixture of deference and aloof dignity. The others he knew, and greeted with casual pleasure. Cosmo and Flora were wide-eyed with interest; Robb looked hostile but managed to be polite.

With four men and two women at luncheon, it was as well that the meal had been laid on a round table. Even so, placing would be tricky, I thought, but Grandfather was equal to it.

"I shall have to forgo having the pleasure of a lady on each side of me," he said. "Flora, will you sit on my right, with Robb beside you, then Caroline, Cosmo next to Caroline, I think, and Mr. Bennet on my left."

"Please call me Julian."

"With pleasure."

Conversation flowed lightly during the meal and I thought that Grandfather and Julian got on surprisingly well. Melon was followed by roast chicken with several fresh vegetables and a delectable stuffing, to say nothing of the usual rolls. Grandfather tasted the golden Rhine wine brought by Mackenzie and approved it, and we finished with a blackberry and apple pie. Mrs. Mackenzie was to be congratulated. The meal was simple but perfect in every detail, her pastry deliciously fragile, a mere paper-thin container for the fruit.

Over cheese, Grandfather himself drew attention to the pewter bowl with the rosebuds and lavender. "Do you know the period, Caroline?"

"Yes, early eighteenth century and by Chamberlain, I believe. I'm sure it should not be used for flowers, but I found it in the flower room."

"Your mother was the first to use it for that purpose and I agree with her view that beautiful things should, on the whole, be utilized. My collection of silver which is of particular value is kept in the strongroom, naturally, for that is my investment. I thought you might like to see it after luncheon?"

We all made sounds of agreement and pleasure, but Robb, I thought, looked mutinous.

Coffee was taken in the drawing room and I was detailed to pour, which gave Flora an excellent opportunity to comment on my ring. I had noticed her eyes on it several times during lunch.

I waggled by right hand, admiring the flash and fire of the stone, but feeling also an exquisite nostalgia for the time when my mother had worn it. "Mother left it with Robb for me," I said briefly, and Flora's eyes grew round with astonishment.

"With Robb? Why should she do that?"

"I suppose she trusted him." It was Grandfather who replied, before I had time to say a word. Flora went scarlet, Cosmo paled and Robb was like a wooden Indian, totally impassive.

I moved to Julian's side, refilled his coffee cup and hissed, "What are you doing here? Why did you come?"

"Am I in the way?"

"No, of course not, but . . ."

"Ah, well, you see, Caroline, Amanda was such a bitch last night that I left her early and began to drive just anywhere. When I found myself batting north on the M1, I thought I might as well cross over to the M6 and pay you another visit."

I shot him a look as I moved on with the coffeepot. *That* for a tale. He had been asked to come here, but it was pretty hard at that moment to think who had invited him, or why.

# 13

"HAVE YOU decided to buy the *Flora* yet, Robb?" My grandfather seemed, as usual, to have a good knowledge of what was going on in Skerran, even if he seldom went out, but then, anything that con- cerned Robb might have been discussed between the two of them.

"Not quite. I intend to take her out to sea before I make up my mind."

"May we come with you?" Cosmo was quick to ask. "Why don't we all go?"

Robb smiled. "Flora has seen her already, I am sure, as her namesake belongs to Drummond. And Caroline has been aboard with me."

"Have you, Caroline? You did not tell me," my grand- father said.

"It must have slipped my mind."

Every time I was acid with my grandfather I felt cross with myself. This was the kind of trap my mother had fallen into and it caused a lot of rasping at the nerve ends without achieving much for either side. A complete waste of time, of use only for establishing the refusal to be a doormat.

"But it would be fun for us all to go together," Cosmo persisted. "How about it, Robb?"

"I'm sorry but I can't go today, and tomorrow I have the vet coming again."

"Tomorrow evening, then?" Flora suggested.

I was busy with the coffee, but after a moment I heard Robb's voice saying, reluctantly, I thought, "All right, tomorrow evening."

The strongroom was the room to which I had been taken by Mackenzie, where the safe held a silver leopard, twin to mine, and cash for household expenses. The drawers, of varying depths, were unlocked by my grandfather, who carried the keys with him but laid them on a chest of drawers after use. Again I thought how inadequate were his precautions. One or two of the drawers were steel-lined, the others were not, and there were many drawers, fitted and cushioned with purple velvet, a splendid fabric for showing off the lovely, soft sheen of silver.

A side table had been spread with velvet, and a desk light shone on the dark pile. We were allowed to lift out and examine any pieces which appealed to us, and Flora did not exaggerate when she called the room an Aladdin's cave. There were lighthouse-form sugar casters, fluted, pierced and engraved, one by Joseph Sheen of London, a great silversmith of the late seventeenth century. There were pairs of silver beakers in cases and even one Charles III beaker, seventeenth-century of course, chased with flowers and leaves and engraved with a crest, a beautiful thing.

Gravy spoons and marrow scoops abounded; there were porringers and children's mugs, coffee and chocolate pots, exquisite silver-mounted crystal claret jugs, George IV meat skewers and many, many snuffboxes dating from 1716 into mid-Victorian times, lovely things with flowers, moths and butterflies, or hunting and battle scenes. Finally we were shown two great epergnes, kept in cupboards and wrapped in black velvet, magnificent with heraldic beasts, twined leaves and pilasters.

Robb handled nothing, I noticed, merely leaned over and looked. Flora pounced on pretty things with small cries of joy; the snuffboxes appealed to Cosmo; Julian handled many articles in a detached, professional way, his long, sensitive fingers feeling for faulty workmanship or recent repairs, smoothing the silken sides of some of the larger pieces with his thumbs and fingertips.

"Well, Julian, what do you think?" Grandfather was watching him and I noticed that there were deep lines of exhaustion scoring the old man's face on either side of his nose and mouth.

"Undervalued, certainly. I shall need a lot more time."

"You may have all of tomorrow."

"To do the job properly I would need longer."

"Yes, well, you may be able to come up with some kind of advice tomorrow and after that we shall consider."

Robb, Flora, Cosmo and I had stood around silent during this exchange, but my own indignation had been mounting. "Julian, have you been engaged to catalog this lot?"

"Not catalog, my dear," Grandfather said firmly. Coldly, with his eyes resting on each of us in turn, he added, "I can assure you *all* that the whole collection is cataloged and the details which I have are duplicated and lodged with my bank. No, Mr. Bennet, a man of repute in the antique world, has been engaged not to catalog but to revalue the collection. I am underinsured and I must do something about it."

Robb said sharply, "I thought Caroline was the silver expert in the partnership."

"She is," Julian said, but Grandfather put in suavely, "Julian has enough knowledge to do this for me. I have taken expert advice on that. And besides, you see, he is the only disinterested person here."

"*I* am disinterested," Robb said. "But I know very little about silver."

"You, disinterested, Robb?" My grandfather drew himself up and prepared to leave the room. "I think not. Oh, I think not."

Robb looked baffled and angry, the rest of us merely confused, aware that some deep game had been laid out, but the pieces on the board puzzled us.

"Aren't you going to lock the drawers again?" I asked sharply.

"Mackenzie will do it directly."

We followed him upstairs, trooping behind in a straggling way, and when we reached the great hall, Grandfather said, "I must rest for a while, but I hope you will not leave yet." He turned to the visitors and shook hands with each one. "Caroline will show you the garden, and Mackenzie will serve you with tea in the drawing room before you leave."

I walked with Julian to the garden and he took my arm. I was glad of it, for, after standing, my knee was playing up again in the usual tiresome way. "So you did not come here on the spur of the moment but were sent for?"

"A bit of both. My answering service supplied me with the information that Ian MacRobert would like an independent valuation of his silver; Amanda at her worst supplied me with the keen desire to get out of London. I did not exactly lie to you."

"H'm. The old boy is up to something."

"Oh, undoubtedly. Is your friend Robb out of favor?"

"I don't know. They seem less than cordial with each other at present." I turned to glance over my shoulder. Flora had taken Robb's arm; Cosmo was walking alongside them with his hands in the pockets of his elegant slacks, and he was kicking pebbles as he walked. He bent to pick up two or three and went to the side of the causeway, where he took aim at a rock and hit it once out of four times.

"You're better with a catapult," Robb said, laughing.

"Of course. You taught me how to use it."

The look of triumph which Cosmo threw at me, his gladness that I happened to be looking over my shoulder at that moment, made me gasp and grip Julian's arm more firmly, my fingers unintentionally pinching. Immediately they were covered by Julian's hand and softly he said, "What significance has that little exchange for you, Caroline?"

There was not the smallest use in denying the significance, so I said, "I'll tell you later. Julian, are you staying at the Castle?"

"No, I was offered a room but declined by telephone. The Drums will do me nicely, and I called there for breakfast and booked a room. They must wonder what the hell we're playing at."

I laughed. "They don't take much notice of the mad English. Incidentally, I saw you this morning, over there." I nodded towards the shore of Loch Branta.

"You couldn't have! I was most careful. There was no one on the causeway and none of the Castle windows overlooks that road."

"Ah, but I was at an upstairs window at one of the garden cottages."

"Of all the rotten luck!"

"It didn't matter, did it?"

"No, except that I meant my entrance to be a spectacular surprise, not a damp squib."

"I wasn't certain. I couldn't read the number of the

car, and if it's any comfort to you, I was certainly surprised." I turned and waited for the others. "Robb, do you
know who is going to occupy the cottage Hamish is
doing up?"

"Hamish, I imagine. And Maggie, if he gets his way,
but for heaven's sake don't tell anyone. Mrs. Munro would
be mortified if she wasn't the first to know."

"Are they engaged?"

"Not formally, but I believe they have made up their
own minds. Maggie is from the islands, though; she will
not take such a serious step without consulting her parents
and getting their permission, and they would have to ap-
prove Hamish, who was a wild lad in his youth, by all
accounts."

"You mean parents still give permission in these parts
and the girls *listen*?" Julian's face was a study.

"I do mean it. Quite seriously."

"For how much longer, I wonder." Flora's laugh was as
light and brittle as glass, and it set me thinking about her
and Cosmo, and about Grandfather. What did he think
of them? I wondered. He had played a part this morning,
that of the perfect host entertaining strangers. My overworked imagination fancied that he was playing a deeper
game as well, but I had no idea what it was.

We lingered in the garden until teatime, Flora and I
in our pale clothes, sitting decorously on one of the benches.
The three men were sprawling on the grass or sitting up
and hugging their knees. The air was cool and pleasant,
bees made soothing sounds among the flowers and we were
at peace for once. Robb renewed his invitation to sail in
the *Flora* on Monday evening and we arranged, all of us,
to meet at The Drums at seven-thirty. Robb promised us
an evening picnic on board, put up by his housekeeper.

Tea was already laid in the drawing room when we went

in, except for the silver teapot wafting the fragrance of Earl Grey behind it and the hot-water jug which Mackenzie brought in and put on a stand.

"Will there be anything else, Miss Westwood?"

I glanced at the inevitable plates full of tiny buttered scones, homemade cakes and shortbread, and shook my head. "Nothing, thank you, Mackenzie. I'll ring if we need more tea."

He bowed and withdrew silently. I had grown to like him, and thought now with faint surprise of my early hours here when I thought his quiet movements almost sinister.

Flora's eyes watched him, and I decided that she was viewing him as a distinct asset. I wondered how long it would be before Quern Lodge had a manservant. Or perhaps she was hoping to move into the Castle.

Immediately after tea Julian left and I went with him to the door. "Have dinner with me at The Drums?" he invited.

"I don't know whether I ought. Anyway, you look all in."

"Which is why I am leaving so promptly. Frankly, I intend to fit in a couple of hours' sleep before dinner. Please come, Caroline. I'll pick you up here. Seven-thirty?"

"I'd like to. Thanks." I reached up and kissed his cheek. This evening would seem flat after having so much company, and I knew that Grandfather would be too tired to want anyone with him other than Mackenzie.

But as I moved back to the drawing room, Mackenzie himself came out of his small room off the hall, an expression of distress on his face. "Miss Westwood, may I have a word with you? I won't keep you long."

He was upset, I could see that, and I listened to what he had to tell me with every sympathy. He had had a telephone call to say that his brother was ill, dying, in Inverness.

He had been sent for and wanted to go as soon as possible, tomorrow morning, if that was all right. "Only for a few days. I'd like to see him before . . ." He fell silent.

"But why not go tonight?" I asked, thinking quickly that I would cancel having dinner with Julian and stay at the Castle. "Take Mrs. Mackenzie with you. Maggie can help me and we shall manage perfectly well."

Mackenzie looked uncomfortable. "I'm sorry, Miss Westwood, I couldn't help overhearing that you are to dine with Mr. Bennet at The Drums."

"I can make my apologies."

Finally, after a long pause, Mackenzie said, "I'll see what the master says. Thank you, Miss Westwood."

When Flora and Cosmo left, Robb stayed behind, saying that he had something to discuss with Grandfather. He went upstairs and came down soon afterwards with a frown creasing the skin above his nose. "What's this I hear about Mackenzie going to see his brother?"

"Just that. His brother is dying; of course he must go."

"But you can't manage here in this great place without the Mackenzies. Besides . . ."

"Besides, what?"

He smiled at me. "Selfishly, I was thinking of tomorrow and the sail in the *Flora*. I very much want you to be at my picnic. It wouldn't be the same without you. I had intended to ask you out to dinner tonight, which was why I stalled Cosmo's suggestion for today, but it seems Julian got in first."

"My, you do keep an ear to the Skerran ground. I shan't be able to go now, anyway."

"Why not?"

"I won't leave Grandfather alone."

Robb pushed a hand through his hair. "Your grandfather has other ideas. He says that so long as Hamish stays in the Castle he will be satisfied. He wants a quiet evening reading a book, anyway."

"He has me to convince that he will be all right. I'll see how he is later."

"I wouldn't cross him, Caroline. That upsets his heart quicker than anything. You'd better go out." Robb rose from the chair he'd dropped into when he came downstairs and towered over me. "But I'm wishing I'd thought of dinner before that partner of yours. He is attractive to women, I suppose?"

"Oh, *very.*" I grinned up at Robb and he made a fist to brush at my chin while he said softly, "Minx."

He left then, and I was in a turmoil, not knowing what to think about Robb Morrison and his relationship with my grandfather. Also, there was the astounding matter of Grandfather's sending for Julian, as a disinterested party, to value his collection. There were a dozen capable men who could have done that for him, far nearer than London. It was a crazy idea. Crazy like a fox, I thought, and without further delay I went upstairs to ask him about it.

In that big bed he looked small and lost again. A book had fallen against his chest, still the Vasari, I noticed, and he was fast asleep, his white hair ruffled, a faint smile curving his lips. He looked, I thought, like a man who had made some plans and was seeing them work out very nicely.

I crept out of the room, went downstairs and rang the bell for Mackenzie. The master had said he and Mrs. Mackenzie must go tonight, he told me, but tomorrow Mrs. Munro would come and live in until the Mackenzies returned. Yes, Miss Flora Cunningham had agreed. It was all arranged. Oh, and the master had said that on no account must I cancel my dinner engagement.

"Yes, Mr. Morrison told me that. What do you think, Mackenzie?"

"He'll be all right, Miss Westwood. He's that much better after the young company and something to interest him."

"Yes, he does seem better. I hope—I hope the news isn't worse for you when you see your brother, Mackenzie. You have a car?"

"Yes, I have a car, Miss Westwood. We'll be off just as soon as Mrs. Mackenzie has packed a bag. I've laid a cold tray for you in case you don't go out."

"Thank you."

Food, I thought. All anyone ever thinks about here is food. Meal after meal.

Grandfather wakened from his nap refreshed, and became decidedly belligerent when I suggested remaining at home for the evening, so remembering Robb's advice I quickly said that if he didn't want me to stay, I would dine with Julian at The Drums, as arranged.

Hamish was around when Julian arrived, and in the cool evening, slanting light on the water made the lochs look beautiful—silver gilt where the wind caught at the water, dark gray in the hollows. I sighed, peacefully happy.

Julian put the car at the track between the trees, and as we soared up the incline he said, "You're beginning to like being here again, aren't you?"

"Yes, I like it. It isn't quite real, though. You know what I mean?"

"Yes, I know. All feudal allegiance—or enmity, with undercurrents between people too well bred to allow them to erupt to the surface."

"That's it."

We plunged into the Forestry woods, and on this Sunday evening there was no machinery around and no trees lay across our track or groaned and creaked, ready to fall, but the scars were still across the track, and chips of wood where the tree had been sawed up. "A tree nearly fell on my little hired car, right here," I told Julian.

"When?" He rapped the word out and turned to look at me, horrified.

"That first time I came. Robb was driving. He drove me back to The Drums in my car because there'd been such a storm and he thought someone had felled the tree on purpose, or rather part-felled it and then released it when my car was coming."

Perhaps subconsciously, Julian put his foot down and the car speeded up a little. "But that would take two people."

"No. There was a chain round something or other on a tractor. It only had to be knocked off a hook at the crucial moment."

"I mean, it would take two people to fell the tree to a point where it would fall *as planned*. They'd use a two-handed saw."

Julian knew all kinds of things, his mind was a ragbag of information. "Are you sure?" was all I could think of to say.

"Yes, I am sure. Whose idea was it that Robb should drive you home?"

"His." I saw the way his mind was working and added quickly, "But it was a spur-of-the-moment thing. He was cross because Grandfather invited me to stay in such a grudging way that I refused."

"To you it may have seemed a spur-of-the-moment invitation, but what if it was planned? And the rope or chain, or whatever it was, round that tree . . . Did you see for yourself what had happened? Did you get out and look?"

"No. I stayed in the car."

"Robb Morrison got out and looked?"

"Yes."

"I'll warrant he didn't see anyone."

"No, he didn't. But it would be easy to hide among the trees." I kept my voice level.

Julian was silent, frowning, and when I began to laugh, he jerked his head in my direction. I said, "I'm sorry. I can see you are worried, and I was, too, but the situation is a bit ridiculous. I mean, while I was driving along this very road right after the accident with Robb, *he* was furiously quizzing me about you and implying that *you* could be behind it."

"So that I could get my hands on your half of the business, I suppose. He's a suspicious devil, or a devious one. I wonder which. Anyway, wasn't I on my way back to London at the time?"

"Yes. Without doubt. I phoned you late that evening, remember?" I allowed my amusement to show, so that Julian would not take it too hard.

"You mean you telephoned on purpose? Checking up on me?"

"In a way. I did not think for a moment that you meant me any harm, but you know how it is, once seeds of suspicion have . . . started to grow." I had been going to say "have been sown," of course, and it was not lost on Julian. He was very cross indeed and mentioned that he hadn't had much opportunity for felling trees.

"Have any other dangerous games been played?"

I thought that as Julian had returned to Skerran, he might as well be in the picture, so I told him about the blocked road when I had wanted to return to Invercorrie, and the fall of stones and earth onto the rough lochside road which I'd been forced to take and the flash of yellow as someone vanished from the clifftop. Lastly, I told him about the worst thing of all, the small bombardment of yesterday with pebbles fired from a catapult. That, I thought now, was when I had felt most truly menaced.

An arm came round me and Julian gave me a warm hug,

but he did not stop the car. "Robb is an expert with a catapult," he said slowly. "We heard that today, didn't we?"

"Yes. He taught Cosmo the art, it seems."

"And the flash of yellow. Oilskins?"

"Perhaps," I said slowly, remembering the fisherman I had seen earlier.

We did not speak again all the way to The Drums. When we drove by the loch, it was calm and beautiful in the evening sunlight, with eddies and currents making dark scribbles across the surface of the water. There were a few yachts in the deeper channel, but they moved slowly, turning to catch each breath of wind and dip before it.

The first person we saw when we entered the bar was Cosmo, and he had been drinking. His fresh complexion was heavily suffused, his blue eyes glittered and he swaggered over to greet us in a loud voice, with laughter and slapping on the back for Julian. I moved out of reach and he shouted something after me about it being time I made up my mind which man I wanted, or which property, a Castle or an antique business. He slurred over the word "business," made another try at it, failed and lapsed into brooding silence, staring at me. I felt my hand go to my throat in a totally involuntary gesture, and I came back to the present when the string of white beads which I was wearing cascaded at my feet, rolling all over the place.

"Caroline, what's the matter? The boy's drunk, that's all. You look as if all the hounds of hell were after you. Caroline!" Julian had taken hold of my arm above the elbow, and he shook me.

"I'm sorry. I'm sorry. He looked so like his father."

"And that frightened you?"

I shook my head helplessly. We were in a darkish corner at one side of the little bar, but Julian took my arm and turned me round gently. "Come, we'll have a drink at our table, shall we?"

Mutely I went with him, and Dan Drummond himself came into the dining room, bending over us too solicitously, full of apologies. "I'm sorry, Miss Westwood. Young Mr. Cunningham is leaving now."

"He's not fit to drive," Julian said brusquely.

Drummond smiled. "I wouldn't know if he intends to drive himself or not. He has a friend or two here. Anyway, I've seen him handle a car impeccably when he's had more than he's taken tonight. Don't you worry about him."

"I was not worried," Julian said with dry distaste, and Dan Drummond straightened up and left us without another word.

When we'd had a drink and chosen from the menu, Julian leaned across the table and took my hand. "Your mother's ring is very beautiful."

"Yes."

"Curious thing she didn't entrust it to anyone in her own household. Do you know why?"

I shook my head. "No idea. It is quite a while since I left home. Flora and Cosmo were young then. Let's talk about you, Julian. Or rather, about the business. What on earth have you done? Closed it down? Put a notice on the door?"

"Yes. Referring customers to Nancy."

Nancy dealt only in antique dolls and she had a tiny shop two doors away from ours.

"But you can't do that. At least, not indefinitely."

"Who said anything about indefinitely? Anyway, your grandfather is paying for this trip. His fee is handsome."

"I'm glad to hear it." I lifted a hand. "And don't tell me what it is. The less I know about whatever deal you've done with him, the better, I think."

"It's all aboveboard, I assure you."

There were not many diners on that Sunday evening, and by common consent Julian and I decided we should cut the evening short so that he could get some rest and come to the Castle early in the morning to start valuing the silver. The road back was deserted and we saw only a few boats on the loch before we turned away from the water and into the dark wood. The windows were down and the call of an owl close to the car made me jump. Julian laughed at me and patted my knee. "Relax, Caroline. I have a notion that whoever has been playing games with you will by now have given up. I mean, here you still are, you haven't been frightened off, and, moreover, I'm here to look after you."

When we said goodnight, kissing gently, he repeated his remarks. "It's over, Caroline, and it was all noise and thunder, anyway. Threats to frighten you off, and they have failed."

"I'm sure you are right."

We had driven across the courtyard after Hamish had opened the gates for us, and now I got out of the car and waved as Julian swung round on the flagstones and went out through the arch, with Hamish closing the great doors by means of the mechanism in the tiny lodge. As I watched the rear lights disappear and heard the muted roar of the engine as the car went up the hill again, I wished that Julian was staying in the Castle. It was an enormous, lonely place to house only my grandfather, Maggie and me, with Hamish in one of the cottages.

Grandfather was well and had settled down for the night, Hamish told me, and Maggie was making a cup of tea in the kitchen. "Would you like a cup, Miss Westwood?"

"There's nothing I'd like better, Hamish. Thank you. Ask Maggie to bring it to my room, will you?"

I was on my way upstairs when I remembered how we had all left the strongroom, with Grandfather saying he would ask Mackenzie to lock up. It had been after that that Mackenzie had received the telephone call about his brother's illness. Uneasy, I thought I would check that the room was safely locked.

When I got to the door I cried out in horror, but there was no one to hear me in that stone corridor. The strongroom door had been closed but it yielded to my touch, and when I looked inside, I was sick with dismay. There was silver everywhere, not thrown about but piled up on floor and table in such an appalling muddle that I knew it would take hours just to gather it safely together. Moreover, without a catalog, I could not possibly find out if there was anything missing. I began to pick up a few things, tiptoeing between small piles, gathering snuffboxes here, scoops there, putting them together and then simply giving up and staring about me. Grandfather's keys were still lying where he had left them.

"Miss Westwood!"

I turned at the sound of a voice, moving slowly as one does in a nightmare, wanting to hurry but unable to. "Maggie," I said softly. "Maggie, look . . . look!"

But she had seen at once, of course. Both of her square, capable hands had flown to her mouth and covered it. Her brown eyes were enormous, filled with horror as she stared about her.

"But who . . ." She gulped. "Who could have done this? We've been together all the time, Hamish and me, or with Mr. MacRobert. All the evening. It wasn't us, Miss Westwood."

"Get Hamish," I said, my voice hoarse with anger. "Get Hamish and come back yourself."

They both came, hand in hand, looking scared, and I

gave them hell, but I did not shake their stories. They'd been together or visiting Grandfather, briefly, for the whole evening.

"Is anything stolen?" Hamish asked fearfully.

"How do I know? How can we possibly know without the catalog? Grandfather has one and his bank the other, I believe, but I don't want to worry him." I chewed my lip, staring at the winking, glittering, forlorn clutter. "If we put everything back," I said. "That's it—if we put everything back into these lined and fitted drawers, we'll know if there is anything missing."

"It'll take forever," Hamish said dully.

"No, with the three of us, it won't."

There was a silence and then Hamish said, "You do believe us? You don't think we did it?"

"I want to believe you," I said, and then I remembered the rope—Hamish's entrance and exit to the Castle.

"Have the gates been locked while I've been out?"

"All the time."

Maggie nodded agreement and shivered. "I'd not stay here with the gates open, Miss Westwood. I'd be frightened."

I did not point out that there was no way of knowing whether whoever had done this was still in the Castle or not, but to Hamish I said, "Maggie will bring tea here and we'll all start to clear up. But first, Hamish, you and I will remove that rope which you have been using and I'll take charge of it."

He flushed but said nothing as he followed me.

Out there in the windy darkness I think I was less afraid than I had been in the vandalized room, and we walked quickly to the archway at the far end of the causeway. There I listened to the night noises, the wind and waves, the slap of water on rock, the cry of a startled bird.

I made Hamish haul up his rope, hand over hand, and coil it over his shoulder.

"Do you think he has gone?" I asked in a hard voice.

"Who?" He sounded startled and very young.

"Whoever came up that rope tonight to do his horrible task."

Hamish stood there with his face turned away from me, looking out to sea, to the islands where Maggie had been born, and at last he said, "I've told the truth, Miss Westwood. I don't know who did that."

"Who knows about your rope, Hamish?"

He was silent.

"I hope he has gone, for your sake," I said savagely.

The great Castle soared above us, black against the sky, a fearsome sight, and I wondered if there was still an enemy within.

We walked back across the causeway, and as we did so, Hamish said slowly, "He will have gone. I do not think there will be any intruders in the Castle now, Miss Westwood. I'd not have left Maggie alone there now if I'd thought there was anyone still inside."

I did not ask again who "he" was. I knew that Hamish was too afraid to tell me.

Before starting on our task, I checked that Grandfather was all right. He was sleeping lightly, his breath coming softly, and the curtains at his windows were open to catch the first of the morning light.

We drank more than one pot of tea as we cleared the room. But finally, with the three of us working methodically, we had everything back in its velvet nest, and not one piece was missing. I could not be sure that everything was in its right place, but the slots each had an occupant. We looked at each other, gray-faced, hollow-eyed but triumphant, and we smiled. The time was ten minutes to three, and my leg was twitching and musclebound.

As we left the room my eye caught a gleam of bright metal between two banks of drawers. I bent and pulled it out. In my palm lay a gold watch, the black strap so worn that it had broken. Robb's watch.

# 14

I SLEPT for what was left of the night, with Hamish's beastly rope in my bedroom, the door locked, and Robb's watch lying on the bedside table, but my sleep was uneasy and I kept starting awake, trying to remember when I had last seen the watch. Robb had not handled the silver when we had gone into the strongroom with Grandfather. I remembered that clearly because his detached attitude to such things was alien to me, but I could not remember when I had first noticed that the watch strap was weak, or when I had last seen the watch. It was hopeless to rack my brains and at last I fell into a deep sleep from which I was awakened by roars of rage from Grandfather. He was giving poor Maggie a dressing down for being late with breakfast. Neither Maggie nor I would be willing to explain why, so she had to endure his rage.

When I was dressed, I went to see him, and chided him gently for being rough with Maggie on her first morning of such responsibility. "You see now how lucky you are with the Mackenzies. I am sorry your breakfast was late. I intended to be up myself to see to it and I overslept."

He looked at me critically. "You may have overslept but I doubt if you've had much sleep for all that. What time did you get back from gallivanting with that young man of yours?"

"He isn't my young man and we were back quite early."

"Then you should have gone to bed like a sensible girl."

I acknowledged that I should have done that, and he was sufficiently mollified for me to go in search of my own breakfast. There was a variety of cereals on the sideboard, which I ignored, but I poured myself a glass of orange juice and some coffee, and Maggie came in with fresh toast and scrambled eggs in a covered dish. Her eyes were red and I said, "Maggie, Maggie, you must not be so sensitive. Mr. MacRobert is not as fierce as he sounds."

She managed a rather watery smile. "I know it, but Hamish was so angry when he saw I was upset, that I thought he would go up to the master himself. Never fear, Miss Westwood, I'll not let it show again."

"I hope it won't happen again, Maggie. I've told my grandfather he must make allowances. He is spoiled." As I caught sight of her startled expression, I added, "Oh, I know I should not say so to you, but just for today, until we get the house running smoothly, we are partners, you and I. Agreed?"

She gave me one of her wonderful smiles and I could see why Hamish was in love with her. She would brighten any man's life.

"Your partner is here, Miss Westwood—your real partner, I mean."

"Mr. Bennet?" I was astounded. Even for Julian, nine o'clock was pretty early to be anywhere, but he had said the fee was good. An inducement, perhaps. "Have you given him some coffee?"

"I offered it, but he said he'd rather have some later, about eleven o'clock. I'll not forget, Miss Westwood."

"Thank you, Maggie. You can bring me some then as well. I shall join him in the strongroom."

Even before greeting me, Julian said, "What on earth has happened here since yesterday?"

"Is it so obvious?"

"My dear Caroline! Most of the silver is covered in fingerprints. If your grandfather had been going over his collection, he would not have left it like this."

I looked bleakly at Julian and said absently, "Thank you for dinner last night. Did you sleep well?"

"Like a log. Eight hours. It's so *quiet* at The Drums."

"While we were dining there last night, it wasn't so quiet here, presumably."

"Someone was mixing this lot around?"

"Yes. That someone emptied the drawers and cupboards. The stuff was piled all over the place, but undamaged. Nothing stolen, I hope. You'll find out about that when you check with the inventory."

"Very likely." Julian's eye was stern as Caledonia itself. "Who did it?"

I shrugged. "I have no idea."

I could not believe that Robb would do something so petty and childish. My mind told me that I did not want to believe such a thing of him, and the thought of his shinning up that rope was absurd. He came and went at the Castle, he could ring the bell for Hamish to let him in and he would be admitted, with no questions asked. An insistent inner voice told me that he would not use the gateway if he wanted to enter without anyone knowing he was here. Robb was a strong, athletic man. Climbing a rope would present no problems.

"May I help you with this?"

Julian sighed. "Not with the valuing, since you are what your grandfather calls "an interested party," but as I now have your grandfather's inventory, I know where each piece should be. If I hand you things, would you rub them up and put them where I tell you?"

"Surely."

"Thanks, Caroline, it will speed things up considerably. But first, tell me what happened."

So I told him what I had found on my return, about the rope, and how Maggie and Hamish had helped me to straighten things up, and how late it had been when we had finished. His eyes did not leave my face as I spoke, and finally he rose and turned away from me, pacing the floor to a bank of drawers, turning and coming back again.

"It's horrible," he said at last. "An act of childish vandalism, and performed to show that someone can get in and out of the place at will. This door was left unlocked, you say?"

"Yes."

Julian's expression worried me. He was too concerned. He came over and stood close, looking down at me, and without warning, he framed my face in his two hands, then slid them round to the back of my neck and pulled me against him. His mouth found mine in a long kiss, such as I had never had from Julian, and I tried to push him away, but his hands slid lower, holding me tightly. I was fond of Julian, even loved him, but I was filled at that moment with a mixture of sorrow, affection and regret, because the kind of love I had for him could not respond to the desperation in his kiss. Poor Julian, he wanted a stable love at last, but I was not the one who could give it to him.

"Oh, Julian."

He still held me with one hand. With the other, he touched my lashes, first on one eye, then the other, and his finger traced the curve of my brow. "I was going to ask you . . ." His voice was husky and he cleared his throat. "I was going to ask you to marry me."

"Julian, Julian." I bowed and put my forehead against his chest, sorrowing.

"A most suitable match." His voice lilted with forced gaiety.

"I know. And I would be very lucky, but . . ."

"But the answer is no?"

"I am truly sorry, Julian."

He sighed. "It's Robb Morrison, isn't it? It has always been Robb Morrison."

"I don't know," I said. "Julian, I don't know. Sometimes I wonder if I shall ever love anyone in that way."

Julian, who always had a quick and easy response, was for once silent. Perhaps he, too, was beginning to think I would never love anyone. Tears pricked my eyelids and I tried to be light-hearted, to coax him back to his customary easygoing, philosophical attitude. "What about all the Amandas of this world?" I asked. "You can't desert them so soon."

He smiled with his mouth but his eyes were somber. "Quite right," he said and he gave me a little hug and a shake before he let me go.

We were still checking and carefully avoiding personal matters when Maggie brought the coffee. We drank it without breaking off. Finally all was in order and Julian settled with his list, reference books, the Silver Auction Records, a pad of paper and his pen. As I prepared to leave he looked up at me and said, "Make up your mind what you want to do, Caroline. It is time."

Julian knew me better than I knew myself. I'd had the sensation of waiting for something momentous to happen, but perhaps I must make it happen. It is time, he said. It is time. And I knew that he was right.

The time that day was very well filled. Grandfather was irritable—a reaction from the previous day's excitement, no doubt—and there was plenty to do with preparing meals for everyone, and trays for Grandfather, and keeping the absorbed Julian supplied with coffee at frequent intervals. Mrs. Munro had not arrived, but she had telephoned Hamish to say that she would be ready after tea at Quern Lodge, so would he fetch her at five o'clock.

Julian would not join us for tea, preferring to work on in the silver room, so when I had drunk a cup with my grandfather, I went outside and walked to the arched gateway to try out the mechanism. It worked perfectly and I myself closed the doors behind Hamish when he had driven the truck through. Without that dangling rope at the causeway, the place was impregnable to anyone without a key to this door, but all the same I checked that there was still no rope at the causeway.

When I returned to Grandfather's bedroom he asked if Mrs. Munro had arrived, and I looked at him, frowning, with something stirring in my mind. "It always seems to me," I said, "that you know what is going on at Quern. Could it be that Mrs. Munro keeps you informed?"

"I don't gossip with servants," he said sharply. Then he added, "But Mrs. Munro is Mrs. Stockton's sister and I have been able to help her from time to time."

I digested the information that she was related to Mrs. Stockton. It did not seem to have any particular significance. "You helped by employing Hamish, for instance?"

"I owed her that much." The voice was tired again. He tipped his head back against the piled-up pillows and there were two deep lines between his brows as he frowned. "And now I owe her more. He's a good gardener. I hope he will stay at Invercorrie."

It was on the tip of my tongue to say that it might not be wise to put complete trust in Hamish of the dangling rope, but I kept silent. It would be cruel to sow doubts if

Grandfather took comfort from having the boy here. I would wait and try to find out for myself what it was that made Hamish devious and evasive at times.

"Are you sure you don't mind if I go sailing tonight?"

The blue eyes were steady on mine, and after a silent moment he replied, "I don't mind. You go and enjoy yourself, but take care, Caroline. If I were younger, I would come with you."

I bent and kissed him, knowing that an accident at sea lurked at the back of both our minds.

Hamish had a key to the gateway and when I went downstairs the truck was parked in the courtyard with Mrs. Munro getting out of it and Hamish taking a case from the back. It was years since I had seen Mrs. Munro out of uniform—today she wore a tweed coat of soft heathery tones, with a silk scarf tied loosely around her neck and her head bare. The black hair was slightly ruffled and her round black eyes sparkled. She and Hamish were laughing together, and the boy looked very like his mother, but also like someone else. I caught again a tantalizing glimpse, so brief that it vanished before my mind could provide the link. I remembered my first visit to the Castle on Friday and the feeling I'd had then of having seen Hamish before.

Mother and son moved round to the back of the Castle and I went to the drawing room. Ten minutes later there came a knock on the door and Mrs. Munro entered, wearing a dark dress and looking again the excellent housekeeper.

"May I see you for a minute, Miss Westwood, before you go out?"

"Yes, of course. It is good of you to come to the rescue, Mrs. Munro. I did not want to leave my grandfather here with the Mackenzies away."

"Quite so. Though he will not be disturbed, Miss Westwood." Her eyes met mine impassively but with such intensity that I knew she intended to convey her own conviction. I felt relieved and less uneasy.

"I brought you this." Mrs. Munro was holding an envelope in her hand and now she held it out to me, dropping her excessively formal manner. "I haven't had an opportunity to give it to you before. Your mother was very insistent that I should hand it to you in private, Miss Caroline." Almost as if she herself was responsible, she added apologetically, "You must forgive the writing. It was in the last days, you see."

Mrs. Munro slipped silently from the room, leaving me holding a gray envelope with the one word "Caroline" scrawled on the cover, the final *e* trailing away into a faint scratch, as if my mother's strength had given out at the very moment of writing the last letter of my name.

Slowly I opened the envelope and took out a single sheet of paper covered in the same shaky handwriting. "My dearest Caroline," I read, "I know you find it hard to understand why I married Angus, but it is so simple. He loved me, I loved him and I was very lonely at the Castle. Also, I felt it would be good for you to have a father again, but I chose the wrong father. You saw that it did not last, but I ask you to believe that we were happy at first.

"I wonder why I have never been able to tell you this and talk it over. It is too late now but do not blame yourself, Caroline. I love you very much and hope that one day you will find the enduring happiness denied to me."

My mother must have been perfectly lucid when she wrote, despite her weakness, and her letter moved me so much that after reading it through twice I stood holding it in both hands, seeing through unaccustomed tears a young and lovely woman with a demanding small child and a crotchety, elderly father but no one on whom to lavish the womanly love she had in such abundance—no man to love and fulfill her, or to laugh and be young with her. Oh, yes, I could understand. Besides, Angus Cunningham could be very persuasive.

Thinking back, I pitied us all. There was nothing I could do about the past, but I hoped I could be happy in the future, as my mother wanted me to be. My mind became filled with clear images of Robb Morrison, and then it clouded over with doubt and dismay as I remembered a gold watch with a broken strap, lying now on my bedside table. My ears heard again the vicious cracking of a pebble striking rock, flying true from a well-aimed catapult. There had been many attempts to frighten me away from Invercorrie, but I was still here.

# 15

JULIAN DROVE me in the Volvo to the jetty behind The Drums, and in the dark wood, branches stirred softly in a whispering breeze. Flora and Cosmo were already aboard the cruiser when Robb picked us up and whisked us aboard. "I thought we might moor among the islands and picnic there," he said.

The engine growled to life and Flora became very busy, opening hampers and chilling champagne in the refrigerator, mentioning that she had done this before, during Dan Drummond's ownership. I thought she sounded wistful.

Cosmo was everywhere at once, running catlike on sneakered feet, examining everything and having a wonderful time. He had missed his father's boat, I was sure, for Mother had sold it after the accident.

Without a good deal of effort on everyone's part, this evening could become a wake, I thought bleakly. Mother had been dead so short a time and the death of my step-father must be vivid in the minds of everyone who had been there, which meant everyone except Julian. I watched Robb at the helm, apparently totally absorbed in what he was doing. If they were looking for a reaction from me tonight, they would not get it. I was aboard for the sail and a picnic supper, nothing more. When I moved to the side and leaned over, Julian joined me and it occurred to me that he was sticking close.

"You are wearing your white pullover, I see."

"I am very glad of the warmth." I smiled at him, grateful for the casual way he had accepted my refusal to marry him. Probably he had quickly regretted the impulsive proposal but I hoped very much that he was not hurt and that we would be able to continue in business together. "It will be cool once we are out of Loch Skerran."

"You mean cooler than this? It is freezing *now*."

"But very beautiful. Even you must admit that." I spoke softly, looking first back at our creaming wake, then forward at the stretch of green water with evening light lying along it in bars and tipping the waves with brilliant, shimmering gold.

Julian grunted. "Give me the Aegean. Subject to storms, but warmer."

We emerged from sheltered water into a stiffer breeze, the islands magnificent crouching beasts in the distance, resolving themselves into hills and glens as we drew close, with the heather purple and brown, and cliffs with great plumes of water cascading off them. Some of the isles had a rough track or two, a huddle of houses, hotels, a harbor and ranks of yachts, but these we soon left behind. With the cooler evening, only a few small yachts cruised close to the mainland or played around near the larger islands. No one else seemed to be, as we were, making for deep water and a long sail.

When Robb turned northward my heart began to beat in slow, uneven thuds, and for a moment I wanted to ask him to turn back. I felt as if I would suffocate, for he was repeating the sail we had made on Mother's birthday. But this time there was not a large party as there had been that night, and he would not go so far out to sea, I thought. The *Flora* was smaller, and we were only a makeshift crew. We could all sail, I fancied, but Robb would be by far the most experienced in these waters and was unlikely to need any assistance, provided we did not go too far.

"Do you remember Seal Island, Caroline?" Robb called back to me.

"Very well. We used to swim there." I moved forward to join Robb at the helm; Julian was captured by Flora and taken below to help set out the picnic supper. I could not see Cosmo but he was somewhere on deck. The sea had darkened to a color between slate and purple, and the final rays of the setting sun blazed over the Western Isles and died.

"Are you warm enough? I can find you a windbreaker."

"No, I'm fine, thanks."

Suddenly Robb gave an exclamation. "How careless of me! I ought to have provided everyone with life jackets. There are plenty on board."

He was dropping anchor, the weather was good. As the boat pulled on her anchor chains and steadied, I said, "Oh, let's wait until after supper."

The meal had been put together by Robb's housekeeper and she must have thought she was providing for a naval expedition. There was hot soup in flasks, various meats, game pies, salads in marvelous variety as well as fresh fruit and a creamy dessert. Flora produced the chilled champagne and Robb opened one bottle while Julian opened another. Julian liked champagne but Robb probably hated it, so I was not surprised to hear that it had been contributed by Dan Drummond himself—a gift with the *Flora*, Robb explained.

"So you have decided?" I asked.

"There's nothing signed." He glanced at me quickly and changed the subject.

We had supper in the cabin, Flora, with a glitter in her blue eyes, becoming feverishly talkative. She was not affected by the champagne, for she drank only moderately, and I thought she was trying to cover up an underlying sadness. Flora became garrulous in an emotional situation, Cosmo silent, as he was silent now, watching us all in turn. He began to drink more steadily, to look at me more intently, his mouth twitching at one corner, eyes moving from my face to Julian's, and then to Robb's, the fingers of one hand plucking incessantly at his sweater. The two older men were absorbed in a discussion about catamarans.

I hoped with all my heart that Cosmo would not repeat the scene we'd had to endure at The Drums, Julian and I. Tonight it would be more than I could stand. When we had cleared away the food, we went on deck to finish our drinks and watch for the moonrise. Someone had started a cassette, and with nostalgic pain, I recognized the tape as one which my mother often played. I moved to the bow of the boat, hoping to hide my emotion, but Cosmo followed me. "This guy's in love with you" came clearly from the cabin in a gentle, honeyed tone.

"Mummy loved this," Cosmo said with a catch in his young voice.

"I know."

"Dad gave her this tape, that last birthday. It was playing on the boat, actually playing, when he . . . You remember that, don't you? You are bound to remember." His voice had hardened.

"We all remember, Cosmo." I was trying to calm him.

"But you most of all, you most of all." He was muttering now, with vicious anger, completely sober. "I saw you push him, Caroline."

I felt as if I had been punched. "You could not have seen what happened, not possibly. There was no one anywhere near us."

"I saw. I was there, behind a ventilator."

"Spying!"

"If you like."

"Then you know why I pushed him."

"What does the reason matter? Nothing excuses murder. Murder, Caroline. Murder."

His hysterical, repeated use of the word horrified me. I wondered how long he had been uttering it to himself as he remembered the events of that night, and how much damage had been done to his young mind. At the moment he looked crazed, and I turned to leave him, to hurry away from the menacing voice and join the others. What happened then took place so quickly that I was unable afterwards to be sure of any details. I only know that I fell, and as I went overboard I heard running footsteps on the deck and thought I felt a hand between my shoulders, either grabbing to save me or pushing me over.

The moon had not yet risen, the water was becoming choppy and there was a strong current. I let myself go under and allowed the current to carry me away for a short distance before surfacing and turning to swim out of it, for I knew it flowed south and west and would carry me too far from land for me to be able to swim back on a cold night, hampered by clothes.

Voices came from the boat, carrying clearly across the water, Julian's sounding frantic as he demanded that Robb should circle around and look for me, Robb's replying more steadily, telling him not to be a fool. "Do you want her chopped in pieces? If we could see her . . ."

I wanted to call out, but I dared not.

A searchlight came on and swept the sea, settling on the current, beaming down it, then fingering away and coming towards me. I ducked beneath the water, stayed down until my lungs were bursting, then surfaced. The light had moved away, closer to the route I might be ex-

pected to take if I survived—the route to Seal Island, the
nearest land and the most friendly, with sandy beaches,
small trees and even a huddle of big rocks which might
provide some kind of shelter from the wind. I struck out
now towards the island, wishing that in my busy London
life I had made more time for swimming. I was out of
condition and soon out of breath. I trod water to rest,
watching the light which was again probing the darkness
in methodical sweeps. If I had called out at once, I would
have been hauled aboard, but explanations would have led
to an immediate reopening of all the bitter past and perhaps to further tragedy. I did not know for certain whose
hand I had felt between my shoulders, but of the male-
volence of Cosmo's accusation there was no doubt. If I
could reach Seal Island, I would take my chances there
overnight, call for rescue by the first fishing boat or yacht
to pass in the morning, and when I reached the mainland
I would go straight to the police. This time I would hold
nothing back about the night of my mother's birthday
party. With a dull ache I knew that the renewed investigation would mean misery, but it might bring eventual relief.

My thick new jersey was heavy with water. It had
brought me little luck, I thought, and began to wriggle
out of it. I allowed it to float free, and as it drifted towards
the current, I heard with wry anguish the shouts of my
former companions as they caught a glimpse of it and held
it in the beam from the searchlight. I heard a splash, then
another, as someone dived overboard, and was followed
by someone or something else—a life belt or the *Flora*'s
inflatable dinghy, perhaps. When they found the jersey
they would know I was trying to swim for it. I unzipped
my trousers, rolled them off with difficulty, then struck
out with smooth strokes in a rolling, powerful crawl, making no splashes, in a way which would have delighted those

who had taught me to swim. I heard the dinghy then, and the stutter of an outboard motor, but it seemed to be staying close to the cruiser. I swam on and the sounds fell away behind me, until all I could hear was the splash of water and my own breathing, rhythmic but harsh, becoming noisier as I tired. I might be followed to the island, but I remembered every detail of that place from my childhood and I could hide. Only the cold would defeat me now.

I had not allowed myself to think of how far I had to go, or how long it would take me, so it was with a feeling of dull surprise that I bumped my knees and knew that I was coming ashore on a sandbank which lay only about two hundred yards off the southern shore of the island. I stumbled over the sandbank, struck out again in a channel of deeper water and at last found myself on the island. Unfortunately, I caught my weak knee on a sharp edge of rock, and in making an involuntary recoil I pulled the muscle. Limping slowly and with blood flowing down my leg in a steady trickle, I clambered up the sloping, sandy beach. I wiped the leg with a finger which felt spongy with water, and as I licked my fingers I tasted two kinds of salt—water and blood.

Completely exhausted, I wanted only to fling myself down on the sand and rest, but I felt certain that Seal Island would be searched, and I did not know who would be the first to find me. I left the beach, and on legs which felt like rubber, began climbing upwards into the rocks which fringed the bay, then over them somehow, and skirting a dune which I knew to be slashed with razor-sharp grass, I reached at last a hollow, lined as it had been in my youth with close grass and thrift, soft and cushiony. It was a haven, and never had I been so thankful of simple sanctuary. I lay and closed my eyes, scarcely aware of the cold, for I was drying quickly with only a bra and tights clinging to my body, and in this hollow I was out of the wind. I breathed deeply, great life-giving lungfuls of clean, damp air, and that was salty, too.

It was a long time before my breath came normally, easily, and as the effect of my exertions wore off, I began to shiver. All the time I had been listening for the cruiser or the sound of the outboard motor on the rubber dinghy, but the first thing I heard was my own name being called, thinly like a reed in the wind. It was a voice in the distance. Quickly I rolled over on my face, ear to the ground, listening. No vibration, no approaching footsteps, only the voice calling, "Ca-roline, Ca-roline. Are you there?" I longed to reply, but felt threatened, surrounded by danger, my sanctuary invaded. The island had been beached in silence and this hollow would not hide me if the searcher came near. The moon was rising now, but the sky was heaped with pillows and featherbeds of cloud. I watched the moon and stars and an approaching dark bank, and when the moon hid behind it, I came to a crouch, climbed the bank of my hollow and slipped out, running awkwardly with my limp towards a group of remembered bushes.

Despite the scouring wind, they had grown since I had last played among them and were larger than I remembered, so I found them easily. What I sought was two rocks beyond, leaning against each other, forming an inverted V which would provide a hiding place. Yet I knew with sick clarity that if I knew of it, so would anyone else who had grown up in Skerran and sailed to Seal Island for swimming, and we had all done that—Robb, Flora, Cosmo and I. But only one end of the rocky hiding place could be guarded by one person, and from the other end I could break free and run, if my injured leg would let me.

I found the rocks, and the space was as I remembered it, so narrow I could barely squeeze through. A cold wind whistled through it and turned my skin into gooseflesh. Or perhaps it was fear which was doing that. Certainly I was afraid, with that awful, griping terror which is so difficult to control. The calling voice had fallen silent, but at last I heard footsteps, a slither of stones on rock and a voice almost whispering my name. "Caroline. Caroline? I know you are there between the rocks. You might as well come out." It was Cosmo's voice. A shadow blocked one end of my rock tunnel, and against the faint light coming from a starry sky I could see legs, braced against the rock.

It was useless to pretend. He knew I was there. He could probably smell my fear, like the animal he was. I thought bitterly, and pretended shyness. "I'm not exactly fully dressed. Where are the others?"

He laughed then, and the sound was hideous, bubbling with saliva, rough with the intention of vengeance and rising in triumph as he answered, "What others? There are only the two of us here, Caroline. The *Flora* is out beyond the sandbank, the dinghy lost—I saw to that. And I saw to it that I, the youngest and strongest, should swim ashore to look for you. They are waiting for news of you out there, but too far away to hear you, if you should think of calling out."

He was right. If the *Flora* was moored beyond the sandbank, a voice crying in the wind could be anyone's— Cosmo's own, a seagull's, an illusion. Strained ears would hear nothing definable.

"You pushed me off the boat."

"No, you fell. As my father fell."

"You don't know what happened at the party that night."

"Oh, yes, I do. He made a pass at you, *because you encouraged him*. It was your own fault."

"I did not encourage him," I interrupted furiously, but

his voice sharpened with hysteria and he said, "Shut up!"

What puzzled me was the long silence since that night. Not my own, but Cosmo's, if he had known what happened. I asked him why he had never spoken.

"It was my word against yours. They might have believed you. If you had stayed away from Invercorrie, Caroline, there would have been no trouble now, but you came back for Mother's funeral, which was to be expected, I suppose. If only you had gone away afterwards without making up your quarrel with Grandfather." He sounded regretful and very young. "When I saw you go to Invercorrie, I decided to get rid of you one way or another. But you don't frighten easily, I'll give you that."

"Was it you who watched from the trees that day?"

"Yes. With binoculars. I rode over." He was rather proud of it.

I ought to have remembered that he was a skilled rider.

"And the tree—what about the tree? You couldn't have felled that on your own. It took two people."

"Hamish was easy to persuade." Cosmo spoke with contempt. "I took the silver leopard from the bureau some time ago and hinted that Maggie might have taken it, or Hamish. Maggie left and Hamish followed her, as I knew he would. Besotted oaf! After that, I had a tool inside Invercorrie. If I threatened exposure for Maggie, innocent or guilty, Hamish would do what I wanted. So he returned the leopard to Grandfather when I told him to. I thought that would finish you with the old man, but no, you got round him. You must have some kind of hold over him, Caroline. What is it?"

"Nothing. I have no hold over him." But I had a hold. I loved my grandfather, and in spite of everything, he knew it.

I recalled hearing Hamish murmuring to Maggie that

no one would ever find out. He was talking of his return of the leopard, of course, and with that he must have thought that his business with Cosmo was at an end. Then came the catapult incident and the discovery that Cosmo knew of his rope. Hamish's fear for Maggie's safety must have returned tenfold as Cosmo became more desperate.

"You got into the Castle, messed up the silver."

"That was a joke."

Odd sort of humor, I thought. Bizarre. Perverted. Intended, no doubt, to cast doubt on the integrity of those in the Castle who would be concerned with the strong-room. Julian and me. It was more than a joke. He hoped we would be asked to leave.

I moved, massaging my knee, which was stiffening, and small stones rattled against the rock. Instantly the shadowy legs, which were all I could see of Cosmo, flashed round to the other end.

"Don't worry," I said wearily, "I'm not going to run for it, but I am not coming out, either. Not until daylight, anyway."

The *Flora* would not go away. Julian or Robb would get ashore. Somehow I had to stall Cosmo until help came.

"Suit yourself. You must be cold." The thought amused him. "Anyway, I can get you out anytime."

I knew he couldn't. If I stayed in the center, the longest arm could not reach me.

"Did you know I was the one who was frightening you?" That was something he wanted to learn—his voice was urgent.

Feigning indifference, I replied, "I found your games more annoying than frightening," and he flew into a rage, as I had hoped he might.

Hate came from Cosmo in a stream and, with it, disclosures. He and Flora had planned to approach their grandfather. With me out of the way, there was a good chance that they could heal the breach which had opened between our mother and Grandfather MacRobert. With that healed, they might hope to inherit Invercorrie. "Soon we'll have it," he exulted. "Soon now. The old boy is ill, he can't last long. And if Flora marries Robb, we'll own the whole of North Skerran. All of it."

He was the true son of Angus Cunningham—arrogant, boastful, certain that might was right.

Faintly, from a distance, there came a sound. It was a voice through a loud-hailer, and it called, "Cosmo. Have you found her?" The anonymous call trailed away in an echo among the rocks, "Her-her-her." Cosmo did not answer. Instead he said, coaxing me, "Listen, they are calling us. Wouldn't you like to come out?"

I laughed through chattering teeth. "You have told me too much, Cosmo. You must be mad if you think I am coming out now."

He caught his breath. "*I* have told *you* too much! You're the murderer! You're the one who can't afford to get caught, but you will be caught. You are coming out of there *now*!"

"I'm *not* a murderer," I said with tired vehemence, and dropped my face on my knees. I was so desperately cold and so tired. I doubted if I could hold out in this cramped position until daylight, but what else could I do? If Cosmo got hold of me in his present state, I doubted if I would live till morning. He would throw me off the only cliff on the island—it wasn't far from here—and I had no strength left for another swim. It would be so easy for him just to return to the *Flora* and say he had not found me. I would be a statistic in police records, like my step-father. Accidental death. Death by misadventure.

My side felt warm. Puzzled, I lifted my face, sniffed,

choked and began to cough. Cosmo had lighted some dead bracken or heather and was thrusting it into one end of my hiding place, pushing it between the rocks with a stock so that I had to get onto my knees and scramble away in the other direction.

"Now are you coming out?" he asked. "I can do the same thing at the other end if you prefer it that way."

"You daren't!" I gasped, tears streaming down my face from the smoke which was filling the confined space.

"Perhaps you are right. We don't want anyone to find charred remains, do we? Come out, then, and run for it."

I had no option but to leave my safe cranny in the rocks, for it was a refuge no longer. It was too hot for comfort already and the smoke was choking me. I went out, but I did not run. For one thing, my leg would not get me very far.

Cosmo stood there, tossing something silvery with one hand, catching it again and looking at me, smiling. "Wonderful things, these waterproof lighters." He was wearing swimming trunks with a zipped pocket and he could not have been any warmer than I was.

"You came prepared," I observed.

"Ever the optimist. Though Seal Island was not on the agenda—only a midnight swim. Lucky I'd left this in the pocket of my swimming trunks." He caught the lighter one last time, put it away and lunged for me.

I twisted away then, refusing to stand there like a rabbit hynotized by a stoat. If I took only a few steps, I would at least be making an effort. I stumbled for the cliff, preferring the sea, after all, to a violent death among the rocks. Cosmo followed, gained on me rapidly, and just as I saw a shadow detach itself from a rock I felt Cosmo's hand on my shoulder, took one longer stride and fell. I lay shuddering, too spent to get up, half dazed. Afterwards,

I was not sure if I had lost consciousness or not. I heard voices shouting, and one sharp scream, and the next full awareness was of being lifted up and carried against someone who was miraculously warm. It was Robb. He cradled me against his bare chest and said my name over and over. "Caroline, Caroline . . ." When I lifted my head and looked at him, the moon burst from behind the clouds and I could see that his face was ravaged with grief and emotion.

"Are you all right?" he asked.

I nodded wearily. I could not speak.

"We have to go into the water. Trust me?"

I nodded again. I knew I would not survive being left here, so I might as well try to swim again. But I did not have to swim. Robb turned me over onto my back in the water and towed me out to the sandbank, carried me over it and towed me again, shouting to those on board. I did lose consciousness before being hoisted aboard, then found myself being wrapped in blankets, piles of them. A mug of black coffee laced with brandy was held to my lips. I sipped some and slid backwards into a merciful darkness.

# 16

THE DECISION to get me back to Skerran was taken while I was asleep, so the *Flora* returned to her mooring near The Drums. I was told later that when they reached the entrance to The Drums, with Julian carrying me this time, I began to struggle and refused to be taken inside. Perhaps I remembered last night's scene with the drunken Cosmo. That was Julian's theory, anyway, and I was whisked in the Volvo to Invercorrie Castle, where Mrs. Munro put me to bed with hot-water bottles.

When I opened my eyes briefly later on, I was terrified by the sight of a blazing fire, but it was in the grate, with flames leaping up the chimney, and no smoke. I could still smell smoke from Seal Island—it was in my hair—but after staring for a bewildered moment at the bright fire, I closed my eyes again and slept. The next time I awakened, it was morning; the sun was well up, and outside my bedroom door I could hear my grandfather's voice saying, "Mind you examine her thoroughly, now. She has had a very bad time. Exposure and all that."

"I shall examine her thoroughly."

It was young Dr. Staines, blue jeans and all, and he was thorough but reassuring. "A few days' rest," he said, smiling, "and you'll be all right."

"How is Grandfather?" I managed, in something of a croak.

"Stronger than I'd been led to believe. You have been good for him."

I smiled, but regretfully, wishing that my presence might continue to be of benefit, knowing it could not.

Maggie brought me a breakfast tray and I drank the coffee she poured, but could not eat. Mrs. Munro brought flowers cut by Hamish and clucked at my lack of appetite. Grandfather came and stood by my bed. On the bedside table he put my silver leopard where I could see it, then blinking very quickly and touching my shoulder, he walked out again, throwing gruff phrases of encouragement over his shoulder. Julian came and went. I slept again and awakened feeling much better, with my mind filled with images which were all too clear. I thought then of Cosmo and Robb. Robb had saved my life and had got me back to the *Flora*, but what had happened to Cosmo? I had resolved to tell the police all I knew about the birthday party, but there was a sequel now and I did not seem to know the plot.

I rang the bell, and when Maggie came in I said, "Maggie, I need to talk to the police."

"The *police*, Miss Westwood?" Her eyes widened, she flushed and then went pale.

"Don't worry. This has nothing to do with you or Hamish."

"You know, then . . . ?" Her voice trailed off.

"Yes, I know that Hamish was compelled to do certain things, but he has nothing to worry about." I smiled reassuringly and shook my head as she began to thank me. A knock came on the half-open door and Robb came in. "I'll handle this business of the police, Maggie," he said, and she fled thankfully.

I lay looking up at Robb and wondered why he was frowning. Everyone else who had come to see me had been smiling and kind.

"So you think I killed Cosmo?" he asked abruptly, his dark-gray hooded eyes boring into me. "Is that it? Is that what you are going to tell the police?"

"Is he dead?" I asked fearfully. I had not dared to allow myself any coherent thought about my half brother.

Robb nodded. "But I didn't kill him, though I might have if I'd got my hands on him. I was trying to catch him when he lost balance and fell over the cliff."

"But there is water below."

"Almost everywhere. There is one ridge of rock, if you remember, and he fell on it. I climbed down and got him out of the water onto a ledge, but he was dead. The police have brought him back."

"Poor Flora," I whispered. And then, "If you climbed down and got him out of the water, I must have been unconscious. It didn't seem long before you took me to the boat."

"You were unconscious." His eyes had darkened. "How are you, Caroline?"

"I am all right." I spoke stonily. "I want to talk to the police about my stepfather's death, not about Cosmo's. I have been bottling it all up for so long, because of my mother, you see, and because it was, it still is, so hazy, so horrible."

Robb sat down on the side of the bed, facing me, and took one of my hands in his in a firm, warm grip. "Suppose you tell me first, to help get it straight, and then we can send for the police if you want to."

"I do want to! I must. I have to get everything cleared up. There is no one to be hurt now, except poor Flora. Poor Flora," I repeated, thinking of Cosmo, her brother, whom she had loved.

"Try not to worry about Flora. Dan Drummond will take care of her."

"Drummond? I thought you . . ."

Robb smiled down at me, keeping it light. "Not my type. For a short time, she thought there might be advantages in joining Ardnacol to Quern—I'm not so sure that she was keen on having me thrown in. Anyway, when Dan Drummond began visiting Quern Lodge, she soon saw what she really wanted. That was what tipped Cosmo over the edge of reason, I think. He had his father's delusions of grandeur, and a local hotel owner, however well endowed with money, did not fit into his schemes at all."

I digested this. "You know it was Cosmo who did all those things? The frightening things?"

"I heard a little last night and guessed the rest. Now tell me about Angus Cunningham's death."

So I told him about being pursued by Angus Cunningham, my mother's husband. About how I had eluded him for most of the evening and had gone to a quiet place in the bow, believing that he had lost sight of me or given up. But then he had appeared, more drunken and determined than ever, and in utter disgust I had pushed him and seen him fall and strike his head.

"I ought to have gone to him and helped him up—he was nearly incapable anyway, but I didn't. I left him lying there, but he had moved. He was up on one elbow, glaring at me, shouting abuse. And, Robb . . ." My hand left his grasp and I put both hands on his upper arms, clinging, as I said, "Robb, I am sure I saw him later that evening, talking with others, but it was all so hideous. Afterwards I wondered if I had remembered correctly or if I had made that part up, to save my mother's feelings. I even wondered if, later on, my mother had pushed him. I would not have blamed her, but imagine the headlines . . ." I gave a short laugh that was half a sob. "The papers would

245

have made a meal of it. They'd have thought the whole thing was a drunken orgy, but it wasn't. He was the only one . . ." I stopped, shuddering. "What I fear most is that maybe I wasn't thinking of my mother. Maybe I wanted to save myself the unpleasant questions, the *exposure.*"

"Maybe," Robb said firmly, putting his arms round my shoulders and pulling me against him in a brief, reassuring hug. "But maybe your overworked imagination has spent far too long going over that one push, magnifying it into something which never happened. Now lean back and I'll ring for Mrs. Munro."

I leaned back, but try as I might, I could not think why he wanted Mrs. Munro here just now. However, she came at once, as if she had been waiting for a summons, and she stood at the foot of my bed, pale and drawn, looking not at me but at Robb.

"You'll have to tell her, Mrs. Munro," Robb said briefly.

Before Mrs. Munro could say anything, Grandfather came into the room, went over to the fire and lowered himself stiffly into an easy chair. "Now tell my granddaughter everything," he said, and Mrs. Munro nodded.

After one startled glance at Grandfather, Robb kept his eyes on my face. I could feel them but I couldn't look at him. Mrs. Munro's story was startling, and it supplied the final link to all that had happened.

With dignity, her round black eyes resting on me with sympathy and regret, Mrs. Munro said, "I had no idea that you were troubled about what had happened that night, Miss Caroline. You saw Angus for a minute or two sometime after you had pushed him. He was all right then. You must have brooded over it later until it was all mixed up in your mind."

She had used his Christian name, Angus.

"Mrs. Munro—" I began, but she interrupted me.

"Housekeepers are traditionally addressed as Mrs.," she said with a flash of disdain, "so I wore a wedding ring, buried my imaginary 'husband' and had Hamish. He is half brother to Flora and Cosmo, but not to you. He is Angus Cunningham's son. Your mother knew and she was very good to me." The poor woman swallowed. "After I had Hamish, there was nothing more between Angus and me until that night on the boat when he was mad with rage and drink. After going for you, he came after me again. I couldn't stand the humiliation for your mother, Miss Caroline, and I pushed him. God knows, I didn't mean him to go over, but he fell and later we found he had disappeared. If anyone killed Angus Cunningham, it was me and not you, but I think it was the will of God."

The relationship explained so much—most of all, the care with which my mother and grandfather attended to Hamish's welfare when he left Quern Lodge, though they were not aware of Cosmo's treachery.

"Did Cosmo know?" I asked.

"We don't think so." Robb said.

"You knew?" I asked him. "All the time?"

"No, Caroline. Your mother told me when she entrusted the ring to me. She wanted me to explain to you if it ever became necessary. Mrs. Munro told Mrs. Stockton, who is her sister, and Stockton told Mr. MacRobert."

Grandfather said from his armchair, "The man was an obvious blackguard. Can't think why my daughter married him."

"She was lonely," I said.

"Nonsense," said Grandfather, and I knew he would never understand why she and I had felt lonely, each in our different ways. I looked at Robb. He knew. But then, Robb had always been remarkably perceptive.

"And now there's Cosmo," I said. "What are we to do?"

"Cosmo's death, like his father's, is accidental."

I sighed. "The police are going to think it very strange."

"The police can think what they like, and they can try to prove differently. They won't succeed." It was the master speaking, the Invercorrie himself, and I knew that he was right.

Almost without my realizing it, everyone had melted from the room suddenly, except Robb and me, and Robb said gently, "Do you think you can sit up?"

I nodded and he put his hands under my arms and lifted me upright, shaking the pillows in an inexpert way and putting them against the bedhead. Then he made sure that I needed no pillows by pulling me against him and wrapping both arms tightly round me. That stern mouth of his became loving and tender as it found mine, and the hooded eyes were filled with light. I put my arms around his neck and held on to him as we kissed.

Later, laughing down at me, he said, "I hadn't imagined that our first passionate encounter would be in bed, and you're not at all embarrassed. You are more experienced than you used to be, Caroline."

"And so are you." I was weak with love and, no doubt, with last night's adventure, but that seemed strangely far away now.

Robb stroked my hair, pushing it behind my ears. I could just imagine how awful I looked. He would certainly have seen me at my early-morning worst—only, it wasn't early morning. His eyes went past me to my bedside table and widened. "What is my watch doing there with your leopard? Where did you find it?"

"In the silver room after it was wrecked." Teasing him, I added, "I knew at once, of course, that the watch was a clue to the criminal."

"You couldn't possibly have suspected your future husband even for an instant." He saw the laughter in my eyes and bent to kiss me again. I did not tell him otherwise, that I had for a while suspected even Robb, such was the state of my confusion.

"Caroline, you don't need to go back to London before we get married, do you?"

I pushed him off and sat up. "I'll have to talk to Julian about that. Where is he?"

"Valuing silver again, I understand."

"I wonder why on earth Grandfather sent for *Julian* to do that."

"Didn't you guess?"

"No."

"He didn't entirely believe your protestations about Julian being only your business partner, and Stuart, who last valued for him, has died. So he decided to kill two birds, as it were."

"Do you mean that Grandfather thought I might marry Julian and was looking him over?"

"That's it."

"How old-fashioned of him!"

"Oh, I don't know. If Julian had been a prospective suitor, he'd have wanted to know him better."

This was not the time, I thought, to mention that Julian had recently become a suitor. These hard-headed Scots might imagine it had something to do with the silver, but I knew otherwise. Dear Julian. I felt an overwhelming fondness for him, but not love.

I did not need to go back to London, I supposed, but I would go if necessary, in order to transfer the business or whatever we decided. I owed Julian that much, and I hoped he would find another, more permanent Amanda. As for me, I still wanted to work with antiques.

"There are differences between your way of life and mine," I told Robb, frowning.

"Nothing which can't be solved by discussion or argument or a battle."

I laughed. Our marriage would have all of those, I thought, but most of all, it would have love.

Later, when we told Grandfather, he was as pleased as if he had arranged the whole thing himself. "Where will you live?" he asked. "Here or at Ardnacol?"

I caught my breath. So he intended me to inherit the Castle. "What about Flora?"

"Yes," the old man mused, still scheming. "She might marry that Drummond fellow. Now if Quern Lodge were to come on the market, you could end up . . ."

"Owning the whole of North Skerran," I finished for him. "Grandfather, that is sheer greed."

"It's good sense. Flora doesn't love Invercorrie as you do, but I'll see she's all right, don't you fret."

That made me feel a little better, and my spirits rose still more and I dissolved into laughter when Robb said thoughtfully, "I could commute from here to Ardnacol by boat, maybe, but I don't think I'll buy the *Flora*. We'll choose another and call it *Caroline*."

"As to where we live," I told Grandfather, "it will be at Ardnacol for many years yet, I hope. But we shall come to Invercorrie often, to visit you."

We smiled, the three of us.